City Ash and Desert Bones

Laurel Myler

D⬤G STAR
BOOKS

City Ash and Desert Bones © 2016
by Laurel Myler

Published by Dog Star Books
Bowie, MD

First Edition

Cover Image: Bradley Sharp
Book Design: Jennifer Barnes

Printed in the United States of America

ISBN: 978-1-9357388-79
Library of Congress Control Number: 2016947116

www.DogStarBooks.org

for everyone who ever told me I was capable
you know who you are

1

Reesa did not know it yet, but when she stepped from the coach she was putting her foot down in the dirt where she would die, or that she was many different pieces of seven people who already had. The crystal white sole of her shoe set down on the ground with a crunch. The sound made her feel like she was stepping out of a time machine to the past. Away from the skyscrapers, away from the lights, away from everything she knew, to a tiny desert town too far west to warrant a dot on a map. Big City was certainly not what its name implied.

Spots of darkness from the dim, drawn-curtain coach ride cleared from her vision as she squinted in the afternoon sun. She gasped when she got her first look at the town. To think that just *yesterday* she'd been celebrating Christmas in the snows of the city! Shivering with the excitement that rippled through her body, Reesa snatched her hand up to get ahold of her partner's collar as he stuck his blond head out of the coach.

"Oh my Lord, Joule, look," she said, scanning around with wild, gleaming eyes. "It's just like a movie set!"

And it was. After a three hour rumble through the desert from the train station, over the Nevada wastes and the low-lying scrub, she and Joule had finally arrived at Big City, their new home. The coach had come to a stop at the top of a wide, curving dirt road shaped like a lightbulb and ringed with buildings. At its head was the town hall—a dilapidated, squatting structure which a single breath like blowing a birthday candle could have toppled over. It was flanked on either side by a jail and a bank, then the livery and stables, post office, blacksmith's, newspaper shop, the saloon, hotel, general store, seamstress's, and finally the church and barbershop. There the commercial buildings turned into houses and the lightbulb curve straightened out. Each was made of wood and stone, collectively looking like some Cowboys and Indians playset dropped out of the sky and covered in Christmas lights. At the center of it all was a white marble fountain, burbling as it shot clear water into the air. The longer Reesa studied the sun-bleached buildings, the stronger she felt something tugging at her brain—something she knew she knew but couldn't bring forward to recall.

"I really don't think you should say, 'Oh my Lord,'" Joule replied, breaking her reverie by prying her hand from his collar and smoothing the wrinkles.

She ignored him, as she usually did. "I feel like I'm in *The Quick and the Dead*." Her mouth fell open in delight and a laugh burst from her throat as she turned circles to take it all in. "Do you think Leo DiCaprio is waiting for us inside the saloon?"

Her partner regarded her with a flat look. "Ha ha."

"It was a joke, Joule."

"That doesn't make it funny," he answered. "He isn't in the saloon. He's been dead for three hundred years."

Reesa bit her tongue. DiCaprio had been dead for exactly two hundred and fifty years that May. She knew because she'd held a candlelight memorial for him in the middle of the night in her dorm at the Apostle Training Center. Alone, of course. She had to admit it was a little weird in retrospect, but all her friends found the actor too old fashioned to be handsome. She didn't share this information with Joule. Sometimes she forgot he was her husband, but husband or not, she figured he wouldn't understand. Even if the Theocracy's infallible computer had matched them together.

Quite suddenly, a suitcase rocketed over the side of the coach. Reesa jumped to dodge it, and Joule narrowly missed a beheading by the second as he squawked and sucked himself back inside. Their coach driver, a young girl in a too-big jacket whose face was framed by limp braids and a ratty straw hat that tied beneath her chin, grinned at Reesa as she dusted off her hands. She'd introduced herself as Randy when she'd come to pick them up from the train station, or at least that's what Reesa *thought* she'd said. The girl's voice had been so primeval and scratchy and her accent so thick—or maybe just different—that Reesa was still unsure of her exact words, even having puzzled over it during the three hour coach ride. The girl couldn't have been more than thirteen.

Joule poked his head furiously through the doorframe and scowled up at her. "What are you doing with our luggage?"

"Getting it off the coach," Randy replied, spitting a wad of tobacco onto the ground. "And if *you'd* get off the coach I could get a move on."

Grumbling, Joule obediently disembarked and went to collect their suitcases from the dirt. Randy gave her horses a hearty slap and sped off behind them, kicking up a mighty cloud of dust that set Joule to coughing. As Reesa stepped forward to assist him, a large shadow fell upon her and she turned her head to get a look at the large man who cast it. Beneath a wide, black Stetson, a sunburnt face with a moustache like a bleached rib bone smiled down at her.

"Welcome to Big City, Apostles." The man extended a beefy hand. "Mayor Big City at your disposal."

Reesa recognized him from his picture. She and Joule had been provided with a folder detailing Big City and its prominent figures before their departure. The mayor, one Hicks Grey, had been the only one on the list. As apostles—liaisons from the Theocracy to coordinate between the local government and the national one back east—she and Joule would be responsible for working closely with him. Big City had never been a part of an Apostleship before. It had never warranted one until now, but the world had never been quite so desperately thirsty for oil. The Big City reserves were rumored to be some of the largest on the continent, though they had yet to be accessed. She and Joule were out there for the oil, but it was Reesa's duty to insist otherwise. That in mind, she flipped around and happily held out her hand.

The mayor's expression faltered when he got a better look at her. "I know you," he said, brows drawing together.

A frown flicked across Reesa's features. Randy had reacted in a similar way when she and Joule had stepped off the train and into her coach. Hicks gave her a thorough looking-over, but still shook her hand, and Joule's as well when he stepped forward.

"I trust your ride was pleasant?" Hicks asked, tucking his thumbs into a thick leather belt that sat snug below his beer belly. "That scrub can be devilish prickly. Been a long time since we had to cut a path to the train station."

Reesa latched onto the small-talk topic, as she had been trained to do. "Why is that?"

He chuckled. "Why do you think, Apostle? Those who can afford to leave Big City can't afford to go by train. And those who can afford the train sure as spit ain't stopping in Big City. You're the first visitors we've had in nigh on a hundred years."

Out of the corner of her eye, Reesa saw the color drain from Joule's face. She knew he had been hoping for an assignment in Alaska—somewhere with cities and technology. Somewhere still a part of civilization. When they had received the documents issuing them out to Big City, Reesa had never heard the end of it. Joule had even gone to the doctor for prescription antiperspirant in preparation. Reesa put on a smile extra bright to make up for her partner's lack of enthusiasm.

"Are all these buildings that old?" she asked.

"Hm? Oh, no." Hicks glanced around him. "Older."

Joule very nearly fainted.

"Big City's built over another boom town: Austin, founded in 1862," Hicks explained. "Moved some of the original buildings into the formation you see here today. Others of 'em we used as materials." He waved his hand about casually at the four-hundred-year-old structures. "Big City's coming up on its Bicentennial this week. December thirty-first. Ain't that nice." He smiled proudly, his cheeks puffing up around his moustache.

Reesa returned it, steadying Joule who had begun to tip over. "I'm glad we'll be here to celebrate," she said.

With a start she noticed a sudden crowd had gathered. About a hundred people, silent as the crypt, just staring with their arms tucked at their sides and their faces expressionless. They watched, wary, from balconies and porches, saying nothing, and making no sound. Almost imperceptibly, one of them slipped from the crowd and gamboled up to the group.

Hicks turned as the newcomer—a short, skinny fellow with black hair like a brillo pad—approached. The mayor smiled and slung an arm around his shoulders.

"Apostles, this is Gig Sullivan. Deputy-Sheriff Big City. Couldn't do without him."

The deputy-sheriff held out a dusty hand, nails and knuckles caked with dirt, and the apostles shook, Reesa with pleasure and Joule with the least amount of reluctance he could manage.

"Pleasure to meet you," Gig said. "Never seen apostles before."

He took a long, uncomfortable survey, eyeing the sprig lines of their identical white uniforms, the three gold bands on their shoulders that marked them as ordained apostles, the polished appearance of their hair and faces. He started when he came to Reesa.

"By god!" he cried. "Don't she look familiar!"

Hicks whacked him on the back. "I thought the exact same when I first saw her. Who do you reckon she looks like?"

Together, the pair of them peered into Reesa's face. She leaned back slightly, shifting her gaze away. They proceeded in their study in spite of it. After several long seconds, Joule came to her rescue.

"We'd like to get settled if you could show us to our room?" he said, easing Reesa away from the mayor and the deputy.

Hicks smiled kindly. "I bet you would. Deputy, why don't you—"

A chorus of shattering screams from the crowd split his sentence in half and a single voice cried above the din: "Lord and Saints, *it's on the roof!*"

The apostles spun around following the direction of a pointed finger to the roof of the Big City Hotel across the street.

There was nothing.

When they turned back around the street was empty. Reesa's bones could have leapt right out of her skin. The little army of walking corpses was gone. Had anyone even been there in the first place? She glanced at Joule. He shook his head.

Mayor Big City reappeared, returning from around the side of the town hall, scuttling across the dirt, swearing all the way. *"Damn, damn, damn."* He reached Gig, who came from the opposite direction, and gripped the deputy's shoulder. "You keep everyone inside until that thing is dead. I'll take the apostles to their room." He scurried to Joule, yanked the suitcases out of his hands, and flashed the apostles a stewardess smile. "If you'll follow me this way…"

The pair of them had no choice but to trail Hicks across the street to the hotel, the very building at which everyone had pointed and screamed. As soon as the three of them were on the porch Hicks practically shoved the apostles into the lobby and dumped their luggage in the entryway. Slamming the door behind him, the mayor disappeared.

It was as dark inside as it was bright outside and Reesa and Joule stood blinking for several moments before they could see. A diminutive clerk looked up from behind a front desk as if he had not heard the door slam and was only just now becoming aware of the presence of guests in his establishment.

"You must be the new apostles," he said. His mouth tried to smile and failed. In the half-light, his oily skin looked made of candlewax. He slid out from behind the counter and produced a set of keys from an aged pocket.

"If you'll follow me this way," he said softly, gesturing to the staircase and shuffling toward it. "And do please bring your bags."

He ascended the stairs without any more ado and had trundled all the way up before Reesa and Joule even had ahold of their luggage. He surveyed their progress from the top step, eyelids half shaded like the bust of some disapproving emperor.

"Did you hear that commotion out on the street?" Reesa asked, glancing up at the clerk as she lifted her bag from stair to stair in slow advancement.

"Commotion, ma'am?"

"Yes. All that shouting. You didn't hear it?"

"I'm afraid not, ma'am."

He turned abruptly and shuffled swiftly down the hall. Reesa rolled her eyes, hefting her bag up in front of her chest and taking the stairs two at a time to catch up. The clerk had already reached the end of the hall by the time Reesa made it to the top. The two of them stared at each other for a moment before he spoke.

"I hope you'll be comfortable here." He inserted a key into the lock on a door at the end of the hall. "It's the best Big City has to offer."

Smiling, Reesa started down the hall. "Thank you, I'm sure we will."

He scooted away before she could reach him, leaving the key in the lock, and sliding by her in the cramped hallway.

"I didn't catch your name," she called after him.

"Shay, ma'am."

With that, he descended the stairs, passing Joule and returning to his post behind the desk. When her partner reached the top step, Reesa raised her eyebrows.

"Don't look at me," Joule grumbled.

9

He gestured for her to lead the way down the hall, and she did, dragging her suitcase behind her. She pushed open the door to their room and peered inside. A quick glance around made it quite clear that the best Big City had to offer was not much. The wallpaper, which would have been ugly in its prime, was peeling or torn at every seam. Alternating stripes of yellow-once-white and roses were patched at the corners with cadet blue, poorly disguising the water stains from the bad drainage on the roof. A full-size bed made of twisting metal slathered over in white paint to hide the rust was home to a stiff, rosy bedspread. What she would have given to have seen a pair of twin mattresses instead. It was going to be a long ordination sharing that thing with Joule. The only other furniture in the room was a small dresser to which Reesa went instantly. She couldn't dwell on it. Had to keep busy. She began unpacking as Joule stood cold in the doorframe.

"This is hell," he whispered. "We've been excommunicated and this is hell."

"I really don't think you should say 'hell,' Joule," Reesa retorted, tugging on the top drawer of the dresser which refused to open. She glanced over her shoulder to smile at him and he all but glared back at her. The drawer popped out and Reesa chirped with pleasure, laying her suitcase on its side and undoing the latches.

Her partner flopped down on the bed and the frame let out a terrible groan under his weight. "I don't know how I'm going to live here for the rest of our ordination," he said, rubbing his left temple as she'd noticed he did whenever he was getting a headache.

"Stop complaining." Reesa folded her undergarments and set them in the drawer. "They're doing their best."

"I wish someone had warned us," Joule grumbled. "I would have brought more with me."

She turned to look at him. "Like what?"

Joule did not reply with words, only flung his hands up in a general frenzy of frustration, so she came over and climbed onto the bed beside him, folding up her legs beneath her. He barely consented to crack an eye open. The gesture made her sigh.

"Do you want to go over our ordination instructions again?" she asked.

"Absolutely not," Joule replied. "I've read that ghastly manual a thousand times."

She scowled at him and when he finally opened his eyes and noticed, a little flash of guilt flitted across his face.

"But maybe I would like to say a prayer," he amended.

Smiling as he sat up, Reesa scooted herself over on the bed to give him room to kneel just in front of her. They joined hands, shut their eyes, and bowed their heads.

"Our hallowed, holy Father who resides in Heaven with all glory, sacred be Thy name and works and blessed servants upon this land. May Thy will be done through humble hands. May Thy plan for Thy children come to pass. May we, your

obedient apostles, be given the strength to aid in Thy divine labor. Hallowed, holy Father, help us to—"

A scream from the street ripped through the speech. It hung long and curdling in the air, alone for a moment until it was joined by a strangled, inhuman shriek, coming from right outside their window.

Reesa shot to her feet and rushed over. She pressed her face against the warped glass, but could see nothing aside from blurred colors. Her hands flew to the latch, but the window wouldn't budge.

"What *is* that?" Joule gaped.

He scrambled from the bed to help Reesa push against the window, but even with the two of them it hardly moved an inch. The air outside filled with the paired screams and Reesa shoved urgently against the window, hungry to get a look. The distinctive whir of a weapon as it powered up reached her ears and was followed by a snappish hum as a shot was fired. Mid-yowl, the shrieking cut off. Reesa looked at Joule, her eyes wide.

In the next second the pair bolted from the room, flinging open the door and flying down the hallway to the staircase. At the bottom they hurtled into Gig coming up.

"Oop! I was just about to check on you, Apostles," he said, adjusting his hat which had been knocked slightly askew in their collision. He stepped conspicuously to the side to prevent both Reesa and Joule from coming any farther down the stairs. Reesa craned her neck, pushing onto her tiptoes to get a look out the front windows, but Gig popped up to block her view.

"How are you finding Big City?" he asked, grinning into her face.

"What is going on out there, Deputy?" she demanded.

"I'm sorry?"

"Outside. We heard a gunshot."

Gig pursed his lips in thought and paused a moment before shaking his head. "Hardly anyone round here even *carries* a gun, Apostles. I don't know what it is you could have heard."

Joule stepped in. "What about the screaming?"

"Screaming, Apostle?"

"Yes, screaming. We distinctly heard screaming. Out there. On the street."

"Hm. You don't suppose it could have been something else?"

Joule's mouth hardened into a line. "No."

"Why don't you show me your room? I'd like to see it..."

Stretching out his arms to gather them under his wing, Gig started to sweep his way up the stairs, but Reesa ducked beneath his left and made a dash for the front door. Her fingers had just closed around the knob, turned, and begun to pull it open when Gig materialized and flung himself against the wood, slamming the door closed again.

"I'd *really* like to see your room, Apostle Reesa," he said.

"*I'd* really like to go outside," she countered.

"*Get off me!*"

The pair of them regarded each other with surprise at the sudden entrance of a third voice from out on the street. Reesa seized the opportunity, yanking the door open and sending Gig tumbling into the lobby. Lifting a hand to shield her eyes, she rushed onto the front porch and took a look around.

There was hardly anything to see. Just a young woman who sprawled in the middle of the dirt road, her skirts gathered up around her legs, and the tall figure of a man who stalked away and out of sight behind the church. Not far from the porch was a thick, blackish puddle of peculiar liquid. Several men were sweeping at it with push brooms.

"What on *earth?*"

Joule stumbled out the door then, followed by Gig. The three of them watched as the men continued to push the liquid into a dusty pile. Some exchanged their brooms for shovels and began scooping the stuff into a dog cart.

"Looks like that dung buggy overturned," Gig commented, gesturing at the cart and the men around it. "Do you think that could be what the two of you heard?"

Reesa raised her eyebrows at Gig; he put up his hands and shrugged in response. The shrieking had most certainly not been human, so it was *possible* that it could have come from the cart as it tipped over, but she was certain that the sound was organic, alive. And if that was manure it was the most bizarre manure she had ever seen.

"I'm sure that must have been what it was," Gig said, finally managing to get his rope arms in a pair of nooses around their necks and shoulders. "Come with me, Apostles. I've got a job for you in the office."

Reesa could not escape him now. The deputy practically dragged her and Joule across the dusty expanse of the square to the town hall. Reesa tracked that puddle with her eyes the whole walk over, her borrowed bones trembling in remembrance.

2

Three hours, nine minutes, twenty-six…twenty-seven…twenty-eight seconds since the mayor had popped up on Huxley's property line and asked him to shoot Ben Greeber. He hadn't used those words exactly, but the implication had been clear enough. Hicks Grey was a master of subtext. Now, crouching down beside Callum's smith shop, Huxley watched Ben's body as it clawed at the side of the hotel.

"Ben Greeber's been taken," Hicks had said.

Huxley had been checking a breach in his fence, and had set down the wood post he held in his hands before he straightened. "When?"

"Last night sometime. Had the graveyard shift out at the hole."

That was a dangerous one. Hard to see the takers in the dark, but keeping an eye on the hole was a duty Big City had to keep sacred. Huxley took more shifts than anyone.

"Was he alone?" he'd asked.

"No. My boy Shane had the other slot in the shift."

Huxley had simply nodded. Hicks knew well enough that the gesture meant he would take care of it. Of course he would take care of it. His hands had long stopped shaking at the prospect of shooting one of his neighbors though that didn't make it any easier. No matter how many times he'd done it.

He'd picked up Ben's trail out in the desert, a set of slippery footprints that led back to town and followed them until he'd found Ben—though he hardly qualified as *Ben* anymore—behind the post office, just a moaning shell of a man, the toxin having taken hold of his body completely. That was what happened when the takers touched a human: a body would break itself down into a mess of half-digested skin and organs in a matter of minutes. Big City had been dealing with takings for the past two years. And by Big City, he meant himself. *He* had been dealing with takings for the past two years. Nobody else had the stomach for it.

Ben continued to paw at the planks of the hotel, trying to get a purchase and clamber up, looked like. Huxley pulled his gun from its holster, ready to power-up and shoot anytime. He would have just done it, but Hicks had made it clear that when the apostles arrived, they were to be told nothing of the takers, and Hicks himself was standing in the middle of the square with those very same apostles. Damned idiot.

Huxley looked past them. He didn't give a rat's ass about the Theocracy and its cohorts. Someone taken was on the loose and he didn't want to shoot any more people than he had to. Unfortunately, the apostles' arrival had drawn a crowd. Everybody filed out of their homes and stood and stared like dumb sheep.

"Shit," Huxley grumbled.

"You find him?"

Huxley jumped—there was Gig, staring down at him with doe eyes.

"He's across the street," Huxley replied.

"You didn't get him then yet?"

Huxley gritted his teeth. *Gig* was deputy-sheriff, *he* should have been the one with the gun, but Huxley and Freddie Dunstan, the old sheriff, had only ever been the ones to carry guns. With the high cost of shipment, Hicks's demand for control, and superstitious natures nobody else in Big City had dared buy or borrow one. And with Freddie gone, the job of taken-hunting had fallen to Huxley.

Gig sniffed. "Them the new apostles?"

"Evidently."

"Huh." Gig scratched his chin. "I'm gonna go say hello."

He patted Huxley on the shoulder and moved away, right up to Hicks and the apostles. Putting himself at risk. Ben had climbed halfway up the hotel by then and was making his way toward the awning above the porch. Hicks and Gig chattered away. Huxley took aim at their heads, but lowered his gun. The gesture was hardly cathartic.

Ben made it onto the awning. Somebody was bound to—everyone *screamed*. Rachel Rice's voice cried above the others, "Lord and Saints, *it's on the roof!*"

At the cry, Ben scuttered back around the side of the building, climbing into a window frame just as the apostles turned to see what all the commotion was about. Everybody else, since they knew what they were dealing with and apparently hadn't lost entirely *all* of their common sense, rushed back inside on silent feet. Gig came scurrying back to Huxley's watching point when everybody went running.

"You see him?" he puffed.

"Yes."

"You gonna get him?"

Huxley looked up. That cold fire in his eyes burned hard. Gig swallowed, licked his lips, and took a step back. Don't ask again. That's what his eyes said. Eager to escape, Gig flipped around and returned to Hicks and the apostles.

With him gone, Huxley focused once more on Ben. He could just make out the edge of his body, lingering still in the window frame on the side of the building.

In the square, Hicks grabbed the apostles' suitcases and started for the hotel. He pushed the apostles through the front door and, as it slammed shut behind him, came flying across the square, a fine trail of expletives hovering in the air behind him.

"I thought I told you to *take care of him*," he hissed, grabbing one of Huxley's sleeves and yanking him to his feet.

"That's what I'm *doing*," Huxley replied, pulling his arm free and sending Hicks stumbling. "You don't like the way I work, you can do the job yourself." He held out his gun. Go ahead. Take it.

Hicks shifted uncomfortably, pulling at his belt loops and staring at the dirt.

"That's what I thought."

"Now don't you say—"

"*Shit.*"

Chivalry was standing out in the street. In the middle of the square. Ben had reemerged and she was watching him, paralyzed. Huxley started to move. Ben saw her. He was going to attack. Huxley came out of the shadows and into the sun. Chivalry screamed.

The sound of it reverberated off the buildings in a thousand echoes—for a moment lost to space and time. The sound of a dying planet. Ben joined her, opening up his jaws and sending up a shriek that pierced the air. He fell to all fours, his neck twisting his head around and garbling the sound. Huxley had heard it too many times. The sound a body makes when it's been taken.

Huxley's feet carried him across the square. His fingers flipped the switch on the gun in his hands. His eyes—they watched Ben, watched his bobbing head as it weaved inhumanly through the air and searched for the signs, the indications of attack. Ben would jump if Chivalry moved.

There—a lifted arm—Chivalry picked her foot up from the dirt, began to turn to flee, and as she did, Ben leapt from the awning, snarling, and Huxley caught Chivalry around her waist, holding her in place as he raised his gun, took aim, and shot Ben through the head.

Chivalry fell over his arm. Ben fell into a pile at the foot of the porch.

At once the others were back on the street. Hicks found his way into the middle of them, giving orders, sending men out for shovels and commandeering a nearby cart. "Gig, you keep the apostles inside 'til we're all cleaned up," he said. "This all went to hell in a handbasket quick. Quietly, now. Quietly."

Big City went to work. Shovels arrived. Ben Greeber was scooped into a cart. Chivalry still hung limp over Huxley's arm. He tried to help her stand.

15

"Thank you, Tombstone," she whispered as she found her feet.

Tombstone. He'd never really felt the nickname had fit him until recently. Until he'd become the one responsible for sending people to their graves.

"You're welcome."

She clung onto his arm.

"You saved me."

"It's nothing."

She clutched tighter.

"It's *everything*."

He stepped back, but she followed.

"Get off."

She stared up at him, her eyes glittering and wild and still glazed with terror. He'd just killed a man. A father. A husband. And she pressed against him in a daze. It was abominable.

"Get off me!"

He shook Chivalry to the dirt. A swift gait carried him across the square. Had to get away. The hotel door swung open, the apostles came onto the porch, but he didn't look back. He wasn't ready to see them. A shadow fell over his back and he found himself beside the church. How fitting.

Huxley leaned against the holy planks and slumped to the ground. He set his gun down and put his face in his hands. What was he going to tell Ben's family?

3

Them apostles were sure slippery little fellers. Gig had had to wrap his arms around their necks and haul them like a couple of hogs across the square to the town hall. It was a good thing the comm needed fixing, else how would he have been able to pull the pair of them away from the puddle that used to be Ben Greeber? That woman apostle—Reesa, she was—she kept her eyes on it the whole walk over. But Mayor Big City had said the apostles weren't to know about the takers, and as the deputy-sheriff, he would see to it that the orders were carried out. He was a good man like that.

"Deputy-Sheriff Big City…" The woman began saying something more, but Gig got caught up on the way she said his title—like it meant something, like it had real authority. He liked it. Made him tingly. "…where is everyone?"

"Huh?"

"Why isn't anyone outside?"

Well, that was on account of the taken Ben Greeber crawling his way up the side of the hotel and trying to take others along with him, but he couldn't say so.

"Heat, ma'am," he replied. "Folks got work to do."

He bit the bottom inside of his lip. Them two things weren't exactly related, but the answer seemed to satisfy Apostle Reesa. She kept quiet the whole rest of the way up the steps and into the town hall. He finally slipped his arms from around their necks. Getting kind of tiring, that.

Going to the door, Gig opened it and held it to usher the apostles inside. "Right this way," he said. "It's just through here, in Mayor Big City's office."

They went in first, and Gig followed, taking in a deep gulp of air. Smelled like warm, warped wood inside, like dust and ghosts. It was his favorite smell in all of Big City. This was what authority smelled like.

He led them down the short hall to the door marked Office and pulled that one open too, revealing the cozy little room filled with filing cabinets, his desk and the mayor's desk, a couple of chairs, and the comm unit. Apostle Joule stopped dead in the doorway when he saw the comm upon Mayor Big City's desk.

"That's the latest model," he whispered.

Apostle Joule approached the comm like it was a wolf asleep and he wanted to catch it. When he got to the desk he ran his hands all over it—all over the plastic screen, all over the scan pad, the telegraph printer, and the thick silver wire that connected the whole thing together. Looked like he was in love.

"Will it recognize me or will you need to scan me in as admin?" Apostle Joule asked.

Gig wasn't sure what "admin" was, but he did know the thing would let anybody use it. "It'll recognize you," he replied. "Don't have much security on it."

Apostle Joule nodded and set his hand down on the scan pad. The screen lit up in yellow when he did. A second or two ticked by before the comm went *bing* and the screen switched to blue, displaying the menu. Apostle Joule flipped through the glowing circles rather quickly, eventually settling on one called *Options* where he pulled up the settings.

Gig had looked there too, but hell if he knew what he was doing. This always happened with their comm units. The settings looked perfectly fine, but the static interference was something else entirely. He'd long since figured it was an outside problem, but it didn't hurt to have a professional take a peek.

"Look okay?" he asked, craning his neck to see what Apostle Joule was doing on the screen.

"Looks fine," the man replied. "The code is meant to be simple. Anyone can rewrite it if something goes wrong. This is perfect."

"Which means?"

"It's not a problem with your unit. Here, let me try something."

Gig smiled privately to himself as the apostle pulled a little handheld out of his jacket pocket. He *knew* it hadn't been a problem with the unit, and the Theocracy just kept shipping them the latest models like it *was*. He'd outsmarted the government for once. The Big City comm started ringing and Apostle Joule tapped on the *Incoming Call* circle as it popped up on the screen.

The call clicked in with a lot of unholy yapping from both devices. Signal was fuzzy as always and Apostle Joule frowned at the double image of himself displayed on both screens and the Joules on the screens frowned back. A screech and three loud pops and the signal cut out, the call disconnected.

"Always does that," Gig supplied.

"Strange..." Apostle Joule murmured.

"I don't think we've seen anything like it," Apostle Reesa said.

"Happens all the time," Gig said. "The unit goes screwy after a few months, so the Theocracy sends us a new one, then after a while the new ones break down too."

"That would explain how you got your hands on a Gen-27," Apostle Joule grumbled, ferreting away through the code again.

"You're very lucky, Deputy-Sheriff Big City," Apostle Reesa smiled—by god, she looked familiar when she did that, too. "You have the best piece of tech you possibly could."

Who was it the apostle reminded him of? Where had he seen her face before? Lord and Saints it was going to drive him mad if he didn't figure it out soon. Mayor Big City burst into the office. Gig yipped in surprise. He'd forgotten to tell Hicks his plan for distracting the apostles with the comm, and he was already on the mayor's shitlist for having failed to keep the apostles inside in the first place. He'd have to get them out of the office ASAP. The look in Hicks's eyes said so.

"Let's don't worry about it anymore for today, Apostle," he said, taking hold of Joule's elbow and pulling him slowly away from the screen. "It's your first day here after all. No need to put you to work so soon."

He grabbed hold of Reesa too and led the both of them to the door, then out into the hall. He released his grip, then slipped back inside and closed the door softly behind him.

Gig Sullivan was a goddamn fool. Hicks would have given a limb or three to have had Freddie Dunstan back, but he wouldn't get his hopes up. Either the takers had kidnapped him or Tombstone had killed him, and no matter which he wasn't coming back. He glared fiercely at Gig, his sad sorry excuse for a deputy-sheriff.

"How's it on the street, sir?" Gig asked.

"Cleaned up," Hicks replied.

"That's good."

"I need to report the incident."

He would do no such thing, but this was his failsafe. He'd filled out an official report for every kidnapping, every killing executed by the takers and/or Tombstone. He'd never sent them, but he could blame that on the static. If the Theo found out about the takers, he could claim they should have always known. He could claim he'd told them and maybe still retain his position. Even if Russia rose from the dust and rained down another nuclear thunderstorm, Hicks would hold onto Big City. It was in his blood.

He nudged Gig out of the way—the office was just too damn small—and sat down at their new machine. He eyeballed it for a second. Would this one cut through the static? If it would his failsafe wouldn't be much for safety.

"Lord and Saints!"

Gig's exclamation nearly toppled Hicks out of his chair. He glared fiercely at the deputy-sheriff. Didn't like being spooked.

"I'm sorry, sir, it's just that I remembered who that woman apostle makes me think of."

Hicks raised his eyebrows.

"Merrick."

"Huh." She did look something like Tombstone's wife.

"Weren't she kidnapped?"

Hicks pulled up a fresh telegraph document on the screen, began to type. "Kidnapped or killed," he replied. "Hard to be sure with Tombstone."

Gig sat, plopping into the chair in front of his own desk. "Still, it's strange though."

That it was, but Hicks was too deep into his report to reply. He made an affirmative grunting noise instead and called that good enough. Gig would understand.

"Maybe it ain't just Merrick, though," he continued, taking his hat from his head and whirling it around on a finger.

Hicks stopped typing. He sat up. "What do you mean?"

Gig shrugged. "Maybe it ain't just Merrick she reminds me of."

"Who else?"

"Dunno…maybe Cassandra."

He gave Gig a flat stare. Another one of the kidnapped women. The sun had finally fried Gig's mind. Hicks said nothing, and returned to his typing. He would not be including such strange speculations in his fake report. The document had to at least *look* real.

Darling could have burst right out of her skin. It weren't everyday Big City got new apostles. It weren't *never* Big City got new apostles. She had planned a special party just for them.

She'd been waiting their arrival on pins and needles since Mayor Big City had shown them all their pictures. The man—he was *so* handsome with that blonde hair, and the woman, well, she was just about the most beautiful thing on the planet, and they were both so *stylish* Darling just couldn't wait to have them in her life.

Soon as Ben was cleaned up, she went door to door gathering everyone who wasn't already out on the street. She weren't about to let a killing ruin her party. She was Darling Shank and Darling Shank *always* kept people happy.

Nearly everybody had found their way to the square, and the ranchers should have been coming in any second, and Darling only had one more door to knock on. She rapped her knuckles on Doctor Fencer's door and waited. She looked pretty. Didn't think he would say no. She'd been to his house so many times to check the town genealogy records as she was wanting to get married soon and you couldn't be too careful in Big City, seeing as everyone was so close. She'd figured out that way that she and Doctor Fencer himself were the farthest related and she'd been eyeing him ever since. Imagine *her*, a doctor's wife. Made her giddy just thinking about it.

Fencer pulled open the door and looked at her through the blonde hair that fell into his eyes. Once they were married, she would see if she couldn't get him to trim it.

"Party's starting," she said. "We're just about to go greet the apostles. They're in the town hall with Gig."

"I'll put my shoes on," he replied.

"See you soon, then."

With a little giggle she turned and hopped down from his porch. She was about to go, but he called her back.

"Darling?"

"Yes?"

"You look lovely tonight."

She flashed him a smile. "Thank you." He knew as well as she did that she was his best candidate for marriage. And she knew he knew.

Darling dashed back up to the square. Fencer could find her later if he wanted, though she would be serving at the saloon and would be busy and would want to talk to the apostles every chance she got. Her brother met her as she reached the fringe of the crowd.

"You get Fencer?" Seth asked.

"Sure did," Darling smiled. "Now let's get the apostles."

She looped her arm through his and led him expertly through the crowd up to the front. Her other brother Junior and their father Edward Shank spied them as they went and latched on to follow. Darling was in charge of this party, and Darling would see to it everybody had fun. Having a little trail of people follow her every move and command was all rather exciting.

Once she reached the front of the crowd she released her hold on Seth's arm and placed her hands around her mouth before calling out, "Let's get to the town hall, everyone!" With a wave of her arm she started off and the whole of Big City followed her.

As they reached the bottom of the steps, the apostles appeared in the town hall's front windows coming down the hall and a hush fell over the crowd. Darling, too. She couldn't help it, they were just such beautiful people—like celebrities almost. They came through the door, and they were talking.

"That was odd," Apostle Joule was saying.

"You think?" Apostle Reesa replied.

"I've never seen anything like—"

They looked up simultaneously and noticed the crowd. Big City stared at the apostles and the apostles stared at Big City. Darling's heart beat fast in her chest. She stepped forward.

"We want to welcome you to Big City," Darling said.

"…Thank…you?" Apostle Reesa kept her gaze on the crowd like she expected them to eat her up.

"We have a little something planned for you. Follow me."

Darling turned and the crowd turned with her, all at once. It made her giggle. She was the master of ceremonies, the leader of the circus. She'd never seen a real circus, they never stopped in Big City, but she'd looked at plenty of picture books and she figured this feeling right now, that was how a ringmaster felt every day.

The apostles did not follow, so she paused at the bottom of the steps and waited for them. Apostle Reesa first came down and Darling smiled brightly.

"I planned a party the *minute* I heard we were getting apostles in Big City," she said, and grasped Reesa's hand. "I know you're not allowed to drink, so I had Marty order seltzer water for you."

Darling couldn't help herself; she took off, towing Apostle Reesa through the crowd. They lost her partner somewhere behind them.

"I'm Darling, by the way."

"Apostle Reesa."

She beamed back at her. "I know."

Apostle Reesa was going to have the best time at this party that she'd ever had in her life or Darling Shank wasn't Darling Shank.

4

In the hubbub of the mass exodus to the saloon, Reesa had lost Joule somewhere among the other citizens as the two of them were swept along with the crowd. Blessedly, the citizens were all more interested in obtaining their alcohol to pay much more attention to her and Joule once the party reached the saloon. Darling seated Reesa at the bar and scurried off just as Joule reappeared, gasping and popping his head above the crowd like he'd been carried away on a rip tide and was swimming back to shore. He waded his way over to Reesa and collapsed on one of the stools.

"Glad to see you could make it," she said, smiling down at him.

"At least it's a welcome party and not a hanging," he replied.

"It could still *be* a hanging."

He glared up at her and she laughed. King of can't-take-a-joke, that was Joule. Grunting, he hauled himself up onto the top of the stool he'd collapsed on and sat next to her like a human being. They turned their gaze to the interior of the saloon, packed from floor to ceiling with the Big City population. Most had found their way to tables by then, others continued to weave between the chairs, lean against the walls or against the banister of an upstairs balcony. What the saloon might have looked like empty was unimaginable it was so full of people. One hundred and six, well, one hundred and eight now. Didn't sound like much until you tried to pack them into a single room.

A pocket of space hung around herself and Joule, a little no man's land, a buffer between apostles and flock. The stools on either side of them stood empty. Reesa looked into the crowd and smiled, but those her eyes fell on turned away. At once, Darling popped up in front of her.

"These are for you," she said, gingerly handing them each a glass of seltzer water.

Joule eyed the glass like it was a dead snake, held it between two fingers. "Thank you."

Darling laughed a twittery, giggling laugh, her brunette ringlets bouncing as she did. "This has just *got* to be the most exciting day of my life," she cooed. "Apostles in Big City!"

"Darling! Gin here!"

"Coming!"

With a squeal, she flitted back to her duties, hurrying from table to table, to a back room, to the upstairs carrying beers and gins and all sorts of liquids of varying shades of brown to her customers. Joule set his glass down on the counter and scooted it away.

"How late are we obliged to stay?" he asked, glancing at Reesa.

"I'd say until you're no longer enjoying yourself, but if that were the case we'd have to leave now." She gave him a sideways smile.

"You're hilarious."

"Relax, Joule," she said and nudged him playfully. "This is a good place to get to know people, start putting names with faces."

"If they're all going to be names like Darling and Hicks and Gig, I don't care to put them with any faces at all," he grumbled, placing his hands over his eyes, rubbing for a moment, and then dragging them down the length of his face while letting out a great sigh. "But I suppose you're right."

"I'm always right."

"Hardly."

In front of them, a couple stepped across the line into the no man's land. Both Reesa and Joule looked up at the stubby gentleman covered in a thick forest of wiry copper hair, a long shiny ponytail of which spilled from his head down his back, and the woman, taller and built sturdy with wide hips and working hands. Reesa smiled. Joule did not.

"Hello," the coppery fellow said.

"Hello," Reesa replied.

"Name's Callum." He stuck out a meaty hand. "Blacksmith. This is Nana. Wife."

Reesa sat forward on her stool and shook Callum's hand, then Nana's. Joule was forced to follow suit, barely masking his reluctance.

"Apostle Reesa, and this is my partner, Apostle Joule."

Callum gave a curt nod, *understood*, it seemed to say, and gestured with a flicking finger at the seats on either side of them.

"Mind if we join you?"

Reesa perked up. "Please do."

No sooner had Callum lumbered into the seat beside Joule, and Nana plopped down in the one next to Reesa, than Darling had appeared to take their orders.

"Hello, hello," she trilled. "What'll it be?"

"Seltzer water," Nana gushed. "It's been *ages*."

"An ale for me, Darling," Callum said.

In a flash Darling bounced away, still giggling and grinning like a mad gull. Had Nana said it had been ages since she'd had seltzer water? Ages? What constituted an age around here? It was carbonated water, nothing special. Just how tight *was* the Big City budget? Reesa's grip around her own glass tensed unconsciously. By her side, Callum struck up a conversation with Joule about the price of beef in the city.

"Darling's a sweet one," Nana said, leaning into Reesa in that motherly way older women have when they talk about the young. "Keeping everybody happy."

"That's admirable," Reesa replied.

"But impossible."

"Oh."

Reesa's eyebrows lowered a little; she waited for Nana to continue but the woman did not, just sat with her hands tucked up in her lap and looked out on the crowd. She'd backed Reesa up against a wall whether or not it was intentional, and Reesa had no choice but to let it sit until she could think of something else to say. Which, for the moment, she couldn't.

Instead she joined Nana in her scan of the crowd. What sorts of people were these dusty, sun-dried individuals? What did living in such a small town do to your brain? She looked over all the faces in her field of vision, noticing among them common traits: Big-City-blue eyes, wide rim noses, a particular bend in the jawline. Probably everybody in Big City was at *least* cousins with everybody else. They'd been isolated for, what? Two hundred years? Such a long time in such a limited gene pool...

Her gaze fell upon the corner to her right and upon a figure in partial shadow. He sat alone in a bubble not unlike the one formerly surrounding herself and Joule, sipping at a honey-brown liquid in a short glass. He must have sensed her eyes on him because he looked up, and looked right at her.

His was the most beautiful face she had ever seen.

"Reesa?"

She snapped her attention back to Joule at the sound of her name, releasing a great gasp of air and the grip she had on her stomach. Cold wetness spread across her lap. She'd been spilling her seltzer water on her legs.

"Oh!"

Righting the glass and ditching it on the counter, Reesa took the napkin Joule passed her and began mopping herself up. He tried to catch her eye as she pressed the square of fabric into her lap.

"Are you all right?"

"Oh, um, yes, fine. I'm fine." She let her hair fall in a curtain around her face to hide her blushing. She could still feel that man's eyes on her from the corner.

"Are you sure?"

"*Yes*, Joule. I'm sure," she replied, suppressing an eye roll. That was one of the worst things about Joule—the double question asking, just to be "sure."

He frowned, but sat back on his stool and got out of her face. "All right…"

Though the napkin was soaked through and her pants still mostly un-dry, Reesa continued to wipe absently until Joule resumed his conversation with Callum. She did not listen, she waited until she could no longer feel those eyes on her and glanced up, ever so slightly, from her lap the moment she felt their scrutiny lift.

Her stomach turned over and so did her heart, a strange twisting feeling like tightening a rope. Again, that absolute beauty struck her. She had a clear view of the man, peeking up from her lap, and she let her eyes wander across the fine curve of his jaw to the radiant brown of his eyes, the white hat atop a head of fantastic coffee-colored curls. He was different from the others—a little brighter, a little less brow-beaten, perhaps. Tall, and confident in his isolation. He was familiar to her. Her eyes *knew* him.

Darling returned that moment with drinks for Callum and Nana and before she could even set them down, Reesa darted out a hand and grasped her arm.

"Darling, who is that man?" she asked, her voice barely audible in her own ears.

The girl leaned over slightly to follow Reesa's line of sight, and once she saw who it was, she straightened and set the ale and seltzer on the counter.

"That's Tombstone," she answered.

"Tombstone?"

Darling shrugged. "Everybody calls him that. A rancher. Lives out on Little Hadham."

Reesa did not know where Little Hadham was. She nodded, prying her eyes, which seemed desperately to want to cling to Tombstone, away from the corner. She focused on Darling instead.

"Why isn't anyone sitting by him?"

Callum let out a snort, took a sip of his ale, then pointed a thick finger at Reesa. "Because they're afraid of him, Apostle."

Her attention flicked to Callum. "Why?"

"He's the only one to escape the takers."

A shiver passed through her. "Takers?"

Sipping again, Callum nodded. "His wife and him got snatched up. He came back. She didn't. Some say he did it."

"Did what?"

"Killed her."

Joule, who had finally deigned to take a drink of his seltzer water, choked and sprayed the liquid everywhere, spluttering and coughing.

"*What?*" he gasped.

Callum only shrugged. Joule turned his horrified expression on Reesa, but she could only shrug as well. Her eyes ached, wanting to gaze back at the corner where Tombstone sat. She kept them in check, but only for a few seconds before her heart began winding up inside her chest again.

"I'm going to go introduce myself to him," she announced, and stood up immediately.

Joule grabbed her and yanked her back. "What? No. That is a potential *murderer*, Reesa." He had always been paranoid about being stabbed to death in his bed by serial killers. Then again he was paranoid about most things.

"Don't bother with Tombstone, Apostle," Callum said. "Ain't gonna bring you nothing but trouble."

Reesa looked at him, blinking, but he made no additional comment. Nana picked up the thread and continued where her husband left off.

"Tombstone's a godless man, Apostle Reesa," she said. "Stubborn and sticky and not wanting to do with anyone."

"All the more reason to reach out to him then."

She prized her elbow from Joule's grasp with a triumphant, holy smile. She was going no matter what they said. Hell, she probably would have gone to talk to him even if he'd been waving a gun above his head and frothing at the mouth. Her heart demanded it of her. Though she technically was no longer allowed to say "hell" now that she was an apostle. Regardless. Grabbing her glass of seltzer water, she departed the bar, leaving Callum and Nana shaking their heads and Joule scrambling to think of something to stop her.

As she made her way through the crowd, she tried to think of something to say, but she arrived at Tombstone's table long before anything came to mind, so she just stood there, puzzling. He did not look up at her approach.

"Apostle Reesa," she said eventually, extending a hand.

"I know what you are, *Apostle*."

He spat the last word out like it was a bad taste. It stung. Quite a lot, actually, though his voice sounded like honey. She cleared her throat and tried again.

"Do you mind if I join you?"

"Free country."

A lump formed in her throat and she swallowed at it as she pulled out the chair across from him and sat cautiously down. Tombstone said nothing, sipping his drink. He was *supposed* to be happy for her company, right? A little kid at a lunchroom table all by himself on his first day at a new school halfway through the year? No, Reesa was the new kid, the intruder. This was *his* territory.

"Isn't this the part where you tell me your name?" People said stuff like that, right? She tried to look coy as the words tumbled out, batting her eyelashes though it didn't come naturally.

"It's Tombstone."

She pretended she didn't already know that, letting out a laugh that sounded forced. "Nobody's parents are *that* cruel," she replied.

"You haven't met Chivalry and Honor, then."

"Hm? Honor's not so bad a name." Chivalry she would have to agree with.

"It is if you were castrated for raping your sister's best friend."

She still didn't—wait…castrated? Reesa opened her mouth to ask if she'd heard him right, but Tombstone had already moved on.

"Why are you here, apostle?" he asked, turning his eyes on her in a hard stare. She squirmed. "To introduce myself."

"No, in Big City."

"We were ordained here."

"Clearly. Why?"

"The Theocracy never discloses information like that to civilians," she snipped, bristling, though she should not have. Shifting in her seat, Reesa smoothed her ruffled feathers. "Apostles are sent where their skills can do the most good."

"And what are *your* skills?"

She didn't like the way he raised his eyebrows at her, the forward little smile that pulled at one side of his mouth as he leaned on an elbow and propped his chin up in his hand. In a huff she folded her arms and fought to keep down a blush.

"Why are *you* here?"

"I live here, Apostle."

"Very long?"

"You'd do well to realize now that those of us who live in Big City are trapped. We're all born in the same dirt we'll bleed and die in until the in-breeding takes its hold and a disease wipes every last one of us out."

Reesa blinked. Tombstone sipped his drink. The loud mumble of the crowd crept in at the corners of their silence. At least *someone* else had noticed the in-breeding. Who was Tombstone related to in particular? And why, if everyone was practically family, did they steer so far away from him? She wanted to ask, but she didn't dare. Still, she was not quite ready to leave the table. Thankfully Tombstone spoke first.

"Your partner at the bar. Apostle Joule, right?"

Reesa nodded, a friendly smile finding its way onto her face. "Yes."

"How does that work?"

"How does what work?"

He gestured between herself and Joule with a waving hand. "That," he said, making no clarification at all.

"You mean our relationship?" she asked, her eyebrows knitting together.

"Sure."

She still didn't understand the question. "Joule and I were matched to each other about three months before the end of our apostolic training," she explained. "After that we went through our matrimony and were ordained out here. This is our first assignment."

"So you *are* married, then?"

"All apostles are married to their partners." How could he not know that?

Chuckling, Tombstone sat back once more in his seat, shaking his head in what could only be described as disbelief. Goosebumps rose up on her arms at the sound of it, so dark and lovely. He gestured between her and Joule again.

"Then the two of you have…?"

She cocked her head to one side. "Have what?"

He laughed out loud at that. "You don't take my meaning?"

Reesa shook her head. "I'm afraid not."

Adjusting himself to lean on his elbow across the table, Tombstone drew a little closer to Reesa. She couldn't help but lean forward into him.

"The Theocracy ships you out in couples, all married and ready to go," he said. "Doesn't that seem like a rather intense solution to such a small problem?"

"What problem?"

"Sex, Apostle."

At once a red-hot flush swept into her features and she snapped back away from him, her mouth falling open, her arms folding across her chest, her eyes glaring embarrassed at the floor. Heat rose palpably from her skin. A sensitive topic anyway, only made worse by the fact that the appalling man in front of her presented *exactly* that kind of temptation. She pushed that thought to the back of her mind.

Apparently satisfied, Tombstone sat back and polished off his glass. Darling was upon them before he could set it down on the table.

"Can I bring you another?" she asked, her lashes fluttering rather attractively and not at all like Reesa's as she turned her eyes brightly to her feet.

"No," Tombstone replied, rising. "Thank you, Darling."

She blocked him as he began to go. "You saved us again today. Like you always do."

"Here." He handed her a few bills retrieved from the inner pocket of his jacket. "That should more than cover it."

When Darling separated out the money for her tip and tucked it provocatively away in her bodice, the blush in Reesa's cheeks rose up all over again. The barmaid blocked Tombstone a second time as he tried to take a step around her.

"I took some water to Indie," she said, "so she should be ready for the ride home."

"Thank you, Darling."

"You're welcome, sir."

Dazed, she stared up at him and neglected to move out of his way until he gave her a rather pointed smile, put his hands on her bare shoulders, and scooted her to the side. A little string of trilling laughter slipped out of her lips as she found her feet and moved out of his way, the rest of the way, on her own. Free, Tombstone swept away and quickly disappeared into the crowd which parted like the Red Sea before him.

Darling leaned against the back of Reesa's chair and sighed. "Ain't he beautiful?"

Reesa was about to agree, but she checked herself with an awkward cough. Darling looked down at her and she quickly replaced her current expression for one of piety—one she might give a sinner coming to confessional.

"You'd make a handsome couple, Darling," she replied.

The barmaid's eyes went wide, almost cartoonish. "Me and Tombstone?" She gaped for a moment, as if fully processing the thought, and then erupted with laughter. "He's nice to look at ma'am, but that's all. Ain't nobody ever going to be sweet with him again."

She picked up Tombstone's empty glass and walked away, still snorting and giggling like Reesa's comment was the world's funniest joke. A little trod-on, Reesa rose and returned to her place at the bar, clutching her seltzer water in an iron grip. In her absence, Joule and Nana had switched places so she could sit beside her husband. Her partner eyed her as she climbed into the empty seat.

"How'd it go?" he asked.

"What?"

He frowned. "Reesa, are you *sure* you're feeling all right?"

She shot him a glare, daring him to ask her one more time if she was all right. She could have stone-cold slapped him, but managed to keep control of her limbs. She wasn't even going to answer his question, reinforce the behavior. Apparently she would have to train her partner like she'd train a dog. Tombstone's words crept back into her mind, tingling and warm with attraction but she shoved them away. Joule was her husband. *Joule.*

Her eyes wandered to the corner where he'd been sitting, into the crowd in the direction he'd taken when he'd departed. She knew him somehow. Her heart did, her eyes did. But where had she seen him before?

Curiosity plagued her the rest of the evening.

5

As he stepped out onto the saloon porch, Huxley realized just how dark it had become since he'd gone inside. He hated that—going in some place in the afternoon and coming out after the sun had set, but that was winter: eternal darkness and seasonal affective disorder.

In the interim between his entrance and exit, all the Big City Christmas lights had come on, twinkling. The red and white striped lights that glittered on the saloon cast a long shadow out in front of him. He stood and looked at it for a moment. That female apostle... He'd thought she'd looked like Merrick when the Theocracy had sent them pictures and they'd passed them around the town, but in the flesh it was entirely too much. Her hair. He'd wondered throughout their whole conversation if it smelled the same. Her eyes... A spitting image of his dead wife was hardly the thing he needed at the moment.

"Hey, Tombstone."

The voice made him jump, but he covered it, glancing in its direction and finding Randy standing in front of the hitching post petting the nose of his big black horse. Indie snorted when she saw him and Randy casually wiped the resulting spray of snot from her hands onto her pant leg. The girl smiled when she looked his way. He couldn't help but return it.

"Hey, Randy."

As he came forward she scooted aside to allow him room to untie the rope securing Indie to the post though he didn't do so right away.

"How's things?" she asked.

He shook his head. "Not good."

"Ben Greeber got taken today."

"Yeah."

"You meet the new apostles?"

Nodding, Huxley sighed. "I don't anticipate getting along with either of them."

Randy shrugged. "They're okay."

She was the only one who could stand to be around him. At just thirteen she'd probably experienced more pain than any of the others, himself excluded, having lost both of her parents in the same series of taker kidnappings in which he'd lost Merrick. She'd stuck to him after they'd disappeared, unafraid of the darkness in his eyes, unafraid of his gun. They stood in silence, Randy stroking Indie's muzzle, Huxley staring fixedly at the dirt.

"You haven't been out to see Statia and the little Greebers yet."

It was a statement, not a question, and it stung. Randy must have noticed him flinch because her face fell into an apologetic expression.

"You have to go," she said.

He shoved his hands into his pockets. "I will."

Had to go deliver the news that he'd killed their husband and father.

Randy regarded him for a moment, blinking long and slow as she studied his expression. Gingerly she stepped forward and put her arms around him in a hug. Huxley would have been caught off guard had she not come at him so carefully.

"You're sad about Merrick today," she said. "It's okay to be sad."

A pained puff of breath escaped his lips. The sting of tears threatened his eyes, but he fought it down, patting Randy on the back as she released him. He offered her a pathetic smile.

"I'll ride out to talk to the Greebers tonight," he said, moving decidedly around the hitching post to untie Indie.

"I'll unlock the gate for you."

Together he and Randy walked the horse from the square through the line of lit-up houses to the bottom end of Big City. Randy went to the gate and began fiddling with the lock as he swung himself up onto Indie's back. The horse trotted forward and Randy wheeled open the gate, the only part of the outside fence that wasn't crackling with electricity. He nudged Indie forward and took off as soon as they were clear. The vague sounds of Randy wheeling the gate shut once more echoed across the desert.

Darkness prevailed out in the wastes with the Big City lights left behind. Huxley rode hard. He knew the way to the Greeber ranch, every other sector of occupied land lay in line with Big City itself. One only had to turn left or right once exiting the gate and continue on straight in order to get somewhere. The Greebers owned the tobacco fields three sectors away to the west.

The whistle of wind and the furious buzz of bugs engulfed his ears. The desert came alive at night, howling and hooting and making an echoing din as sleeping things emerged from their holes for the hunt. He'd learned the hard way to lock his animals up at night when a pack of wolves had mauled three of his best purebreds.

Half an hour ticked away while he rode. The McCallister ranch house slid by on his right, then the Hatfields'. Some undeterminable distance away, the wolves made yowling calls to their comrades. Through the scrub bushes, live things scurried out of his path. When he reached his destination and swung himself down, his heart beat fast with exercise and apprehension. The Greebers' cabin was lit up in bright yellow light, great shafts of it pouring out the windows. He walked Indie forward and tied the horse to a staff that held one half of a clothesline in the air. The laundry fluttered in the night breeze.

A scream split the air. A figure flitted across the view through a window, clutching something in its hands. A second shadow lurched after it. Huxley dashed forward, leaving Indie mostly unsecured, and slammed against the door when the locked knob did not turn in his hands. He slapped his open palm against the wood.

"Statia! Statia, it's Tombstone! Unlock the door!"

More shrieking answered him. Nobody came to the door. Lifting his gun from his belt, he grasped the barrel firmly and brought the butt down with a crash against the door knob. He was counting on the aged wood to give way, which it did, but not without a few more solid whacks. He kicked down the door and stumbled into the light.

His eyes fell on a fresh nightmare. Statia Greeber perched on her table in the middle of the cabin's single room, lofting a cast iron pan over her head and feigning swings at a creature Huxley had seen and killed too many times— someone else had been taken. The process had wreaked its full effect on the body by this time. The human to whom the blood and bones used to belong was no longer recognizable. As he powered up his pistol, Huxley wondered how long Statia had been fighting it off.

Tears of fear streamed down the woman's cheeks and she looked at Huxley with pleading, wide-eyed terror. The taken swiped for her leg and she whacked at its arm with her pan. It connected and the creature hissed, spitting mucus and yanking the limb out of her reach.

A chime signaled the readiness of his weapon, but as Huxley shifted to take better aim, something wriggled on the floor. Another body. Taken. It was struggling to rise, shrieking and screeching. Statia must have knocked that one out. Its head was all smashed in. Huxley shot it twice. A jolt snapped through it and it slumped lifelessly on the kitchen floor.

The gunshots nailed the other taken's attention to Huxley. It abandoned Statia in a fit of self-preservation and bolted for the back door. As it tried to claw its way up and out, its flesh caught on a coat hook and it stuck. It wriggled violently, an inhuman scream generating from somewhere deep inside it as it tried to free itself. Huxley shot it in the head. With a final bursting scream, it hung limp on the coat hook.

Atop the table, Statia collapsed into a fit of sobs. The pan slipped from her hand and clattered to the floor. Huxley tucked his gun away and stepped carefully around the taken on the floor. He placed a gentle hand on Statia's shaking shoulder and helped her to climb down, easing her into a kitchen chair.

"It was Ben! It was Ben…" Her fingers fluttered all over her face. "He came and he got them. He got them, too."

She clutched her arms to her middle and rocked back and forth in place. Her mouth was open and contorted in a wail of turmoil, but no sound came out. Every breath she drew in was a gasp, like she'd been dunked in ice water. Huxley tried to take her hands, meet her eyes, but she was unresponsive.

"He came, he came, he got them, my babies, my babies!"

Max and Swan. The taken were her children. Two boys Huxley had known since the day they were born were both dead at his hands—one on the floor, the other at the door. After Ben had been taken he must have made it out to the ranch and caught them.

"Statia, can you tell me what happened? Do you know what happened?"

He worked to catch her eye, prompt her to speak. Statia could only return a glassy stare as tears watered over the lip of her eyelids.

"He came…in the morning he came through the field. I knew it was him. I knew it was Ben. I tried to shout, but Max couldn't hear me. Swan went to save his brother. I ran. I knew there wasn't any hope."

She raised her hand to wipe her eyes and as she did the two of them noticed a smeared mucus handprint on her forearm. Statia began to shake. A few words tumbled out of her mouth:

"Lord and Saints…"

Her eyes flashed to Huxley and they regarded each other in horror. She'd been taken. All at once the shaking overcame her body and her fingers knotted up in her hair. Shooting to her feet she paced rapidly about the room.

"I'm dead, I'm dead, I'm dead. Lord and Saints, Lord and Saints. I'm dead. He got me. He got me!" She dashed suddenly up to Huxley and grasped the front of his jacket, giving him a good rattle. "Kill me! Please kill me, Tombstone!"

Huxley only just managed to shake her off and she sunk into the kitchen chair, sobbing all over again and pleading in a whisper, "Please, please shoot me. I don't want to become one of those things…"

She lifted her begging eyes to him as her bottom lip began to quiver, spilling out *please please please* over and over again. He didn't have a choice. For two years he'd worked on finding an antibody to reverse the taking process. For two years he had failed day after day. Statia was as good as dead. He put on a harder mask of nonchalance than the one he'd already been wearing and raised the gun to her head.

"I'm sorry, Statia."

The bullet left his gun.

Quietly, Huxley abandoned the house, turning off the lights and letting the door swing closed behind him. No one would see the mess he had made; no one would come out to the Greebers' at all. An entire family in one day. He was Tombstone, icon of death.

He mounted Indie, started off, and quite by accident found himself at the gate to Big City. He had not intended to go back to town, but his mind was too occupied by the bullet coming out the back of Statia's head. A scream began to gather inside him, rolling and ready to burst, when he noticed Randy lingering by the gate. The girl was sitting on top of a crate, head propped up on her elbows, waiting for him to return. She perked up as Indie drew near the fence. Huxley did not dismount.

Randy came up to the gate, lacing her fingers in the chain link. "Did you tell them?"

His teeth came down hard on his bottom lip. It took him a moment, but he managed to answer coolly, "Yeah. I told them."

Randy smiled a sad sort of smile. "Good."

A tight nod was all she got in response. He could only see her mother and her father looking at him, dragged away screaming in the middle of the night, himself so far away and powerless. That was two years ago. Felt like yesterday.

Her hands slipped from the fence and she waved at him. "G'night, Tombstone."

"Good night, Randy."

She faded from his view into the shadows and the colored lights of the houses at the bottom of Big City, but when she went she did not take her parents' ghosts with her.

He rode back home through the dark, put Indie away in the barn with the other horses, and trod sluggishly over the gravel pathway to his empty little house. Inside, he fetched a bottle of his strongest whiskey and a photograph of Merry from the mantle and sat down at the table. He took a long draw from the bottle, but he was already trembling before he could swallow it. That night he put his head down on the table and sobbed until he fell asleep.

6

Joule awoke the following morning to scuffling sounds not unlike the thousand and one rats he imagined lived under the Big City Hotel. He opened his eyes slowly—if there were rats, he wasn't positive how badly he wanted to see them—and peeped out from beneath the crusty covers of his horrid bed. It was Reesa—bustling about the room like a bird flown in through the window.

"What are you doing?" he croaked on sleep-coated vocal cords.

She seemed to notice him for the first time, saying, "Good. You're awake," and leaping onto the bed. The metal let out a terrific screech as it nearly buckled under her abruptly added weight. Joule covered his head with the sheets and clutched on for dear life, waiting for the inevitable crash that did not come. Eventually he pulled back the covers and squinted up at Reesa. Why was it so ghastly *bright* in this room?

"How long have you been up?" he asked.

"Since dawn."

An expansive groan rolled out of Joule's throat. Dawn? This woman was inhuman. He buried himself under the cover of the bedspread once more.

"The sunrise is too bright," Reesa said. "We need some thicker curtains."

"We're probably even lucky to *have* curtains in this godforsaken place…" he grumbled into a pillow.

"What?"

"Nevermind." He sat up, looked at her. "You're certainly gleeful this morning."

"I'm excited," she replied, hunching her shoulders up around her ears and grinning. She was like a kid at Christmas, in fact, she *had* been the night before when they'd come out of the saloon and the whole town was lit up in Christmas lights, running down the street and laughing. How did she have the energy? "Today is the first official day of our ordination. I want to make it a good one."

He eyed her, lips pursed. "Did you get *any* sleep?"

She laughed. "Of course I did."

He knew she hated it when he asked her about her health, but he couldn't help but worry, she was such a troublesome woman. "You don't look it."

"*You* don't look it, grumpy."

He scoffed, whipping back the bedspread. "Don't be ridiculous," he said and let his feet hover just above the floor while he sought out his shoes. He slipped them on before standing. God only knew what sorts of molds and microscopic burrowing creatures lived in the wood. He went to the dresser, shaking an image of the floor crawling with bugs from his imagination.

The bed squeaked as Reesa flopped onto her back in the space he'd left. "Do you want to set some goals for today?"

"I think that would be wise," he answered.

The top drawer stuck when he pulled on the handle. He tried again, giving it a good yank, but the dresser maintained its chokehold. How was he supposed to get dressed? How was he supposed to deal with this wretched dresser for what felt like would be the remainder of his mortal life? He braced himself against the bottom legs and *pulled*. The drawer popped powerfully out and his feet slipped in surprise. Reesa snickered. He shot her a dirty look.

"Sorry." She covered her mouth apologetically. "What should we put on the list?"

"I'd like to contact Apostle Tess about fixing the comm in the town hall," he said, rummaging around, finding a fresh uniform, removing the pants and stepping into them with some difficulty.

"It would help if you took your shoes *off,* Joule."

"I'm not putting my feet on this floor," he declared, getting his second leg into the pants with a tough yank. He started to stuff himself into a shirt and jacket. "What would you like to add to the list?"

"I'd like to hold a meeting. Give everyone a chance to voice their immediate needs and concerns, maybe even place an order for supplies tonight."

She was handing him a brush before he could even start looking.

"Should I be writing this down?" she asked.

"I think we can remember two goals."

Nodding, she sat quietly and watched him brush his hair. She'd been doing that a lot lately, watching him get ready like she was going to be quizzed on it later. He didn't know what his hair looked like, seeing as there wasn't a mirror in their room, but he called it quits what with Reesa's eyes on the back of his neck. He set the brush down.

"We can ask the mayor about a good space to hold a meeting," he said as he turned to face her. "He shouldn't be hard to find."

"I don't think *anyone* would be hard to find around here, Joule."

He snorted. She was right. There weren't very many places you could be. "You ready?"

"Mm-hm."

She rolled off the bed onto her feet and gestured for him to lead the charge. He was as ready as he was ever going to be. Heading for the door he braced himself for the heat and the backwards people, for bad breath and dust and dirt, and when he turned the knob in his hands and pulled open the door, there was Shay—pocket-sized hotel clerk—standing smack dab at the end of the hall, half-shrouded in shadow. Joule jumped back. How *long* had he been standing out there?

"Will you take breakfast now?" Shay asked, his lips barely moving.

What was he supposed to say? Did he respond? Did he pretend like it was normal to lurk at the end of a hallway all morning waiting for your guests to leave their room? Joule looked at Reesa for help, that's what she was there for anyway: people problems. She stepped around him to get a better view before she answered smoothly.

"Apostles traditionally fast through breakfast on the first morning of a new week," she said. "We should have told you. I'm sorry, Mr. Shay."

The clerk sniffed and, turning smoothly, descended the stairs, silent as the grave.

"I hope we didn't hurt his feelings," Reesa whispered, glancing at Joule.

He shook his head. "Who could tell?"

Baffled, they followed Shay's trail down to the lobby. He was already standing behind his desk when they reached the bottom of the stairs and he said nothing as they passed him on their way out. Reesa tried a wave, but received only a blank stare in return. She exchanged expressions with Joule as they passed through the front door and nearly toppled over Randy who stood on the other side. What was *with* these people skulking around behind doors?

"Heard you was awake," Randy said and spat on the porch.

Joule could only stare at her, dumbfounded. Randy was disgusting.

Thankfully, Reesa saved him from expressing his thoughts.

"Have you had breakfast, Randy?" she asked. "Apostle Joule and I are supposed to fast this morning and I'm afraid Mr. Shay already prepared something for us. It would be a shame to see it go to waste."

Randy narrowed her eyes, sucking her head back into her throat almost like a turtle before craning her neck out and standing on her toes to get a good look into their faces. Joule drew away, but she kept on staring. Whatever she saw, it must have met with her approval, because she backed off, nodded and mumbled some kind of "thank you," and edged around the pair of them to go inside.

"I like your jacket, Randy," Reesa said.

Both Joule and Randy raised their eyebrows. The jacket? *That* jacket? Joule wouldn't have thought anything of it except for that Reesa spoke with such sincerity and the jacket was so unbearably *ugly*. Randy, too, regarded Reesa with a mix of befuddlement and disdain.

"Thanks," she said, and slipped inside.

On the street, the tinkling of a bolo tie and badge and the crunching of boots on dirt signaled a new arrival. Joule turned to see Mayor Big City, huffing his way up to the porch, a cloud of dust kicked up behind him like a snail's trail from the town hall to the hotel.

"She say anything to you?" he puffed, resting against the porch railing.

"No...?" Joule replied, glancing at Reesa who shrugged. "Should she have?"

Still catching his breath, the mayor waved a dismissive hand in the air. "No, no," he said. "Randy can be impolite is all. Just wanted to make sure she was treating our new apostles with respect."

Randy's respect or lack thereof did not seem to warrant what apparently was a very winding rush across the town square, but Joule made no reply.

Reesa said, "She was very respectful."

Well, he didn't know about *that*, but Reesa walked away from him and stepped past the mayor off the porch and into the sun before he could contradict her. Across the street, the small crowd which had gathered at the saloon grew more subdued as they noticed her appearance.

"We'd like to borrow a room tonight, Mayor Big City," she said, shading her eyes with her hand and turning around to smile back at him.

"Borrow for what?"

"To hold a meeting. To introduce ourselves and allow the citizens to voice their needs and concerns. Do you know of a space big enough to hold the entire town?"

The mayor's eyes shifted from side to side in the shade of his hat as his knees shifted his weight side to side as well.

"Church fits everyone."

"That will be wonderful, then."

"Gets crowded in there," he replied. "Stuffy."

"We'll manage."

He rubbed the stubbly hairs on the back of his ill-groomed neck. "If you say so, I guess the chapel's yours. You want to look at it now?"

Thank heaven for Reesa and her powers of persuasion—or perhaps it was just stubbornness. Joule never would have been able to bend such a burly man to his will. She nodded and Mayor Big City took off at a brisk pace.

Pockets of people had gathered on the street and their eyes tracked him and Reesa as they moved across the town square behind the mayor. Everyone feigned some action, sweeping hay out of stables, tinkering with the bell above the door to the bank, but they all *watched*. It was like being a carcass surrounded by a pack of vultures. It made Joule squirm.

Gig jogged up and interrupted their trek, removing his hat from his head and fiddling with the brim. He waited to speak until they mayor grunted at him.

"Mayor Big City, Tombstone's still here…says he needs to talk to you…"

The group followed the glance Gig threw over his shoulder at the fountain where the dark-haired man Reesa had insisted on introducing herself to last night stood holding the reins of a gigantic black horse. He took its bridle off and encouraged it to drink, then turned his gaze on them, his eyes narrowing almost imperceptibly.

Hicks altered course, offering up, "If you'll excuse me, Apostles…" but Reesa shot him down, following like a magnet and answering, "No need to be excused. Anything he has to say can and *should* be said in front of us."

Joule's mouth fell open. What was she *doing?*

"Fine," the mayor grumbled and stomped away toward the fountain.

Joule tried to reach after his partner, intent on reminding her that the apostle's commandments clearly stated that they were not to contest the local government, but she skipped away after the mayor before he got a chance. This wouldn't end well. Joule tucked his hands into his pockets and followed, dragging his feet.

The silent group arrived at the fountain and Tombstone—what a dreadful name—regarded each of them in turn with uncomfortably perceptive eyes. When he looked at Joule, he looked into his very soul, and Joule could not help but feel a little violated.

"This a private conversation?" Tombstone asked, looking at Mayor Big City.

"Just talk, Tombstone."

He threw an untrusting glance at Joule and Reesa, but said, "I rode out to the Greebers last night."

All the color drained from the mayor's sunburned face. "And?"

"It was all of them, not just Ben."

Mayor Big City suddenly looked as though a piano had fallen out of the sky and missed landing on his head by a hair's breadth. He ran a hand all over his face, huffing and puffing and releasing a great, heaving sigh all while shaking his head continuously.

"I took care of it," Tombstone added. "Just thought you ought to know."

Another heavy puff blew out of the mayor's lips. "Damn…"

"That makes six this year," Gig whispered.

"I know how many it makes, Deputy!" Hicks pounded a boot into the dirt.

"He didn't mean anything by it, Hicks," Tombstone said. "We all know the numbers."

The mayor shook his head. "You took care of it, you said?"

At once a curtain dropped over Tombstone's expression and his eyes went hard, an unfeeling statue. "Yes."

"Good man."

Mayor Big City clapped him on the shoulder and moved away. Gig began to follow, so Joule took his cue, looking over at Reesa to see what she would do. She nodded for him to go. She was going to stay and talk with Tombstone.

As Joule jogged to catch up to Gig, Reesa turned to Tombstone. That strange twisting feeling she felt in her heart when she looked at him had taken over her eyes as well, and her hair, which tingled—crackling—like it was full of static electricity. She opened her mouth to speak, but he interrupted.

"I don't want anything to do with you or your god, Apostle," he said, sliding the bridle back around his horse's face.

Reesa just scowled at him. She hadn't even said anything yet.

He faced her, his brows knotted seriously together above his eyes. "You and your partner should get out of Big City while you can."

A scoff of a laugh burst out of her. "Nice try."

He blinked. "What?"

"Nice try." She shook her head. "That's not going to work on me. You can't scare me away, Tombstone."

His eyes narrowed. He stepped forward. Looking down out of that beautiful face of his, he loomed over her, casting a shadow on her as he leaned in.

"Can't I?"

Her skin sprung up gooseflesh. It was like he *knew*. He *had* to know the effect he had on her, otherwise why should he be so provocative? She blushed and ducked out of his shadow, breathing deep to quiet the frenzied beating of her heart. He laughed a dark and vicious laugh as she moved away.

"Life is different out here, Apostle," he said. "You'll find out soon enough."

A scratchy whoop sounded from the hotel porch and Randy—who had apparently spotted them in the street—came swooping down.

"I was hoping you was still in town," she said to Tombstone. "Saved this for you."

Fringe swinging on her sleeves, she lofted high a scone smothered in butter and dripping honey down the length of her scraggly wrist. Reesa's stomach growled ardently at the sight of food. Fasting was no fun at all.

"Thanks." Tombstone accepted the scone and looked it over before taking a bite. He chewed for a bit and then nodded in approval, giving Randy a thumbs up.

The girl stuck the heel of her hand in her mouth and sucked the honey from her skin. "Cookie's got tons of supplies thanks to them," she said and started on her fingers. "Not every day you get butter."

Tombstone tossed a smile at Reesa. "Maybe you're good for something after all."

Reesa shook her head. "I'm afraid I don't understand."

41

"Ever since the two of you got ordinated out here or whatever, the Theo's been sending us all sorts of stuff," Randy explained as she wiped her hand on her pants. "Started showing up in big plastic boxes."

"The *Theo?*"

"The Theocracy," Tombstone supplied, finishing off the scone.

"Yes, I *know* what she meant."

"You looked confused."

It wasn't funny, but Randy cracked up anyway, laughing a laugh that seemed to shred her vocal cords. Had she always sounded like that or had she lost her voice recently? She settled down as Tombstone made a move to leave, stepping over to his horse and taking the reins.

"Can I bring Messy out to Little Hadham tonight?" Randy asked, trailing after him.

"Of course."

"There's a meeting tonight," Reesa put in. "Apostle Joule and I are hosting it."

Tombstone swung himself gracefully up into the saddle and grinned at her. "I might have a few things to say…" He looked at Randy. "Bring Messy out as soon as you're ready. I think attendance at the Theo meeting will be mandatory."

Reesa glared at him and he laughed, giving his horse a gentle kick and easing her away from the fountain before taking off at a gallop.

"You're friends with Tombstone, then?" Reesa asked, looking down at Randy as the kicked-up dust began to settle.

The girl shrugged. "Guess so."

"You trust him?"

Randy looked up at her with pursed lips and a sour face. What's with all the questions, lady, it seemed to say. Not deigning to answer, Randy started to walk away, but Reesa wasn't done just yet.

"Randy, do you know what a…taker is?" She hesitated over the word itself, not quite sure if she was remembering Callum correctly.

Randy looked back over her shoulder, one eyebrow raised high above the other. "You don't?" she asked.

Reesa shook her head. Randy let out a low whistle.

"I reckon you'd better find that one out for yourself," she replied and dashed off before Reesa had time to think of a follow-up.

7

Gig had suggested Apostle Joule take a look at their busted up comm again and Hicks saw no reason why not, so he led them back to his office as Apostle Reesa stayed behind to talk Tombstone. Soon as they'd arrived in the office, Apostle Joule called one of his other apostle buddies. He worked quickly and quietly, fiddling around with the comm under the desk, on top, and Hicks watched, wondering what it was this city dandy was capable of doing that he wasn't.

Apostle Reesa came in through the door. She looked beat. He narrowed his eyes.

"A little blue, Apostle?" he asked. "Tombstone wasn't untoward to you, was he?"

Hicks'd personally lynch Tombstone if he had said anything to the apostles about the takers. That wily bastard was the only wild card in the whole Big City deck. Couldn't keep his mouth shut.

Reesa shook her head. "Just thinking, Mayor Big City."

Ah, but what about? Hicks cleared his throat and folded his arms and paid attention to Joule again. He was under the desk. His handheld was on top of it, all lit up by the face of some other apostle a thousand miles away. Tess, Joule had called him.

"I can't see anything down here, Apostle Tess," Joule said as he slid himself out and sat up. "It all checks out as far as I can tell."

"Put me down there," the panel replied.

Joule grabbed the handheld and placed it under the desk, holding up a flashlight for it so the panel apostle could see all the wires and things. Tess made hems and haws; Joule looked over to Reesa. He raised his eyebrows and she shook her head. Secret communications. These apostles…they were sneaky.

"I see a wire that *could* be loose," Tess said. "Take a look, Apostle Joule. The two-inch that connects the unit to the battery."

Joule stuck his head back under the desk and hemmed affirmatively. "I see it," he said and shuffled in further, freeing his hand as he reached up. "Let me just—"

Shrieeeek! The comm let out a noise like a shot-down screech owl and spat out a shower of sparks that nearly touched the ceiling. A column of smoke began to rise as well. Joule only just managed to yank the cord out and scramble away from the desk before the thing caught fire. The four of them just stood stupid and blinked.

"What was that?" Tess asked. "Was that the unit?"

"Yeah," Joule breathed. "I think it nearly exploded." He stepped over gingerly to get the panel out from under the desk. "I've never seen anything like it, Apostle Tess."

"It has to be some kind of outside interference," Tess said as Joule scowled at him.

Gig beamed proudly at Hicks. Dumb bastard had said something like that weeks ago after the comm had stopped working again. Hicks gave him a look he was sure would shut him up.

Joule said, "We're in the middle of *nowhere*. Could *that* be an explanation?"

Tess laughed. "No, the signal's strong. It's not your location."

"Well," Joule sighed, "if you think of anything else, let me know. Thank you for your help, Apostle Tess."

"You're welcome. Good luck."

Good luck indeed. Hicks puffed out his cheeks. Middle of nowhere, *ha*. Big City may have been small, but it was ideal. Anybody who said otherwise was a whiner, plain and simple. The comm sent up another shower of sparks.

"I suppose we should put in for a new one," Gig said. "Don't you think?"

"This one won't be working again anytime soon," Joule replied.

"We'll inform our cardinal of the need tonight when we make our report," Reesa added. "He might be able to get a new unit shipped out as soon as tomorrow morning."

Hicks glanced at Gig. City-slicker people and their instant gratification. His deputy-sheriff seemed to agree with him.

"Convenient," Hicks replied.

"Someone will have to ride out to the station to pick it up," that woman continued. "I'm happy to volunteer. Do you think Randy would be willing to lend me her services?"

Lend her services? Woman needed to turn her eager-meter down a solid ten notches. Or twenty. Hicks shrugged in response.

"That's a question for Randy."

"I'll speak with her then."

She smiled at him, but he did not return it, and slowly the smile faded from her face. Something stiff settled into her eyes. She was sizing him up. Challenging him. Dumb animal. She wouldn't win. She had no real authority. He stared calmly back at her.

Joule cleared his throat. "If you'll excuse us, Mayor Big City, Deputy-Sheriff Big City, we ought to prepare for the meeting tonight." He grabbed hold of Reesa and steered her through the door. "We'll see you at seven o'clock."

"All right, Apostle."

Hicks chuckled a little as Reesa tried to barge back into the room and was thwarted by her partner. Dumb, dumb animal.

Darling was just beginning to wonder if apostles had the authority to officiate weddings when low and behold, her very own apostles came stumbling out of the town hall. Standing at the open window of the bank next door—the bank her daddy owned and ran, she was so proud—she could hear every word they said. Apostle Reesa didn't sound too happy.

"What was that for?" she snapped.

"Don't look at me like that. You were coming dangerously close to breaking a few commandments there, Reesa."

Apostle Joule only called her Reesa when he thought nobody else was around.

Apostle Reesa didn't seem to have anything to say for herself about whatever had happened. She opened her mouth and closed it and plopped down on the town hall steps, sending up a puff of dust. She put her chin in her hand.

"Thank you, Joule," she said.

The two of them sat quiet for a minute or two. Darling strained to listen, just in case they'd started whispering or something. Apostle Reesa stared down the length of Big City all the way to the gate at the end and beyond it seemed. She had a look like she was looking into the future. Made Darling's hair stand on end.

"Joule?" Reesa said.

"Hm?"

"What do we do if no one comes to the meeting?"

There was a meeting? Darling would be there, that was for certain. She wanted to ask if they could officiate weddings. Doctor Fencer felt right around the corner.

"We should *plan* the meeting before we worry about attendance," Joule replied. He stood up and brushed off his bottom. "Come on."

He put down his hand to help her up. They were such an odd couple. Darling shifted away from the window as they started down the steps. Everyone she could see out on the street seemed to shift away too, about two steps. They were all wary, even still. The apostles talked while they walked. She could hear them.

"We'll need to make an agenda," Reesa said.

"Right."

"And I think some refreshments are in order…"

"Right."

Then they scurried the rest of the way across the square up the steps to the hotel like kids do when they've turned off the light in the basement and are running upstairs to escape the ghosts that come with the darkness.

Seth came hurtling in through the back door like a bat out of hell. Darling jumped when the door slammed.

"Takers," he said, eyes wide. "We need to call quarantine."

Cookie had been scolded by Shay about four hundred and five times for keeping so many lights on in his kitchen, but Cookie didn't give a rat's tiny fart what Shay did or did not want to pay for, so he kept them all on just to spite him. Besides, he liked the way the lights glinted off his bald, shiny head. Felt powerful.

He had his hands deep in a pile of brown dough when somebody pushed the door open and entered his domain. When he looked up, that woman apostle was standing in the doorway squinting.

"Hello," she said. "Cookie, right?"

What did she want? He had four loaves of funeral bread to bake before tomorrow. One for Ben, one for Statia, and one for each of their children.

"Yes?" he said back. Who else would he have been anyway?

"I'm Apostle Reesa."

She must think he was stupid. Who else would *she* have been? "The one who didn't want breakfast," he said and focused on his work. "Fasting. I've never understood it. Made Randy happy, though."

"I apologize for not informing Shay about our fast," she said, stepping further inside like he'd invited her or something. "But I'm glad the meal went to good use."

"Me too. She doesn't get to eat much with her father dead."

Perhaps that had been too blunt. Apostle Reesa looked like he'd slapped her upside the head. Besides, Hicks had ordered everybody not to breathe a word about the takers to the apostles, and seeing as Randy's father Randall had been kidnapped by said takers, it probably would have been better not to say anything at all. But Hicks was a paranoid power freak and Cookie didn't much care for his wiles. And he wanted the apostle gone.

"Did you want something, Apostle Reesa? It's not too long past lunch?" Maybe if he fed her she would go away.

"Our fast ends at two o'clock," she said as she shook her head. "Lunch would be lovely after that, but that's not why I came down."

"Then why did you come down?"

He pulled the dough he'd been working out flat and sprinkled it over with cinnamon and sugar, a special blend his grandmother had taught him. He rolled it up and set it down onto the bread paddle, coated it with an egg and milk mix, and slid it into the wood-fire oven at his back. Apostle Reesa stared the whole time he was working. He couldn't afford to distract her again, so he didn't start on the next loaf, but instead leaned over the counter and raised his eyebrows.

"Well?"

"Oh! I'm sorry! My partner and I are hosting a meeting tonight, for the town. I wanted to ask if you would be willing to make us some treats. It doesn't have to be anything big."

He shrugged. "Sure." He would be in the kitchen anyway.

"Great. How about more of that bread?"

"*That* bread?" The *funeral* bread?

She nodded happily. "Yes. Would that be too much work?"

The work wasn't the problem. "Well, no—"

"Then it's settled. We'll be sure to replace any of the supplies you use. Just bring a list of what you want to the meeting tonight and we'll get things ordered."

Wait, was she serious? The Theocracy had shipped out quite a bit of the basics, one of the reasons he was even able to make the funeral bread, once the apostles had been assigned to Big City, but their comm was so whacked he couldn't ever put in specific requests. He grinned.

"All right, then."

He wouldn't tell her what the funeral bread was actually for. Ignorance is bliss, as they say.

"You've already had a few deliveries, correct?"

He nodded. "They're out back."

"Would you mind if I took a look at them?"

For free supplies, she could poke her nose around in whatever she wanted. "Go right ahead. Through that door." He gestured with his head to the door that went out back.

"Thank you..."

She weaved around the counter and pushed open the door before disappearing through it. Cookie grabbed a measuring cup and started scooping flour. If the apostle wanted funeral bread, he would give it to her.

Randy followed her nose back behind the hotel—smelled funeral bread. Must be baking for the Greebers. She'd be sure to take a loaf out to their house and leave it soonest chance she got, but as she came around the corner she saw Apostle Reesa digging around in the big white storage boxes Cookie kept outside because they were just too big to take in. Of a sudden she got a wonderful idea.

"Look out! It's a taker!"

She shrieked just about as loud as she could and Apostle Reesa screamed and dropped to her knees, covering her head, and the sight of it cracked Randy right up. She laughed and laughed, laughed her lungs out—so hard she had to lean over one of the boxes to keep from toppling over. Apostle Reesa scowled at her.

"That isn't funny, Randy," she said.

"You should have seen your face!"

Randy pulled an expression similar to the one Reesa had made and let out a muffled scream, falling to the dirt like Reesa had where she laughed some more. The apostle blushed and brushed off her uniform.

"I thought you were taking your horses out?" she said.

"I am," Randy replied. "Just not yet." Nosy cuss. "What are you doing out here anyway?"

"Checking the food supplies."

What a weirdo. "Why?"

"I wanted to make sure they were authentic. Where did you get that jacket?"

Randy frowned. Why would she ask that? How could she know? She'd made some comment about liking it earlier, but still. It wasn't like Randy was about to fork it over. She pushed off the box and straightened up.

"It was my pa's," she said.

Apostle Reesa looked sorry she'd asked. Good. She should have been. They were both quiet. Randy wasn't about to say anything. Apostle Reesa could suffer in silence. She seemed like the kind of person who didn't like silence much. Turned out Randy was right. The apostle changed the topic right away.

"Would you…um, like to show me your horses?"

Her horses? Sure, of course, any day. Randy took every chance she could to show them off. Apostle Reesa was probably too city-dumb to appreciate what specimens they were, but whatever.

"Absolutely!"

She grabbed Reesa by the wrist and dragged her around the back of the hotel and down through the alley between it and the newspaper office. She hurried them across the square, past the fountain, to the stables where she burst the door open and pulled Reesa all the way down the rows of stalls to the pair at the end.

"These two is mine," Randy said, hauling herself up onto the stable door so she could look over the top. "I have four, but I don't have room to keep them all at home, so Messy and Sable stay here."

Their noise had summoned Arthur, the old man who ran the stable. Randy liked him. He was nice. And his daughter, Merrick—Tombstone's wife—had

48

been kidnapped, too, just like her parents. Also, he liked horses. She and Arthur understood each other. He came stepping toward them, a friendly grin on his face.

"You taken Messy out to see Tombstone yet, Randy?" he called. "She's been complaining at me 'bout that hoof...all...morning..."

He was staring at Reesa. Randy figured she knew why. Reesa looked like Merrick. The apostle looked back at him, smiling awkwardly. Eventually Arthur snapped his jaws closed and held his hand out to her.

"Excuse me," he said. "You must be Apostle Reesa. I'm Arthur Capell."

They shook hands.

"Mr. Capell makes saddles and things," Randy said and hopped off the stable door. "And he keeps the Big City horses."

Reesa laughed. "I gathered that."

"Let me show you *my* horses now," Randy said, and unhooked the latch on the stable door to open it. She went inside and motioned for Reesa to follow. "Come on."

Messy lay on the hay in her stable, pretty as ever with her brown and white splotches. She snorted as Randy sat down by her. Reesa stood all lingery by the door.

"This is Messy," Randy said and patted her nose. "Sable's next door."

She pointed just as Sable poked her head over the low wall that separated the stalls. Arthur smiled and leaned against the door.

"These are two of my best girls," he said. "Randy's very lucky to have such fine horses."

"They're beautiful," Reesa agreed, nodding.

"I should get going," Randy said. "Don't want to miss your meeting tonight, Apostle Reesa."

She got to her feet with a grunt and urged Messy to follow, though it was tough with her hurt foot. Arthur fetched a saddle, bridle, and reins from the hook on the wall and suited up Sable for a ride.

"You go slow, all right, Randy?" he said. "Messy doesn't need any more pressure on that hoof."

"Yeah, I know." Bossy old man.

He gave her his serious look and she pulled a face at him. She wasn't stupid. She knew how to take care of her girls. Messy finally made it to her feet and Randy patted her shoulder, but she was still favoring her left front leg, lifting it and setting it on the ground again and again.

"What happened to her?" Reesa asked.

Randy led Messy from her stall and bridled her as Arthur brought over a rope to tie her to the pommel of Sable's saddle.

"Stepped on a scorpion cactus while we was out exercising," Randy replied and swung herself up onto Sable. She took the reins as Arthur handed them over.

"Sounds painful."

Arthur chuckled. "It is."

Someone knocked at the door and then Apostle Joule poked his head inside. "There you are!" he breathed and scurried down the length of the stalls to the end. Hicks and Gig came in behind him like a set of storm clouds. Randy knew that look. That was a quarantine look.

"I didn't know where you'd gone," Apostle Joule said once he reached them. "I was worried."

"Is something the matter?" Reesa glanced at Hicks and Gig.

"Actually, yes, Apostle," Hicks said, stepping forward. "It's been determined that Big City is under threat. I'm calling quarantine, effective immediately. Gig, get that gate."

Gig scuttled off to follow orders. He went out the back of the barn to the fence and the gate that Randy would need to pass through to get out of Big City and head for Tombstone's. Luckily Gig was rubbish with the locks. It would take him a moment yet. She gave Sable the lightest of kicks and tried to edge her away.

"Where are you off to, Randy?"

Hicks stepped into her path.

"Little Hadham," she spat back. "Tombstone needs to look at Messy's foot."

"I just enforced quarantine." He folded his arms across his chest. "Messy can wait."

It was his damn fault she was injured in the first place. "No she can't. She's worse now since you made me run her out to the train station and back." She gave him a fierce glare.

"Go home, Randy."

"I'll be safer out at Little Hadham during quarantine than at home by myself," she replied and urged Sable forward.

Hicks tried to catch the reins as she went by, but she gave Sable a solid kick and took off running so he missed. Hicks called after her, but she paid him no mind. Messy was struggling too much on the tow rope. She had to get out quick so she could slow down and walk her. Gig was just beginning to wheel the gate closed when she shot by him.

"Hey!" he shouted. "Randy! Get back here!"

"I won't do that, Gig," she called back.

"There's takers out!"

She ignored him. The quarantine could have been real or fabricated to fool the apostles, but something told her it was real. The quicker she got to Little Hadham the better. Behind her, the quarantine sirens went off—wailing like demons into the hot, silent air.

8

Huxley caught sight of Randy headed toward Little Hadham, going slow, weighed down by Messy and her injured hoof, but he was headed out in the opposite direction and it was far too late to go back. She could let herself in. She knew where he hid the key. He just had to hope she'd make it there before a taker made it to her. He'd heard the sirens go off and he knew what they meant.

Come out, Tombstone. Come out and kill something.

At least this time it wouldn't be human.

He rode Indie hard and he rode her fast, scanning his horizon constantly. Takers would be easy to see—like Randy. At least Big City had that going for it being so damned flat. Unfortunately it meant they'd be able to sense his approach as well. He'd never quite figured out if they could see or not, but he knew they didn't have eyes and perceived the world through sensory organs in their mouths. He had been studying them for two years, ever since he escaped and Merrick hadn't.

Maybe this time he could bring home another specimen to dissect. Solve that seeing riddle once and for all.

It was difficult to tell how much ground he had covered, but soon Little Hadham was no longer visible behind him. Seth Shank had had the slot in the watch. He must have gone quick back to town because Huxley didn't run into takers until he was halfway to their hole.

They let out a shriek when they sensed him. Six or seven of them, traveling through the brush in a V-shape like geese do. Yet again he was struck by how human they looked from a distance—human height, human shape, longer arms, covered in thick brown mucus, and a hole in their heads, gaping black and multi-functional. They saw, ate, and breathed through their mouths from what he'd been able to gather. Hissed and screamed through it, too. The pack took off running.

Huxley met them head on, slipping his pistol from its holster. It hummed in his hand, powering up, getting ready to fire a shot. Three seconds, and it would be ready… Go.

The point taker's head exploded with a showering spray, black blood bursting through the air. Huxley jetted through their V and turned Indie around just as they were beginning to regroup.

He shot two more before he met the group again. Four left. They hissed and shrieked and made swiping grabs at Indie's legs and tail, but he maneuvered her through the brush away from them and kicked her hard, sending her galloping swiftly out of reach. She was calm, strong, reliable. A little tiff with a taker was nothing she couldn't handle.

With a tug at Indie's reins, he slowed her and turned her round, but as he came about the takers were no longer in sight.

"Damn."

They had dropped into the brush, were using it as cover. They'd be headed away from him. Toward Big City.

He'd poked at a taker brain before. Tried to figure out what made it tick. It ran on electrical impulses not unlike a human brain, but how did those impulses add up to perceptions and controlled movements? Dreams and desires? Why did a taker's brain tell it to attack? Why did such highly intelligent creatures—as stupid as they looked—seem so hell-bent on killing everyone in Big City? Then again, what told a human brain to love? To fight, to kill, to eat, sleep, breathe? Nobody had ever really figured that out either.

He couldn't expect to understand another creature when he didn't even understand himself.

A taker shot up out of the brush right at Indie's legs. She whinnied in a frenzy, kicking back and nearly throwing Huxley. *Damn* it. Pay attention. He gripped the reins, gripped the saddle with his legs and knees, held on and pulled her away. Another appeared on their right. He shot that one through the head.

Numbers three and four appeared behind them. An ambush. He'd never seen them ambush before. Indie got a kick and took off through the opening afforded by the second taker's death. They followed him swiftly, snarling, hissing, picking through the brush like machinery and leaving bits of their sticky mucus behind. Remarkable how fast they could be when they wanted.

Indie galloped forward. He turned in the saddle. Aimed, shot. Missed. Damn it, *focus*. Every second spent here was a second another pack of takers could have been getting closer to Big City. Closer to those few other souls he had to protect. Closer to the people he didn't want to shoot. Out here, it was kill or be killed, and he *much* preferred black blood to red.

The takers dropped into the brush again, but he was ready for them, saw where they landed, saw how the brush shook where they crawled through it. He yanked

Indie to a halt. He raised his pistol. There, right there, just before him. Just a few hundred feet. It was an easy shot. His finger pulled the trigger.

Snap.

The brush stopped shaking.

He aimed at the other.

Snap.

The brush was still.

Huxley blinked. Sweat ran into his eyes. Seven gone but quarantine far from over. Could be more takers. It was hard to say. He'd patrol until he was certain they were all dead. All of those aboveground at least.

The sun set before Huxley made it back to Big City—as much as he would have liked to go home, someone had to decide when quarantine was over, and as that someone was *him,* it was his job to tell somebody else. Indie trotted up to the back gate and waited while he swung down, unlocked it, and went to retrieve her. Taking her by the reins, he led her through the gate and walked into the dark and quiet square. Water gurgled up out of the fountain. The Christmas lights were all ablaze.

He looked at their reflection in the water as he led Indie up to drink. He'd shot and killed twenty-three takers in all, unfortunately all through the head, which made them basically useless as study specimens. If the head was destroyed, the body would rot away within minutes. He'd learned that the hard way when he'd tried to drag one of their headless bodies back to Little Hadham through the brush and had left a trail of taker in his wake.

Probably he should check around the backs of the buildings, in case any had slipped his watch and gotten inside. He left Indie at the fountain.

He walked between the jail and the post office, started off south toward the hotel. Probably there would be nothing. But *probablys* were not things he particularly liked.

Up ahead something was rummaging through one of the delivery boxes Cookie kept out behind the hotel. A taker? No. It was wearing white. An apostle.

Huxley chuckled. He could guess which one.

Approaching quietly, Huxley came right up beside the box. Sure enough, Reesa was bent over the edge, half in half out, digging around for something near the bottom of the box and making an awful lot of noise while doing it. Apparently having found what she was looking for, she let out a little cluck of pleasure and started to tip herself out of the box.

"Hungry, Apostle?"

She yelped, jolting with surprise and throwing a stick of butter at him in defense. He lifted a shoulder for a shield and let it bounce off him to land in the dirt. Not much of a weapon.

Glaring fiercely, she stomped forward and snatched the butter off the ground. "Don't *do* that," she hissed.

He laughed. "Raiding the Big City stores, are we?"

She busied herself with wiping the dirt from the wax wrapper. "Aren't you supposed to be in quarantine?"

"Aren't you?"

Her eyes flicked up to meet his and he raised his eyebrows at her to which she made the strangest face—almost like she was in pain, but she masked it and turned to stomp to the box and close the lid.

"Quarantine's over," he said.

"Good for you."

He rolled his eyes at her. "You're a tad too sassy for an apostle."

The comment brought color into her cheeks. She walked to the back door, the one that led to Cookie's kitchen. Taking a moment, she cleared her throat and looked at her feet. Once prepared apparently, she raised her gaze to him and said, "I apologize. That was unkind. If there is anything I can do to assist you in the future, please inform me."

He laughed out loud. "Why, thank you. Apology accepted."

Such an obedient dog. His response seemed to startle her, but she did not reply, turning the doorknob instead and admitting herself into the kitchen. She held the door with a look of condescension. As soon as he stepped inside the smell of funeral bread overwhelmed him. So many loaves... What in the hell for?

Cookie looked up as they entered.

"Evening, Tombstone," he said. "I take it the quarantine's over?"

"It is."

"Good."

Reesa stood in his way, so he slid around her and picked up a loaf of bread.

"Mind if I take one?" he asked.

"That's what they're for," Cookie replied. "Apostle Reesa requested them for her meeting."

She asked for *funeral* bread? He snorted. How ignorant. You weren't actually supposed to *eat* it. That was the Theocracy for you.

Reesa piped up as if sensing his negative thoughts. "Why do *you* get to decide when quarantine's over?" she clucked, putting a hand on her hip.

He sighed and shook his head. "Apostle," he said, "I'm the only one who carries a gun."

Hinges squealed at the other end of the room and Reesa's blonde, bar-of-soap partner stuck his head in looking worried. He sighed with relief when he saw Reesa.

"You were gone for so long I thought something might have happened. Did you get the butter?"

Reesa lifted the stick in her hands for him to see—the one she'd thrown at Huxley.

"Come on, then," he said, motioning out the door with his head. She obeyed, as ever.

Huxley looked to Cookie.

"You really made her all these loaves?"

"I didn't have the heart to tell her what they were for. I was baking one for Ben when she came in. Hicks told us not to tell them."

Huxley snorted. "And if we do?"

Cookie chuckled but shook his head. "That's dangerous territory, Tombstone. Don't go walking where you weren't meant to."

Huxley pursed his lips. At the back of his mind, something bothered him. It was faint, so faint that if he focused on it, he could no longer sense its presence—like looking at a dim star through a telescope out of the corner of your eye when if you looked directly at it, it would disappear, the receptors in your fovea too weak to perceive it. All the same, the feeling was there. And the feeling told him keeping the apostles in the dark was a mistake.

9

The crickets' night chorus trickled in, creaking through the crack of the open bathroom window, one of those tiny rectangular jobs placed near the top of the ceiling for privacy. It had been open for a while, Reesa supposed, perhaps years, streaks of wind-blown dust decorating the wall just around it in wide alluvial fans. She locked the door behind her and set her toiletries and pajamas on the wooden counter surrounding the sink. Quarantine had cancelled their meeting. She was certain Hicks had planned it that way.

When she turned the water on, it came out orange. She nearly caught a glimpse of the face she made in the warped mirror as she jumped back from the sink, grimacing. She looked into her own eyes as if she were looking at some kind of confederate, another person with whom she could share her disgust.

Letting the water run for a bit, praying it would turn clear eventually, but even then not so sure she wanted to stick her toothbrush, let alone her *face* into it, Reesa undressed and slipped into her pajamas. She waited for the water, studying her reflection—the ski-jump line of her nose, dark ruby waves of hair, smooth nearly-tan skin. She'd never really supposed she was pretty before, but the lilac desert light of twilight that filtered in through the open window made her look supple, healthy. She liked the reflection that looked back at her.

The water finally emerged clear from the faucet and Reesa brushed her teeth, and decided after rinsing and tasting metal in her mouth it would probably be best not to wash her face. She packed away her toothbrush and toothpaste and departed the bathroom, offering herself a final quiet smile in the bathroom mirror.

Joule scurried off as soon as she returned to their room, his own bag of toiletries in his hands. Would Shay allow them to leave their things in the bathroom maybe? If this was going to be their home, carrying their stuff to and from the bathroom every night was impractical. Also not very homey. Besides, the likelihood of other guests was astronomically thin.

She set her uniform down on top of the dresser and tucked her bathroom supplies away in her suitcase. A breeze flitted through her hair as she bent over the luggage and, looking up, she discovered their window was open. She rose, went to it. Joule must have somehow forced it up. Her fingers ran around the frame as the smell of the night settling over the desert sailed in on the breeze. She looked out, and somehow in spite of herself, felt her heart soar at what it saw. The rickety wooden shops and homes, the trodden dirt road—they sang to her, creaking as the wood compressed in the cool from its expansion in the heat. It was all familiar. All like home.

Footsteps tickled her attention and she looked down right below her window just in time to see Tombstone step from the hotel porch, unmistakable beneath his wide, white hat. So he had not gone. He remained, the spark of a powered-up weapon faintly visible at his hip.

He turned around and she shot out of the window frame, tucking her body up close against the wall. Had he seen her? She didn't dare look. She waited, her heart pounding, for several minutes. Should she look? What if he *had* seen her? What would he think she was doing? Spying?

She ducked low to the floor and hurried over to the bed. Crawling in, the frame squeaking, she tucked herself tight in the covers and set her head down on the flat pillow. Tiredness began to creep into her muscles and bones now that she'd relaxed them, laid them down. A yawn escaped her and she settled into the mattress. It was finally dark out, the Christmas lights coming on one building at a time. She fell asleep before Joule even returned from the bathroom.

She is standing in front of a sturdy, handmade well, barely more than a simple circle of sunbaked clay enclosing the rim of the deep, deep shaft down to the aquifer. She hums to herself as she lowers a bucket down into the cool, shadowy depths to draw the water for his bath. He worked hard today.

All around her the desert is boiling as usual, and she hopes the water will be cool enough. A warm bath on a hot day is hardly a comfort. The ranch is quiet, the sun about to head over the horizon for other shores. The ground releases its heat in near-invisible, wriggling waves. Some distance away she hears her horses galloping into their stables for the night. Perhaps she will detour on the way back to the house and see them.

A pair of arms encircles her waist and a pair of lips touches her neck. She is not startled. Instead she smiles and begins to pull the bucket back to the surface.

"How's the fence coming?" she asks.

"Well," he answers, holding her close. "The south section's nearly finished. By tomorrow we should be able to let the horses back on that part of the land."

"They're hardly cooped up," she laughs.

"The more space the better."

The bucket reappears at the top of the well and she takes a few steps forward to retrieve it, but he pulls her back. Laughing, she tries to swat him away.

"Stop it," she says. "You're going to make me drop it."

"Think you can get enough water out of there to join me?"

He spins her around and she comes face to face with Tombstone. The rope slips from her hands, but thankfully it is long enough not to have been taken into the well by the bucket which lands with an echoing splash upon the water at the bottom. She rests her hands on his chest.

"I told you you'd make me drop it," she says.

He only smiles at her. She wraps her arms around his neck to receive the kiss he declines his head to give her. Their lips meet and—

Reesa snapped awake with a gasp. Several deep gulps of air followed. Joule could surely feel the frantic beating of her heart as it rippled through their bed. It pulsated in her ears. Her eyes flicked to the clock on the bedside table. Nearly four AM. Almost too late to go back to sleep. Though now she wasn't sure she wanted to. Red and green spots of light danced across the bedspread in succession.

She shut her eyes, took a breath in through her nose and let it out through her mouth. Again, in and out. In and out. How could Joule still be asleep? Her very breathing sounded like an overhead plane coming down to land, but he snored peaceably beside her. He only snored when he slept on his back. She would have rolled him over, but that might wake him up, and then... She didn't want to talk to him about her dream.

She shouldn't have been thinking about it. Definitely shouldn't have been thinking about it. She ought to stop thinking about it, but of course when you try *not* to think about something, that's all that comes to mind.

Sighing, she opened her eyes, stared at the ceiling and searched for pictures in the water stains—browns and greens and yellows that spread out across the paint in puddles, overlapping one another, a record of every rainstorm ever to fall on Big City. It didn't work. The feeling of Tombstone's lips on her neck... She focused on Joule's breathing.

She'd been one of the first to receive her match documents in the mail. Three months before the completion of her training, three months from graduation. That was when the letters were always sent. That was when apostles found out who it was they would be spending the rest of their mortal life with.

She'd opened her letter surrounded by a sea of eager friends and peers, classmates—some who would graduate with her, others a year or so away. As she'd read Joule's name her breath had caught in her throat and all the girls had let out a gasp, then a cheer, or a croon of one kind or another. What they knew about him was only speculation, rumor, as the male and female classes of apostles never trained together until after their match. But Joule had been at the top of his class, already a well-respected tech in the oil industry. Everybody knew him. And everybody had been jealous of her.

Reesa was just grateful that the pair of them could get along.

She turned over onto her side and propped herself up on her elbow, studying Joule through the half-shadow. She supposed he was handsome by anyone's standards, but all she could see when she looked at him was an ordinary man, a little neurotic, who chewed his nails and hated shellfish. He was no Tombstone—*no*. She had no business comparing the two.

Joule rolled over; Reesa collapsed quickly onto her back and made a bad show of feigning sleep in case he woke up. He didn't, and slowly his snoring quieted before ceasing altogether. The scratch of that rope in her hands. It was so visceral it could have been a memory. The smell of the dirt, Tombstone's familiar kiss...

Sleep swallowed her again.

She is standing by the well, kissing him. His hands are warm and strong around her back. She loves him so much it hurts.

"I'll bring you another bucket," he says.

She nods and he moves away toward their little cabin of a house. Bending, she reaches for the rope and begins to haul the bucket back to the top of the well. It arrives soaked and dripping and she takes hold of it, untying the knot at the top of the handle, and heads for the house. The cool water sloshes over the sides onto her cotton dress as she walks. She is grateful for it.

She meets Tombstone halfway and gestures with her head at the well.

"Trade me," she says.

He takes the heavy pail from her arms and passes the empty one over. She smiles and turns to go back to the well. In the distance, something tall and dark and lurching catches her attention.

A wave of terror wrenched her out of the dream, trembling as she woke. What time was it now? She turned over, looked at the clock. Five fourteen. A tiny, miserable moan slipped out of her. There was no point in going back to sleep now. The thought simultaneously distressed and relieved her—she was exhausted, and wanted to sleep, but if she was going to dream of Tombstone then perhaps it was better if she didn't.

Boots on gravel. Three sets of footsteps. Someone was out on the street. It was nowhere near dawn. She got up, crept to the window. As she got closer, voices drifted up to her ears as well. She shut her eyes and listened hard.

"I wouldn't put any stock in the apostles. Theocracy's got no idea what's going on out here. Those two are here for the oil. Plain and simple."

The voice was still fresh from her dream. Tombstone. Had she and Joule truly been so transparent? Neither of them had even *mentioned* the oil.

"All the same, it might be worth a try." That one sounded like what she remembered of Gig's voice, small and deferent. "They've got resources. Guns and things."

"No. I don't trust them." Definitely Mayor Big City.

"They wouldn't give us guns even if we said please," Tombstone replied. "They have a non-aggression policy."

"It's a Big City problem and we'll deal with it the Big City way," Hicks replied. "Meaning me?"

Tombstone's voice went dark and fierce and neither Gig nor Hicks answered him. Reesa strained her ears in case they had dropped volume, but that didn't seem to be it. The other men were silent. She imagined them unable to meet Tombstone's eye. Even after a moment, he was the one to speak.

"Maybe we *should* ask for guns. You two could do some of the dirty work for a change."

"We can't start carrying guns, Tombstone," Hicks hissed. "What kind of message would that send?"

"The truth?"

"Which is?"

"This will be the end if we don't act quickly."

"We can't all be you, Tombstone. We can't all carry a gun and play Wild West. The people need stability. Leadership."

Tombstone laughed a dark laugh that was not at all amused. "If I sat around on my ass like *you* seem to be so fond of doing, they all would have been dead by now."

"Well, they're scared shitless of *you* and what you've become!"

Silence for a moment. A slow *crunch, crunch, crunch* as Tombstone must have moved closer to the mayor. When he spoke, his voice was low, empty-sounding. Reesa almost didn't hear what he said.

"I wish you could know what it feels like to be scared shitless of yourself."

His footsteps moved away from the hotel. Hicks and Gig scurried after him, whispering furtively to each other. Eventually their voices were lost to her over the distance. What in the hell had she just overheard? Not *hell*. She gritted her teeth. She would be hard pressed to kick her swearing habit in this town. This town that had seen right through her ruse. It was no wonder their welcome had worn so quickly. They weren't wanted.

In the cities, the Theocracy was a shining presence—a beautiful beacon of uprightness and purity. Status. You were respected. But out here, things were different. How strange, how alien she and Joule must appear. She could not be surprised that they did not trust her.

Leaning against the wall by the window, she mulled it all over and over and over in her head until the alarm went off at seven.

10

Reesa hadn't even had her whole request for a ride out of her mouth before Randy was saying yes and running to hitch up her horses. That girl was eager to serve, and eager to get the entire loaf of funeral bread Reesa had been holding in her hands for doing so. Since the meeting had been cancelled, about a hundred loaves of bread were sitting in the Big City hotel kitchen. Reesa had seen no reason to waste them, and she figured she would need a bribe to get Randy to drive her out to the train station to pick up the new comm.

It was three hours there and three hours back, extended even beyond that as Randy was down a horse with Messy still out at Little Hadham. Reesa watched the scrub fly by, bit by bit, in the frame of the window as Randy's coach and horses tore through it. Only a day and a half had passed, but already the plant had grown over the trail. You would think being torn up and trampled by horses would be enough to stop it. At least for a little while.

The new comm had been ordered yesterday evening when she and Joule had reported to their cardinal during quarantine before they'd gotten ready for bed. Cardinal Cyatan did not like to be greeted by apostles in pajamas. They'd learned that one the hard way.

He'd given them a few goals for the day: to pick up and assemble the new comm unit he would ship out, and to assess the situation regarding the drill site. Reesa couldn't remember if there had been more. Hopefully Joule did.

Reesa had asked the cardinal about the takers as well. He didn't know either.

The coach began to slow, then came to a stop right up next to the station platform. There was the new comm, snug in an enormous white box that was blinding in the sun. Reesa's view of it was interrupted as Randy jumped down from the top of the coach and went flying by the window. Her boots landed with a thud.

"How're we going to get it on the roof?" she asked, looking back.

Reesa got out, went to the box. Standing next to the thing, it came up to her chest. Randy was up to her shoulders in it. There was no way the two of them could get it on top of the coach. Would it even *fit* on top of the coach?

"I don't know," Reesa replied.

"Maybe you shouldn't have told your partner to stay back," Randy observed quite unhelpfully as those were Reesa's thoughts exactly but there wasn't a damn—*darn* thing she could do about it. She glared at the box in consternation.

"Is the new comm thingy really this *big?*" Randy asked. She'd been looping the box and running her hands along its smooth, snow-colored surface.

"No. The containers only come in a few sizes. They ship delicate materials in larger boxes with more air cushioning."

"So if we drop it or it falls off the coach it won't break?"

Reesa nodded. "It'll be safe."

"Huh."

Randy nodded thoughtfully, began circling the box once more. A plan seemed to be formulating behind her eyes. It occurred to Reesa as she watched the girl that the delivery box had been dropped off and left entirely unattended even though it was full of expensive equipment. Was the Theocracy really so careless? Then again, there really wasn't anyone around to steal it.

"I've got a rope in the coach."

"All right."

"We could truss it up like a present and haul it up the side? I don't know."

Reesa nodded. It was as good an idea as any. "Let's give it a try. Help me push."

Together they moved behind the box and braced their feet against the wood before putting their shoulders to either side and pushing to move it toward the coach. Even with the two of them, the box barely budged across the planks at a snail's pace.

"Why's it so heavy?" Randy grunted. "They cushion it with rocks?"

Though breathless with effort, Reesa laughed. They worked the box over to the coach and paused to slump against the side of it. Reesa glanced at Randy.

"You ready?"

"Two seconds," Randy said, holding up the appropriate number of fingers.

"I'll lift, you slide the rope under?"

Swallowing, Randy nodded and pushed herself off the box. As Reesa prepared her box-lifting stance, Randy went to the coach and dug her rope out from the storage underneath the seats in the interior. She nodded at Reesa when she was ready. Reesa gripped, lifted, and Randy threaded the rope underneath. They repeated the process for the other side, Randy crossing the rope beneath the box and bringing it around the other sides like ribbons on a package. Hauling herself up, Randy tied the ends together in a knot, the excess remaining for a handle.

"Now we have to get it on the roof?"

Reesa nodded.

"Ai yai yai."

"You want to push or pull?"

Randy shook her head. "Neither."

"You get on top of the coach, then," Reesa laughed. "And take the rope with you."

The girl obeyed, hopping off the box and clambering up the side of the coach. She took a wide stance with her feet braced against the slight railing that ran around the roof and wrapped the rope around her hands. Ready, she gave a nod to Reesa and started pulling.

Miraculously the box lifted off the platform. Reesa wasted no time scurrying under it and lifting from below. The box rose steadily, steadily, until it caught on the railing. Randy gave a tug, Reesa a shove, and with a surprising amount of momentum it flipped up over the side and landed with a resounding crash on the roof. Randy toppled off the back into the scrub, only having just missed losing a toe under the box as it had come down. Thankfully the scrub cushioned her fall. She did let out a few choice words, though. Reesa chuckled and plopped down on the platform.

Randy waded through the scrub and pulled herself back onto the planks like she was getting out of a pool. She sat alongside Reesa and began picking briers from her pant legs. Once she'd finished she looked over.

"You ready to go?" she asked.

Reesa did not answer. There was something she wanted to see, something she wanted to do, but the thought evaded her when she tried to pin it down. It was a place—no, a name. A name that had passed from mouth to ear like a secret password. What was it?

"Greeber."

A jolt went through Randy. "What?"

That was it. Reesa grinned at Randy as the girl paled, staring back at Reesa's rather manic expression.

"Randy, do you know where the Greeber ranch is?"

Randy got up and went straight to the coach, climbing atop it and taking the extra length of rope into her hands to tie it off. She set about her work with her face down, completely ignoring the question. Reesa rose and followed her.

"I said—"

"I heard what you said—ma'am."

Her eyes flicked up to meet Reesa's for but a moment, narrowed and glaring, then she went back to work. Reesa watched, waiting. Even then Randy did not answer.

"Well?"

The girl threw down the rope she was holding and it cracked like a whip against the roof of the coach. "I *know* where it is."

Reesa nearly bounded for joy. "Would you take me there? Right now?"

Randy just stared at her—something like how Reesa imagined people stared through the little window on the door to a padded cell. She didn't mind. She'd figured it out. She'd remembered the name and now she was going to expose whatever secret the mayor and Tombstone had been hiding from her. It didn't matter how long it took, she would convince Randy to drive her out there.

"We really should get the comm back," Randy said.

"It can wait."

"It'll take longer to get there, with the box weighing the coach down."

"We have time."

Meticulously, Randy checked every knot she'd tied, circled the box, circled it again. She went to the driver's seat atop the coach and did everything but sit down, checking the reins and brushing off her cushion and checking the reins again.

"Randy, it's very important that I see the Greeber ranch."

Randy looked at Reesa in a huff. "Do I have to do what you say?"

No, of course not. Reesa was an apostle, she had no authority. "Yes."

She regarded Reesa, searching for a bluff. It was one of the central commandments not to lie, but not technically part of the apostolic vows, so it was all right to bend the rules this once, right? Reesa wasn't going to make a habit out of it, but she *had* to see that ranch. She smiled pleasantly back at Randy, just waiting for her affirmative answer.

Eventually, the girl caved. "All right then, ma'am," she said with a sigh. "Let's go."

Reesa wriggled with excitement. "Great!"

She climbed into the coach and shut the door behind her while Randy rolled her eyes and took a seat on her driver's bench. The reins slapped and the coach struggled and squealed as it pulled away from the platform, making slow progress at first through the brush until the horses were able to pick up speed. She was going to the Greeber ranch. She was going to solve a mystery.

All the excitement died on the three hour coach ride. The ranches lay in line with Big City itself, extending outward east and west parallel to the train tracks. She and Randy had to go all the way back before they could even start for their destination. They headed west after reaching town.

Acres of crops flew by on the right. Patches of green like an endless sea, waving in the desert breeze. Corn, barley, wheat, row after row of low-growing vegetables. An awful lot of food for a hundred people, and they passed only two houses as they went. Two families owned all that land. In the city you were lucky if the rent for your studio apartment was under a thousand a month. She had shared a flat with five other girls until she'd married Joule. What must it be like to look out on several hundred acres of land and say, this is mine, this belongs to me? It sounded wonderful.

In front of the third house, Randy came to a stop, walking the horses and the coach through and opening in a shambling wire fence. As soon as the wheels stopped rolling, Reesa popped open the door and hopped out.

A squat log cabin sat just beyond her, flanked and backed by an undulating expanse of verdant knee-high plants with large leaves. A line of laundry stuck up out of the ground near the house and was hung with pairs of leggings, shirts, and a long cotton dress. The clothing billowed out though there was no breeze to take it into the air. The atmosphere was stuffy, oppressive somehow. It was too quiet.

"Not much to see, ma'am," Randy commented.

Reesa turned round and shaded her eyes to squint up at Randy on her perch. "What kind of plants are those?"

"Tobacco, ma'am."

Reesa smiled. "I've never been one for smoking."

"They do chew as well. Are you ready to go?"

"We came all this way," Reesa replied. "I may as well introduce myself."

She waved a nonchalant hand and started toward the cabin. Randy scrambled down and scurried across the dirt to catch up, clinging to Reesa's shadow. A wind whipped through the laundry, sending all of it flapping madly. Randy jumped, so Reesa jumped and they were about to laugh at each other when a second more powerful gust blew the cabin door open and slammed it with a bang against the outside wall. The two of them nearly left their skins behind. A pale stink crept into the air.

"Please, ma'am. I don't think we should go inside…"

Though Randy grasped the back of her jacket and gave her the subtlest of tugs in the opposite direction, curiosity pulled Reesa like a magnet to the house and propelled her forward to the open, swinging door. She went in, dragging the girl behind her.

Dimness met her on the other side. She paused just inside the doorway for a few seconds to allow her eyes to adjust, but hardly before the most terrible stench assaulted her nose—hot and putrid and burning and hanging in the air like humidity—vomit mixed with rot and excrement. It actually made her reel and she stumbled forward to catch herself on a table.

Her hand sank down into what she'd thought was the surface of the table. She pulled it back. It stuck. She lurched backwards, gagging, and pulled her hand free. From her new vantage point, the source of the smell became abundantly clear.

Sitting in a kitchen chair, with what might have been a head lolled back at an unnatural angle, was a corpse, its mangled teeth and empty eye sockets grinning at her through a liquid coating of sludge that spread from its arm over the table. That. She'd put her hand in *that*. She backed up, but she was angled away from the door now. Her foot crunched down into something warm and gooey. Trembling, she looked and discovered a second body sprawled across the ground with her leg protruding from its back.

Her stomach tried to spill its contents, but she swallowed it down, yanking her foot out and staggering away. She was soaked up to her ankle in black-red liquid, thick and sticky. Her breath stuck in her throat, gasp after gasp, but no air. Her eyes flicked around the room. Her heart stopped. A third carcass, mostly emaciated, hung from a coatrack in the corner. Drip, drip, drip.

"Oh my lord..."

Flick, flick, flick, from corpse, to corpse, to corpse. That was—they were—who had? What was going on? That was not a normal state of decomposition. The smell—like a noose reaching for her neck and nose. The liquid sludge on the bodies seemed to ripple, crawl and creep in rhythm. Digesting the bodies?

It—she—he—she had it all over her hand and foot. The sink! Water. She scrubbed furiously under the running stream. Clean hand, she hauled her foot up over the lip of the sink, shoe and all. She worked furiously until she had rid herself of the slime.

Turning from the sink with a dripping foot, her eyes fell on Randy in the doorway, just an outline of a girl hanging her head.

"You shouldn't have come here," she said to the floor.

Reesa was somehow in front of her.

"Randy, what is going on here?"

"You shouldn't have come."

Snatch—Reesa grasped Randy's shoulders and the girl looked up finally with a jolt of fright. Reesa's nails dug in, and she began to peer down into the girl's face, a bid for intimidation but Randy wriggled out of her grasp and slapped her hands away. She made a dash for the coach. Reesa nabbed her wrist.

"Randy. *What* is going on here?"

Slowly Randy turned and slowly her eyes fell on Reesa in a hard stare. She yanked back her arm and said, "Takers."

Takers? Reesa looked back. Back at the dead, the rotting, grinning. This was the takers' handiwork? Why hadn't anyone buried them? This wasn't real. This was a theatre—a haunted house. It was a plot, to scare her. This wasn't real. A deranged smile crossed over her lips.

"I'm ready to go," she said, and left.

Her sudden departure startled Randy and the girl had to hop to and catch up after taking care to shut the cabin door behind her. Roll the stone across the tomb, though if what lay within rose three days from now, it would be more a zombie film than a resurrection.

Reesa climbed into the coach. They wouldn't rise. They were plastic. They were fake. Hicks and Gig and Tombstone had placed them out there, giggling and hooting with boyish glee at how good they were going to scare somebody. The real Greebers were burrowed away in a neighbor's basement until the prank was complete. She'd put her hand down in that... Her spine snapped with shivers. But there was no call for it. Because it wasn't real.

Randy slapped the reins and the coach took off. Reesa glanced out the back window. The cabin door had blown open again.

11

So help him, if Reesa was at the bottom of a pit out there in that godforsaken desert he would have somebody arrested for assaulting a government official. Where was she? She had been gone *far* too long, even factoring in extra time to get the delivery box on the coach despite her serious lack of upper body strength. He'd told her to use heavier weights, but would she listen? No. When did she ever listen to him?

Mayor Big City stood on the front steps of the town hall with Joule, watching him pace back and forth and fret. It was a bad habit.

"There they are," the mayor said, raising a swollen hand down the length of Big City.

Sure enough the coach was coming through the bottom gate. Joule's lungs let out an enormous sigh of relief. He trotted down the steps to meet the coach as it rounded the top of the square and came to a stop. When Reesa got out, he couldn't help but grab her elbow.

"Where have you *been?*"

She appeared to be in one piece—no evidence of having been trapped in a pit or attacked by wild wolves. She did look—he wasn't sure—*flustered* somehow. Something had happened. She'd seen something, or…something. Either way, she smiled at him.

"We—"

"Move."

Joule looked up to the top of the coach just in time to see Randy untie the delivery box and give it a good shove over the side. He grabbed Reesa and pulled her out of the way as the box came crashing down. He glared up at Randy, fanning away the rising cloud of impact dust.

"Hey! You could have killed someone!"

"That's why I told you to move."

She hopped off the coach, went to the box after landing in the dirt, and started to push it toward the town hall without another word. Reesa detached herself from

Joule and went to help. The box stuck when they reached the stairs.

"Tip it on its side," he said. "The steps are narrow and short enough that it should just slide right up."

"Yes, thank you, Apostle Joule," Reesa replied. "Your instructions are much more helpful than actually helping."

He glared at her and she laughed. Was she determined to make a fool out of him in front of these people or was she just insensitive? Her comment worked on him regardless, and, a little irritated with himself for falling for her tricks again, he braced a shoulder against the box and helped the two of them push it to the top of the stairs, through the doors, down the hall, and just outside the office. The door there was too small to admit the box inside.

"Thank you, Randy," Reesa said, puffing and leaning against the box.

Randy did not reply. She simply turned to go.

"Apostle Joule and I will need a ride out to the old Big City drill site this evening. Would you like to take us?"

Randy turned around. Her eyes said no, but her mouth said, "Sure. Anything else?"

Reesa looked at Joule, her eyebrows raised to direct the question his way. He wrinkled his nose. Randy was not their gopher. What exactly had happened on that coach ride?

"I think that's a no," Reesa chuckled. "Does five o'clock work for you, Randy?"

"I'll meet you at the bottom of the steps," Randy answered, then departed, braids swinging in her wake.

Mayor Big City passed her on the way out, glancing at her as she went, but focusing on the new comm unit as soon as she was gone.

"Seems awful big," he said, peering around the box.

"It's not as big as the box," Joule replied.

"Air cushioning," Reesa added. "Would you like us to unpack it?"

The mayor shrugged. "May as well, I 'spose. You need help?"

Reesa shot Joule a furtive look that he guessed implied something along the lines of get rid of him, we need to talk. He was never very good at reading faces, but he turned to the mayor and shook his head, saying, "Apostle Reesa and I will handle it for you. I'm sure you have plenty of other things to do."

The mayor grunted, rolling his eyes in such a way that confirmed he felt he had a lot on his plate. Joule suspected that plate was probably rather small in the mayor's case, but he did go, thanking them and making a lot of noise with his boots on the wood.

"Well?" Joule said once the front doors had opened and closed.

"Well what?"

"Well, what happened?"

"Let's set up the new unit like we said we would," Reesa replied, going to the box and opening the lid.

Had he misread her? Hadn't she wanted him to get rid of the mayor? He went to the box as well and as she began pulling pieces out and setting them on top of the lid, he studied her. Something was definitely—wait, was that a Gen-28?

He snatched up one of the pieces Reesa had removed.

"Oh my *lands*."

Reesa frowned. "What? Is it broken?"

"No, this model…It hasn't even been released yet."

He looked inside the box. The screen panel was sleek and thin, rounded edges and gold detailing. This was a luxury item. They must have been among the first to get one. It would look ridiculous on the Big City desk.

Wait, wait, wait. Something was going on with Reesa. He wasn't going to let her distract him with the comm.

"Tell me what happened when you went to pick this up," he prompted, still digging pieces of out of the box and trying to sound supportive, or at least nonchalant.

Reesa slowed to a halt. "I asked Randy to take me to the Greebers' ranch."

Greeber? He'd heard the name before of course, but couldn't place it. Or remember why it was important. He simply nodded like he understood and waited for her to continue. The comm was out of the box now. He went to work assembling it on the desk. Reesa did not answer for a moment, so he glanced at her.

"And?"

"There were bodies out there, Joule. Three of them."

The section of casing he was holding slipped from his hands. Bodies? He just managed to catch it before it went sailing to the floor. What did she mean *bodies?* Like actual bodies?

"*What?*"

She shook her head. "I'm not sure if they were real or not. There were just these, I don't know, *things* covered in slime, shaped like people, but—I don't know. I can't describe it."

"Well, *try*." She couldn't just tell him she'd seen three dead bodies and expect to get away without telling him anything about it.

"I think the mayor put them there. To scare us away."

"Why?"

"I don't know, but it's pretty clear nobody wants us here."

He picked up a section of tubing, the power exchange cords. He agreed that their welcome had been a strange one, but one more of mixed messages. Mayor Big City was plainly protective of his turf, but some of the others—Darling, for example—seemed happy to have them. He connected the power exchange to the

70

screen and the telegraph printer, set them both up on the desk.

"I'd like to see it for myself," he said.

"Randy could take us. Tonight, after we investigate the drill site."

"All right."

The pieces became a comm unit as he worked dexterously to set it up, connecting the screen to the scanner, the scanner to the printer, and the unit to the wall. The panel lit up in a sparkling gold some seconds later. Reesa stared at it, mesmerized.

"It's beautiful," she said.

"We'll have to make our report from this unit tonight," he replied.

"What's wrong with your handheld?"

"Jammed up. Same static as the old comm here was getting."

Reesa frowned. "What do you think it is?"

Joule shrugged. "Just distance, or else some other outside source. I'll send a message to Cardinal Cyatan, let him know we've got the unit up and running and that we'll report on the drill site later tonight."

"Did you get those lists of requests for supplies?"

"I finished those ages ago," Joule replied. "I've been waiting for you to get back so we could type them up and send them out. Couldn't do that without a comm."

He smiled, it was supposed to be a joke, but for whatever reason, it didn't work out. Reesa just nodded and crossed her arms, her gaze falling to the floor. Whatever had shaken her up, whatever was out there, had certainly done a number. It was no matter. He would find out for himself soon enough.

Randy was leaning against the front window, chewing on the end of her braid like a teething hog when Hicks came down the hall. She peeled herself off as he went for the door and trailed alongside him down the steps.

"That woman made me take her out to see the Greebers," she said.

What?

Hicks halted immediately, stared down at Randy, bugged his eyes out at her. That fool girl! What was she thinking?

"Why in the *hell* would you ever do that?" he growled.

"She made me." Randy spit on the steps. "I didn't have a choice. You think I *wanted* to go out there?"

Hicks combed his fingers through his moustache. This was bad. "So she knows now. About the takers?"

Randy shook her head, thank god. "No," she replied. "I didn't say nothing, just took her out there. She saw the bodies, that's all. Don't know what kind of conclusions she's concocting in that head of hers, though."

No, no, this was all wrong. They had all agreed—the apostles wouldn't be in the know. They would be expressly *out* of the know. Otherwise just how was Big City supposed to protect its way of life? They couldn't let bigger city people come in and meddle. It just wasn't right. He wouldn't let them take his power from him. *He* was mayor. Not Reesa. Not Joule. Hell, he only ever called them "apostle" to their faces.

"You didn't say anything to her?"

"I'm on your side, Hicks. Else why would I have told you I took her out?"

He winced. She should have called him Mayor Big City, but all the same, she was right. She could have kept the apostle's little sniffings around a secret and he would have been none the wiser. Then what? Big City *really* would have been at risk.

"Thank you for telling me, Randy. I'm glad I can count on you."

"Any time, Hicks."

She looked up at him for a moment, but scampered away soon enough. Good for him too because his blood had begun to boil, its redness reaching the surface and coloring his cheeks. He would take care of this. He would take care of it *right now*.

12

The problem with leaving at five o'clock was that she wouldn't get to watch all the Christmas lights come on. Reesa was looking out the front window of the town hall, hoping, maybe, that the festivities would start before they had to go, but when the hour rolled around, so did Randy, bringing her coach right up to the bottom of the steps.

"She's here Joule."

Tidying up sounds trickled out of the office and soon Joule appeared, swinging his jacket on over his shoulders. Together they descended the steps to Randy and her waiting horses.

"Hello, Randy," Reesa smiled.

Randy tipped her hat, but did not deign to say hello. She looked a little waxy, to tell the truth. Joule climbed into the coach, but Reesa lingered.

"You know where the drill site is?"

"Everyone knows, ma'am."

Just get in the coach, she seemed to say. What had she done to offend her? Reesa obeyed the wordless command and climbed in, clicking the latch on the door closed behind her. Joule knocked on the ceiling below Randy's seat. The team started off. Reesa was getting to like riding by coach. It was familiar. She smiled out the window as they cleared the outside fence and then picked up speed.

Joule shifted in his seat. He was going to say something. He always squirmed around when he was going to say something to fill silence. She'd never understood why he couldn't just leave it alone.

"How are you feeling?" he asked.

"Fine," she answered, and honestly, though he didn't seem to believe her.

"Are you sure you want to go back out there?"

"Yes, I think you ought to see it. Like you wanted."

She looked at him, and he looked back, his eyes narrowing ever so slightly as he tried to discern her expression though there was nothing to discern. She only just managed not to roll her eyes at him.

"You're sure you're all right? You should be in shock."

"Lord, Joule, would you *stop?* You're such a hypochondriac."

"That's not a diagnostic term anymore."

A fiery glare shot from her eyes and he shut right up. Where had that come from? Why had she reacted that way? The brush scraped and tossed outside the window, foiling the silence. Ten long and awkward minutes ticked by. She wasn't sorry. She wouldn't apologize. Or be the first to speak.

Eventually, Joule caved. "What a terrible noise," he remarked.

"It is strange, isn't it?"

He was silent for a few seconds, and then, "...I was only trying to help."

She looked at him. "I don't need your help."

They did not speak for the remainder of the ride.

There wasn't much by way of scenery, but Reesa kept her gaze glued out the window regardless. She could sense the hidden life of the desert—rabbits, and snakes, and wolves, thousands of insects. For a moment she had a strange inkling that she was headed back to the beginning. Out in the desert, there was a room waiting for her. A silver room. But she wasn't going there. Not yet.

Horses slid by in the window frame, some distance away, like they were on a conveyor belt. She could have pointed them out to Joule, but did not. He could look if he wanted. She didn't want to talk to him.

After about an hour or so the coach slowed to a stop and with a wash of excitement overtaking her, Reesa practically leapt out of the cab. The fence surrounding the drill site was just ahead. Above her the sky had taken on a new color—orange and red with pink clouds. The sun took ages to set without buildings or mountains or other shadow casters. It would remain light for a while yet. She looked up at Randy.

"You have a flashlight perchance?"

Joule got out of the coach. Randy stood, rooted around in the compartment underneath her seat, and finding something, tossed it down to Reesa. The tube *vaguely* resembled a flashlight, but Reesa couldn't be sure. When she clicked the on button, nothing happened.

"You have to shake it," Randy said. "To charge the battery. Here."

She held out her hand and Reesa tossed the contraption back to her. Randy turned it off, then shook it, like she said, up and down for several seconds. Then she flicked the switch and the little lightbulb came on—dim and dying after only three or four seconds.

"Like that."

She tossed the flashlight to Reesa.

"Thanks." Dumb thing was practically useless. What was she supposed to do? Walk around shaking it once it got dark?

"Let's go, Reesa," Joule said.

She nodded and followed his lead, looking down at the flashlight in her hands as she walked. After a moment she started to shake it, slowly at first, and found there was a weight inside, something that slid back and forth with her motion. She picked up the pace. This was going to be a workout.

They reached the fence, but there didn't appear to be a gate, so as she shook the flashlight, Reesa looked for alternate means of entry. Under or over? Black bastion drill towers in various states of disrepair lay on their backs or stood twisted in the air not a hundred yards away. Zip-tied to the fence just in front of her face was a warning sign bleached completely white after years of sun exposure. DANGER: ELECTRIC, NO ENTRY, KEEP OUT, VIOLATORS WILL BE SHOT AND SURVIVORS WILL BE SHOT AGAIN. She liked that one, and so that's what it said.

Portions of the chain link at the bottom of the fence curled upward toward the sky like wet paper. She went to one decently people-sized section and rolled the flashlight underneath it before wriggling through herself. When she popped up on the other side, her front completely yellow-brown with dirt, she grinned at Joule through the fence. For a second he looked surprised to see her successfully on the other side, but that faded (as most of his positive emotions did), and settled into disgruntlement.

"How are you going to even *begin* to wash that?" His eyelids fell veiled over his eyes.

"There's a laundress next to the hotel," she replied and turned on her heel. She began to walk away, tossing a glance over her shoulder just in time to see Joule start as he realized he would have to follow her. Her lips curled up in delicious delight. Joule would have to get his uniform dirty. In a few minutes, she'd make *him* shake the flashlight.

He caught up eventually and was still dusting his uniform off when he did.

"We could have looked for the gate, you know."

"Gates are no fun."

He grumbled something about gates and civilized people, but Reesa ignored him. It was easy walking in the drill site—no scrub. For whatever reason, the hairy tangles were nowhere to be found this side of the fence, only compact dirt—an embryo rock in formation. Before too long, the pair of them reached the base of the first drill.

Four sturdy steel legs towered hundreds of feet into the air and ended in an enormous bulbous cap from which the drill itself protruded. The twisting, sharp-edged thing spiraled down from the cap into the ground where a hardened mound of windswept dirt covered its entry. It was like a massive water tower that sucked its own liquid out of the ground with a straw. At least, that was how Joule had explained it to her when she'd asked him on their first meeting. She suspected that was also how he explained it to children and animals.

"It's enormous," she remarked, rather pointlessly, the old bones in her neck straining as she titled her head back to gaze up at the top.

"This is the most advanced model," Joule replied. "The drill can go deeper faster than any other." He circled the base as he spoke, pushing against the steel legs with his entire body. She couldn't imagine *why,* but he looked like he was doing Jazzercise or something. Reesa chuckled to watch him lean against the legs and then shove.

"What are you doing?" she asked.

He shook his head. "According to Mayor Big City, this site never yielded oil. If the reserves are as big as he claims, it wouldn't make sense to abandon them like this. By the look of it, this drill has been out of commission far longer than he's even been alive. We're talking hundreds of years."

"And we haven't built a better drill since then?" The best drill they had was hundreds of years old? And Joule called himself an oil tech.

"We haven't had to," he replied. "These drills are still more than sufficient."

"But not in Big City."

Joule pursed his lips and then placed his hand over them in thought as he wandered round the base of each leg one more time.

"Do you think there's even oil out here?" Reesa asked, tracking him.

He bent low to the ground and placed his hands palms down in the dirt. In the *dirt.* It was the first time Reesa had ever seen him willingly touch the stuff. His brow furrowed in thought, then he stood, brushing his hands together.

"I'll be able to do a better survey when my equipment arrives on the train, but I think it's safe to assume the Theocracy wouldn't have spent a dime if the land was dry."

Reesa nodded. How ordinary. Her bones were begging her to leave. She ignored them, trailing after Joule as he stepped away from the first drill and headed for the second.

The thing lay on its side, separated from the bottom portions of its legs that stuck out of the ground like shrapnel. Its drill shaft was missing, and when they went to the cap to take a look inside, there was nothing. The drill had likely tipped over in a wind storm, Joule guessed.

Together they checked each drill in succession, and each drill told the same story: no oil, no oil, no oil, that is until they came to the last one. It lay on its side like the second, but in a twisted scrap heap—the drill shaft stick stuck into the ground, the end of it curved down and toward the south, as though its point had suddenly hit something incredibly hard and sent the whole thing spinning out of control.

Reesa gave a low whistle, still shaking the flashlight. "Well, well, well, what have we here?"

She glanced at Joule. His mouth was hanging open. He went to the drill shaft and circled it though he had to duck under the bent portion as he did.

"Do you have any idea how strong something would have to be to *bend* steel like this?"

Reesa did not have any idea, but she nodded anyway and tried to look impressed.

He placed his hand on the shaft. "It would—" He cut himself off, gaping.

"What? *What?*" Reesa scampered toward him, shaking the flashlight faster.

He shook his head, put up a hand to silence her before replacing it on the shaft. He shut his eyes, crinkled his brow in concentration. Reesa eyed him wriggling, waiting for him to tell her the secret. She couldn't hold it in for long.

"What is it, Joule?" she whispered.

In reply, he reached out, took her hand, and placed it on the drill shaft.

"Vibrations," he said. "Someone is drilling down there."

She had to focus, for the sensation was slight, but the drill shaft shivered lightly underneath her hand. A tiny gasp escaped her. "Who?" she asked.

Joule shrugged, scowling. "It would seem we have a lot of questions to ask our friend the mayor."

He pulled away from the drill and began walking back south toward the coach. Reesa, distracted for a moment in touching the shaft again, scurried to catch up to him.

"You think he lied to us?"

"Obviously," Joule replied. "He claims the site failed, that not a single barrel was ever shipped out of Big City. The records support that, but all the same, *someone* is out here, and *someone* is drilling."

"Any hypothesis as to the culprits?"

"No. We'll have to do some research, look into the town history."

"Or we could just *ask.*"

She noticed him roll his eyes out of the corner of hers.

"No," he said. "If we ask directly, then whoever is out here will know that we know. They may sabotage the site."

"Who would do that?"

"It's happened before."

"I remember something about the storage of town documents being in our information packet," she said. "I could take a look tomorrow?"

Joule nodded. "This is dangerous territory, Reesa," he replied. "People kill for oil."

They reached the fence.

Reesa crawled under first, followed by a miserably grumbling Joule. Randy sat up as the pair of them drew near, an obvious wave of relief filling her limbs. Reesa paused to look up at the girl once she reached the coach and tossed back her flashlight. All that shaking and it wasn't even dark yet.

"Take us to the Greeber ranch. I want Joule to see for himself."

Randy went rigid—the relief gone in an instant. She stared at Reesa in disbelief, but when Reesa started to get into the coach, Randy snapped back to attention.

"But—ma'am, I-we—we can't go back!"

"It wasn't a request, Randy."

She threw a warning glance—or what she assumed was a warning glance, she'd never really thrown one before—and climbed into the coach after Joule. Once she'd settled into her seat, Joule gave a knock on the ceiling and the coach started hesitantly off—Randy's reluctance showing through.

Reesa's bones were tired. The drill site had worn them out, not finding it in the least bit exciting. In fact, they were scared. They whispered at her that there was something to fear, something real and tangible and dangerous, but how could bones whisper? The sensation made her squirm. She couldn't put a name to it. Joule had never understood. She had long since stopped telling him about the different emotions her body seemed to feed her.

Half an hour ticked away, Big City's light bulb ring of buildings came into view, passed on the left. It was another half an hour to the Greeber cabin, the whole of it spent in silence. The coach began to slow and when Reesa looked out the window tobacco fields were waving at her.

"We're here."

She got ready to stand and disembark, but the coach jarred to a halt and sent her flying. She landed in Joule's lap, and they exchanged expressions as she tried to right herself and he tried to wriggle out from underneath her. Suddenly, he paused.

"Do you smell something?"

Together they sniffed the air. It only took one whiff to identify the aroma.

"Smoke," Reesa said.

She reached for the door handle, but Randy ripped it open before she could get her hand around it. "Apostles! Look!" she cried, her voice cracking on its volume. She scrambled out of the way to let Reesa climb down and stood a little ways off her hands clapped firmly on her head, staring in disbelief at the source of the smell.

The Greeber cabin was reduced to ash, releasing a column of smoke into the sky. Hot, grey flurries floated through the air like snow. This was Big City snow. A few days too late for a white Christmas.

Reesa stared at the charred square of burned and burning wood. A house had been there only hours ago. Hardly anything even in semblance of a house remained—just some cast iron cookware, the metal fixtures of the sink, and a standing coatrack. The fire had burned too hot, too fast to allow anything else to stick around. Not even the corpses.

She looked back at Joule and Randy. "It's gone."

Joule stepped forward and circled the square as she had. "Someone must have started the fire," he said as he went. "Nothing natural would be so contained. Or so hot. You said there were bodies here, didn't you?"

Reesa could only nod.

"Nothing here now." He put his hands on his hips, pursed his lips. "The flames would have had to reach well over a thousand degrees to incinerate bone."

Reesa began to tremble. Her haunted house theory crumbled down around her feet. You didn't destroy the spectacle you wanted others to see. Not this completely. How soon after she had left had someone come out and set the blaze? A mote of ash fell upon her nose.

"I wonder who could have done it," Joule said.

"It doesn't matter, it's gone."

"It *would* serve us to know who set the fire," he continued. "It could be connected to the drill site."

Reesa wasn't listening. She gestured at the cabin's remains.

"It's gone…"

"I'd like to ask the mayor directly, but I'm not sure that would be wise."

"It's gone…"

"Reesa?"

"*It's gone.*"

"Reesa, are you all right?"

He stepped swiftly towards her and took hold of her upper arm, but she wrenched it out of his grip immediately.

"I wanted you to see what I saw!" She started to scream, but it changed into laughter. "I'm going insane. I wanted somebody to see what I saw!"

A second bout of the crazed cackles began to issue from her throat, but she felt a slight pressure on her elbow and they were silenced. She looked down to discover Randy looking up.

"I saw it, ma'am," she said. "I saw it."

Reesa stared at her. The trembling began again. Randy patted her arm and gave her a look of knowing—a look like the Greeber cabin was hardly the worst thing she had seen. Reesa did not want to know what those other things might be.

"We should go," Randy said. "Nothing we can do here."

She went back to the coach, leaving Reesa and Joule no choice but to follow. Her partner tried to catch her eye as they walked, but she would never allow him the satisfaction. She eased herself back into the coach and tucked her ever-trembling hands between her knees after she sat down. Joule climbed in after her.

"Are you all right?"

He would never learn. "Why haven't we left yet?"

She peered out the window and caught sight of the delay: Randy scurrying back to the coach, and just behind her, the payment loaf of funeral bread Reesa had given her sitting squat in front of the cabin. She must have placed it there. The coach tilted as Randy climbed atop, and as they departed, Reesa stared out the back window at that bread and the great swirl of ash that took to the sky.

13

Her hands trembled all the way back to Big City, all the way up the steps to the town hall, all the way down the walk to the office, and they did not stop trembling until Joule dialed Cardinal Cyatan on the mayor's new comm when Reesa realized she would have to pull it together. That was difficult to do when your hands did not truly belong to your brain.

The cardinal's triangle face appeared in a great flash of gold like some sort of rapture. He was even more grotesque on the larger unit, every nook and cranny of his craggy face spelled plainly out on the wide screen. He began speaking almost as soon as the call connected.

"I received your telegraphs for supply orders. I take it that means you got the new comm up and working?" He raised the caterpillars he called his eyebrows up into his forehead, smiling a smile that was hardly a smile. "Well done, Apostles."

"We completed all of our goals for the day, your grace," Joule replied.

The cardinal nodded. "That's good news."

"Well…"

"Well what, Apostle Joule?"

A breath entered Joule's lungs through his mouth as he prepared to answer, but he paused, and the air came back out in a sigh instead of words. "It comes with bad news," he said eventually.

"All right." Cyatan sat back, darkening.

Joule glanced at Reesa and she could see in his eyes that he had no idea how to say what needed to be said. She shook her head, equally dumbfounded, but took over the conversation.

"There's been lots of talk around the town, your grace, concerning creatures the locals call 'takers,'" she said. "I can honestly say I didn't believe they were real until today, and even now I'm not certain, but… I've seen what they're said to do."

"And what is that, Apostle?"

"Kill people. And—" It was impossible to describe what she had seen. The words were always on the tip of her tongue—tantalizingly close and moving out of her reach when she went for them. All the same, she continued, "I saw three of their victims, your grace, at the Greebers' cabin. Already dead, but almost completely decomposed. And when Joule and I went back together, someone had burned the place to the ground."

The deep lines on the cardinal's forehead deepened. "Hmm." He placed a hand over his mouth, thoughtful. "And what of the drill site?"

"Two of the drills are unusable, your grace," Joule piped in. "And…I felt vibrations. There's drilling going on at that site, your grace. I just don't know who…"

Joule's words faded from her ears. Those corpses, the smell, the feel of her hand as it sank into the damp, sticky decomposition. All at once, like a crack of lightning, her mind transposed her somewhere else.

Someone is dragging her across a hard, rock floor, downward at a slight decline. Their hands feel wet and slippery around her wrists. She is dizzy from a crack on the head.

Someone is lifting her onto a table, strapping her to it by her arms and ankles. She hears voices that speak to one another in grizzled spurts, a spitting, gnarled language that she cannot understand. She hears beeping—her heart on a monitor— and feels the adamant poke of a needle entering the back of her hand.

In a burst of color, the room becomes clear. She is in some rock-hewn cave, secured to an examination table that angles upwards so she lays diagonal to the floor. It is incredibly cold. Her teeth chatter in her skull. All around her is a sea of monitors and medical instruments like none she has ever laid eyes on. Her head flops sideways and she sees she is not alone. A second someone is tied to a table not far from hers.

"Randall…"

Her voice is harsh and grating, little more than a glorified whisper. She tries to reach out to him, but the bindings on her wrists will not let her.

"Randall."

He does not respond. His body is limp. She can see the blood trailing down the side of his skull. She reaches again and again for him, struggling against her bonds, but it is fruitless. Tears begin to rise in her eyes. She rallies the energy for one final pull toward the body of her husband, crying out, "Randall!"

She falls back against the table. They're going to die. She knows this. She hopes Randy will be all right without them.

Her calls summon another to the cave. A taker appears in the rough entrance to their cavern. It stands in the doorway a moment, the oversized mouth hole that makes up its face gaping at her, skin dripping. It cocks its head, then sound issues forth, and another taker appears in her view. They speak to one another

They are so humanoid in shape—two arms, two legs, a head, all attached to a torso—that she wonders if they might actually be humans under all that slop. Tombstone says no. It's a mucus, a thick slime secreted from specialized organs in their equivalent epidermis. She had never understood what he meant. The takers had always reminded her of Gloppy, the fudge swamp monster from the Candyland game.

Her captors enter the room, leaving slimy footprints where they step, and busy themselves with preparation she cannot see. Tools clink against one another, against trays. The two of them snarl speech back and forth. She wonders what they're saying. She wonders if this is what happened to Catherine Shane when she disappeared in January.

A gloved pair of three-fingered taker hands presses down on her skull. She tries to wriggle free. It snaps her neck—or at least that's what it feels like when it spikes a needle directly into her jugular. She goes limp, feeling whatever chemical they pumped into her bloodstream make its rounds on her quickened heartbeat. She can still feel everything even though she cannot move.

Another pair of hands comes down on her skull. The sharp slice of a penknife slides across her forehead as it begins to remove her scalp. She is still conscious, she is still conscious! She screams.

"Reesa!"

She looked up at Joule from the floor. Her shoulder throbbed. It had struck first when she toppled off her chair, taking most of the impact. The palms of her hands were sweaty and when she tried to sit up, they slipped a little against the wood.

"Apostle Reesa, are you all right?" Cardinal Cyatan's voice called from the comm.

Joule was on his hands and knees beside her in the next moment with more concern on his face than she had ever seen him show. Her heart skipped at his nearness and the kind softness that shone in his features.

"What happened?" he asked, holding onto her elbow to keep her from tumbling back to the floor.

She let him help her to her feet. "I…" she said, but she could not continue. Her fingers went to her hairline, traced it all the way down her face on both sides. That pain. It was real. And all the different parts of her body were screaming at her to remember.

"I…I don't know," she managed to say, staring at her trembling hands. "I think I need to go lie down…"

Gravity began to pull her back to the floor, but Joule caught her and steadied her body against his own. He looked to the cardinal for a prompt.

"We can finish our call once Apostle Reesa is cared for," Cyatan stated. "Get her settled, then call me back. Apostle—" His eyes flicked to Reesa. "—please rest. Take the time to take care of yourself before you care for any others, all right?"

Reesa nodded, pale to the very pigment and trembling as Joule led her out of the office and the town hall altogether. Outside, the sun had set and all of Big City had turned on their Christmas lights. The soft glow of all that green and red and blue and white warmed a little piece of her soul.

The Big City square was busier than she had ever seen. Every citizen was out, chattering and laughing, standing up on ladders to hang streamers and banners from each and every building, setting out folding chairs in neat rows before the town hall. Darling stood at a table laid out with scones and cider for the workers. An ocean of women sat nearby, sewing some enormous quilt. Gig Sullivan was overseeing the hanging of a banner across the square from the stables to the railroad office that read: BIG CITY BICENTENNIAL CELEBRATING 200 YEARS. The fountain was giving him some trouble, very nearly reaching the banner with its spout of water.

Reesa and Joule walked through it all like Scrooge and the ghost of Christmas Past, completely unseen by all in their jubilee. When they reached the hotel and stepped inside, Shay was absent from behind his desk. Joule helped Reesa up the stairs, a particular difficulty with her quivering knees, and down the hall to their room where he eventually deposited her on the bed.

"Do you want to change out of your uniform?" he asked.

She shook her head, tucking her arms against her stomach. "No."

"Is there anything I can do?"

Again, she shook her head. "No, go finish your call to the cardinal. I'll be all right." She gave him an unconvincing smile and, after frowning at her, Joule left.

Reesa collapsed on the bed as soon as the door shut behind him. The threat of tears stung the corners of her eyes, so she shut them. But even as she lay there, trying to forget what she had seen, she saw again.

He is standing at the pulpit of the church, having just uttered the last few words of his sermon for the next morning. Do other pastors practice? He smiles, tucking away his notes and Bible. This is going to be the kind of sermon that changes lives. He can feel it, but the feeling is interrupted by the sound of slurping echoing down the aisle and the stick-stick-stick of distinctive footsteps. They've come for him.

Turning to run, he collides with a long metal bar that comes down hard on his head. Collapsing, his body hits the ground and in the impact, he loses consciousness.

Reesa gasped herself awake. She looked at the clock. Two minutes. That was all that had passed. Joule had only just left and already he felt miles away. Curling up into a fetal position on the bed, she found herself wishing that she had not sent him back. Being alone and afraid was worse than having him there.

She did not dare close her eyes again. She knew what would happen, so she forced her eyelids open—up, back, and practically all the way into her head, determined. Unfortunately the practice worked against her almost immediately as the arid desert atmosphere dried out her eyeballs. She blinked repeatedly in deliberate, slow movements, trying to moisten her eyes without letting them stay closed too long. It wasn't going to work lying down. She sat up, but her arms began to tremble, elbows wobbling back and forth as they made a sorry show of supporting her weight on the bed. Reesa collapsed with a frustrated groan. She couldn't win. Not tonight. Her eyes drifted shut.

She awakens to his shaking her shoulder with enthusiasm. Blinking sleep from her eyes, she turns over, squints up, and tries to distinguish his face in the darkness.

"What?" she grumbles.

"Get up," Tombstone laughs, excited. "Marianne has foaled."

The news sends a jolt to her heart. She whips the bed sheets off and scrambles to her feet. She does not bother with shoes as she rushes out the door and across the raspy gravel pathway to the barn. Marianne has foaled! She can't believe it. This has been their most anticipated birth in several years.

She throws open the door to the barn and nearly launches herself into the pen where Marianne has been kept in comfort for these final months. Surprise and joy flood over her when she sees the little black foal already out and wobbling around on green legs.

Looking back over her shoulder she frowns at Tombstone in disappointment when he finally catches up.

"Why didn't you get me?" she says. "I could have helped you."

"I was going to, but Marianne didn't need my help. I gathered the things and by the time I'd done that, the little girl was already here."

He gestures to an unused pile of blankets, a bucket of water, and several emergency tools sitting in the corner of the stall. Marianne herself lies practically unperturbed on her bed of hay, watching the progress of her foal attentively.

Going to the mother, she kneels at her head, taking the horse's muzzle in her hands and stroking the soft skin of her nose.

"Good girl," she whispers.

Smiling, Tombstone leans against the frame of the stall. "What shall we call her?" he asks, chuckling as the foal takes a tumble to her knees.

She turns to look at the new arrival—the finest, fastest purebred to be produced to date. The foal is gawky and awkward now, but soon she will grow up to be the most magnificent horse anyone could ask for.

"Indie," she answers. "She's already so independent."

A sharp breath in. Joule was beside her now, already snoring. Reesa held her body stock still in the darkness. The apparent motion of the red and green Christmas lights around their window played in tandem across the bedspread. At least that memory had been a good one.

She drew in a deep breath. She wasn't permitted to think that. She couldn't allow herself to regard Tombstone as a lover or a husband. It wasn't fair to Joule— no. That's not why. She was afraid of what she would do if she let those feelings into her heart.

Staring at the digital clock, Reesa counted out each blink of the colon between the first two numbers as it raised to sixty and the display leapt forward a minute. Fifteen minutes passed. She stopped counting, just stared at the final number and waited with anticipation for it to change. It always took longer than she expected. Thirty minutes passed. She was not going back to sleep.

Midnight rolled around and Reesa abandoned the clock. Sitting up, she scooched ever so carefully to the edge of the mattress where she slipped on her shoes. Joule must have taken them off her feet when he came to bed. Thankfully she was still wearing her uniform. A blush swept into her cheeks to think about Joule removing that as well. She shook it out, getting to her feet and creeping across the floor to the door which she slipped through silently.

Down the hall and stairs, through the lobby and out the door, Reesa was halfway across the square to the saloon before she realized where she was going. Laughter and light poured from the windows. No quarantine tonight.

She slid up the steps and through the swinging door, navigating her way to the bar on the back left. Heads turned to watch her progress through the crowd. Reesa ignored them, keeping her eyes fixed on the stool Darling had shown her on her first night in Big City. She climbed onto it, her spine tingling with the eyes on her back.

Darling herself appeared only moments later, dashing haphazardly around the bar counter to greet Reesa. "Evening, ma'am," she beamed. "What can I get for you?"

"Nothing, Darling," Reesa replied. "I was having some trouble sleeping, that's all."

"I can try to quiet down this rabble, ma'am, but it ain't gonna be easy." The barmaid shook her head with wide, expressive eyes.

Reesa smiled. "No, it's not the noise. Just…dreams."

"I'm sorry to hear that, ma'am."

"Don't be. It's not your fault."

The barmaid cracked her fingers in the air. "My mother used to make us kids a glass of warm milk with honey when we couldn't sleep. Maybe you'd like to try that?" she offered. "Big City bees make the best honey for a hundred miles."

Reesa kept a comment that the Big City bees probably made the *only* honey for a hundred miles to herself. Instead, she nodded graciously to which Darling giggled and bounced, sweeping away on her little feet, saying, "I'll just be right back, ma'am," and leaving Reesa alone again with her thoughts.

The apostle fixed her eyes on a chip in the enamel of the bar just before her while she waited. Her fingers ran over the dent as she considered several different bar-fight scenarios—heads bashed with glass, teeth cracked, a heavy mug colliding with the wood. A thousand different occasions passed through her mind's eye so swiftly that she couldn't have said whether they were a part of her imagination or not. Big City was turning two hundred in a matter of days, but this bar was very likely older even than that. All at once Tombstone was sliding smoothly into the seat beside her.

"I thought apostles had curfew," he said. "You aren't breaking a commandment being out this late?"

He grinned and Reesa bristled instantly. She snapped her neck up to shoot back some witty remark directly to his face, but when their eyes connected, seven different voices spouted seven different feelings into her body one right after another. *He ought to be punished for what he's done to this town, buy him a drink, when I grow up I'll be just like that, God pray for his soul, still owes me a hat, he'll care for Randy, I love him.* That one was strongest. It made her want to wrap her arms around him, kiss him fiercely and forever. She shivered.

"No," she whispered.

"Pity."

Tombstone reached across the bar, took a glass from a stack, and served himself something from the tap. She wanted to tell him to go bother somebody else, but her apostolic duties demanded otherwise. He didn't deserve it, making her think those things. She shivered once more. She could feel his eyes on her as he took a long draw from his glass.

"Here's that milk, ma'am," Darling said, reappearing and setting down a cup for Reesa. "Looks like you served yourself, Tombstone." She turned up one half of her lips coyly and placed a hand on her hip. "Anything else I can get you?"

"This will do for now, Darling. Thank you."

The barmaid shifted her weight from foot to foot, looking very much like she wanted to stay, but she was hailed from across the room in a matter of seconds.

"I think she's sweet on you." The words were out of Reesa's mouth before she could stop herself. A jolt shot through her. What was she thinking?

"If she is, she shouldn't be," Tombstone replied. He set his glass down on the counter.

Reesa waited for him to elaborate, but he did not. Her eyes narrowed. "What do you want from me?" she demanded.

He laughed, shaking his head. "Nothing, Apostle. Just a drink. This *is* a saloon."

The color rose in Reesa's cheeks and she gripped her glass of milk in a hurry to bring it to her lips. Some of the milk splashed up over the rim and her cheeks darkened to feel it drip down her hands and onto the counter. She did not look at Tombstone. She knew he would be grinning.

She turned her back to the bar and sipped the milk adamantly, eyes fixed on the floor in front of her. The milk was good. Two pairs of boots wandered into her view. As she looked up, she recognized Callum and Nana, blacksmith and wife. The copper-colored ponytail that spilled halfway down Callum's back was unmistakable. His eyes were fixed on Tombstone in a grim stare, but Nana managed a smile for the both of them.

"Apostle Reesa! What a pleasant surprise to see you out so late, ma'am," she said. "Where's your partner?"

"Sleeping," Reesa replied.

"Greeber place burnt down today," Callum growled.

Tombstone raised his eyebrows. "That so?"

Nana chuckled, tapping Reesa's knee and drawing her attention. "I see, and while the cat's away, the mice will play, hm?" she smiled.

"It's not exactly like that," Reesa replied, trying to smile back. "I couldn't get to sleep."

"Ain't you got nothing to say?" Callum.

"What is there to say?" Tombstone.

"I'm sorry to hear that, Miss Reesa." Nana.

"Listen here, you son of a bitch—" Callum struck forward like a shot and snatched Tombstone up in his fists, pulling him up by his shirt collar into his own face. Reesa nearly toppled over on her own stool as Tombstone's fell to the ground with the sudden loss of its occupant. Nana hopped over, clutching onto Callum's arm. Tombstone did not look surprised in the least.

"Cal, don't!" Nana tugged firmly on her husband's mammoth bicep.

The blacksmith glanced at his wife for a millisecond, and that was all it took for Tombstone to slip from his fingers, draw his gun, and point it directly at Callum's head. A dead silence swept through the saloon.

Callum put his hands up. "I don't want no trouble."

"Sure. You don't want any trouble *now*. Go ahead. Say what you came here to say."

Callum turned his gaze sheepishly to his feet, but the safety clicked on Tombstone's gun.

"Say it!"

Tombstone had Callum's full attention then. The hum of the weapon powering up floated through the quiet.

"Greeber place burned down today," Callum said, a bit of the fire returning to his eyes. "And we all know who did it."

Tombstone's lips curled up, exposing vicious teeth. "Do we?"

"We all know who killed them!" he shouted. He gestured around the room, looking for conformation in the crowd. "We all know who always kills them!" His eyes fell once again in fiery hatred upon Tombstone. "Murderer."

In a flash, Tombstone had gripped Callum not by his collar but by his throat. He held him there for a moment, suspended in the silence, the guttural choking noises barely making it out of Callum's mouth.

"I do what I have to," Tombstone snarled. He tossed Callum back. "*All right?*"

Callum coughing, the two men regarded each other with wide, wild eyes. Then Tombstone swept out of the saloon. A thousand conversations erupted all at once. In the hubbub, Nana went to Callum and Reesa shot to her feet to follow Tombstone out into the night.

When she reached the porch he was already thundering away on that big, black horse. She shouted after him, "*Tombstone!*" but her voice was lost in the gathering wind.

She started for the edge of the porch, ready to leap down and take off running after him, but Darling had followed her out and caught her wrist before she could.

"Let him go, ma'am," she said, pulling her back. "Ain't nothing you can do."

"But…"

Darling tried to lead her back inside, but Reesa kept her eyes on the gap between the stables and the bank where Tombstone had disappeared and anchored herself to the wood. Darling pulled; Reesa resisted.

"He ain't never gonna accept help from you, ma'am," Darling said. "Not looking the way you do."

Reesa stopped pulling. She stared at Darling. "What do you mean?"

"Like Merrick."

Reesa shook her head. That didn't mean anything to her.

"His late wife, ma'am."

Blood rushed instantly to her head and a chill pricked up every last hair into gooseflesh all across her body—even the hairs on her head. Darling said something, but she could barely hear her over the beating drum of her heart in her ears.

"I didn't want to say it, but you look just like her, ma'am. Your hair and eyes… You could be her sister."

His wife. She looked like his wife. She felt her fingers begin to quiver. She'd *dreamt* of being his wife. Sick began to bubble in the pit of her stomach. Why did she look like his wife? What little milk she'd had made a reappearance as she retched over the side of the porch. Darling patted her back.

"It's all right, ma'am," she soothed. "It's all right."

It was not all right. What a stupid thing to say. How could it be all right? She looked like Tombstone's wife and she'd imagined it, too. Was it possible to be more treacherous than that? It was definitely not all right.

Darling helped her across the street to the hotel, up the stairs, and into her bed. Somehow, they managed not to wake Joule for quite some space of time. His eyes fluttered open as Darling was handing Reesa a glass of water, however, and he sat up in a flash, startled by the presence of someone else in their room.

"It's just Darling," Reesa rasped.

"Sorry to disturb you, sir." Darling smiled at him, her bright teeth shining in the moonlight coming through the window.

Joule opened his mouth, but nothing came out.

"Thank you," Reesa said to Darling. She took the water and sipped it.

"You're welcome, ma'am. I'll be going now." Darling slipped away to the door. "Feel better," she said, and was gone.

"What on *earth?*" Joule's whisper hissed harshly through the darkness.

"I couldn't sleep so I went to the saloon," Reesa replied. "It didn't help."

"Are you feeling well?"

He reached out for her, but when his fingertips connected with her shoulder she wriggled out from underneath his touch almost immediately, her spine twisting out and away from him as she got to her feet.

"Don't."

He blinked at her. Her grip flexed over the glass of water. She didn't want him to touch her. She didn't want him to ask her if she was feeling all right. She wanted him to disappear. Tonight, she would never love him.

Without saying a word, Reesa left the room. She went directly downstairs, took a key from one of the hooks around the back of Shay's desk, and showed herself to a new room. She locked the door behind her. Her eyes stung with unshed tears and she slid down the wood of the door to the floor as slow sobs slipped out of her throat.

What a wasteland this was. What a nightmarish misery. She was sick of secrets, sick of being lied to and pestered and steered around like a horse on a bit—and by *everyone*. Sometimes she felt like a machine, some slave robot. She had to get out. How long would it take her to walk to the train station from town?

A shiver stripped her body of its warmth. She couldn't leave, or shouldn't. She would probably freeze to death in the desert if she tried. Joule had touched her tenderly, but she was violated by it. She didn't belong to him. She belonged to—

He's hurting. I wish I could be there for him.

That voice—did it belong to her or not? Had she heard it or thought it? It didn't really matter. The emotion it carried had already swept through her body. Tombstone suffered, same as she. Reesa drew in a shaky breath, setting her head back against the door and letting the last of her tears run down her cheeks.

Wiping her nose on her uniform sleeve, she crawled across the floor to the bed, pulled herself over the edge, and slithered up under the covers. No clock. Not knowing the time was a thousand times more agonizing than watching it change minute to minute. She fought down a second string of sobs rising in her chest. Tomorrow, which was almost certainly "today," she would hunt down every scrap of information there was to know about Merrick. She *would* know. Even if it killed her.

14

Shay had directed her not to the town hall, but to the private home of Doctor Fencer when Reesa had inquired where Big City kept its records. It was overtly inappropriate for a civilian to store sensitive information, but apparently James Fencer was the last in a long line of amateur historians and somewhere along that line someone had decided just to let his ancestors do the dirty work. His house was the last in the line of the eastern edge of Big City. He stored everything in his fruit cellar.

"Was there something in particular you were looking for, Apostle?" he asked, sweeping away the threadbare rug in the middle of his living room floor that covered the trap door down to the cellar.

Reesa gave him a pleasant smile. "No."

His eyes narrowed almost imperceptibly behind the blonde mask of limp hair that fell into his face, but he knelt down anyways and lifted the hatch, exposing a gaping square hole. The basement was black. Two ends of a ladder poked up into the light like a pair of drowning hands reaching out of a dark sea.

"The switch is out back. I'll go flip it for you." He let the trapdoor slip from his hands and land with a crash against the floorboards. "Go ahead and start down."

As he departed, Reesa stared into the little black pit. Anything could have been waiting at the bottom. Taking a deep breath, she began her descent, easing herself down onto the ladder. Cool air greeted her legs as they entered the darkness, wrapping around her ankles. It was almost like stepping into a shallow pool. She stepped down, and again, and again, until her head dipped under the lip of the hole and submerged in the darkness.

It took a moment to adjust to the lack of light, and as soon as she did, Fencer flipped on the switch. Her eyes shut up in a squint. She froze on the ladder, blinded, feeling around with a foot to see how close she was to the bottom. Nothing. Why was that damn light so bright? She reached a little father, straining her thigh, and slipped. God in heaven!

Thankfully she was nearer to the bottom than she thought, landing only a second later on the foot she'd been using to reach. It twisted painfully against her ankle as it met packed dirt. She bit back the curses that sprang to her tongue. Swearing only counted if you said it out loud.

Wriggling her ankle around in tiny circles, Reesa turned her head to get a look around the room: dirt walls, a ceiling just a few feet above her, squat and square and lined with row upon row of metal filing cabinets. The cabinets tilted slightly at various angles, not one of them sitting flat. Bumpy dirt floor. *Painful* dirt floor. A shelf ran around the ceiling, stocked with jars and boxes and cans of who-knows-what.

Footsteps from above signaled Doctor Fencer's return. His shoes squeaked their way down the rickety ladder and soon he was standing beside her.

"It's all organized by decade," he said, "starting there. More recent history's in these cabinets. Current citizens' documents and the rest." He stepped over to two tall cabinets and tapped the side of one, a metallic echo answering back. "Any questions?"

She shook her head. "No, thank you, Doctor Fencer. It's good of you to let me look."

He shrugged and took two large steps over to the ladder, his tall frame hunched somewhat under the low ceiling. "Help yourself to any of the food. I'll be within yelling's reach if you need anything."

Reesa nodded, smiling diplomatically as he squeaked back upstairs. She would most certainly *not* be helping herself. Not to those unlabeled, indistinguishable jars on the shelf. She squinted at some of them. Tomatoes? God knows.

Going to the cabinets Doctor Fencer had indicated to contain the earliest history of Big City, Reesa placed her hands on the worn silvery handle and yanked it open. She was there for the Theocracy and not for herself. If she collected information regarding the drill site it was all right to dig into the private life of Merrick while she was there, right?

She hadn't said a word to Joule when she'd left that morning. She had risen, groomed herself in that warped bathroom mirror and gone immediately downstairs to ask Shay about the records. She hadn't even eaten breakfast. Her stomach growled at her, but she still wasn't ready to deal with her partner. She couldn't.

The cabinet drawer was stuffed full of file folders like a turkey full of breading. Each little label on the lip of every folder was carefully penned in blue ink, a month and a year. At the back the line began January, 2101, and ended with December, 2101. Reesa pulled open the drawer beneath it. January to December 2102. Below that 2103. She turned to face the room. Two hundred drawers, at least, if not more. She had two hundred drawers to sift through, excluding the ones that contained information on the town's current residents. The task sprawled before her like a great sphinx. She didn't know the answer to the riddle. She reached to the back of the 2101 drawer and gingerly removed the two-hundred-year-old documents inside.

Nearly three hours passed before Doctor Fencer's shoes squeaked once again down the ladder. His top half appeared this time bearing a sandwich on a paper plate and a glass of milk. Reesa sat in a mountain of paperwork, newspaper clippings, interview printouts, sorting and sifting through it all. She smiled at Fencer as he turned from the ladder and smiled a little more when the color drained from his cheeks at the mess she'd made.

"It's all still organized, I promise," she said. "And I'll make sure everything gets back to its proper place."

The man could only swallow in response. He didn't even hold out the sandwich.

Reesa took it from him anyways. "Thank you," she said. Her stomach rejoiced at the sight of food. Her eyes wanted to roll, but she checked them, lest Doctor Fencer think she was ungrateful.

"Is there something in particular you're looking for?" he asked.

Reesa could see his hands twitching, itching to get a hold of every last paper and whip it all back into those neat little folders. He could probably do it in the time it would take her to finish eating. She bit into the sandwich.

"No. Just information regarding the drill site. My cardinal has a vested interest in the oil out here."

That was the first time she had ever said "my" instead of "our." Felt good. She chewed the bread and ham, the lettuce and tomato.

"Well good luck to him," Fencer replied, shaking his head, hair shifting back and forth like the skirt on a hula dancer. "Big City's given up on that a long time now."

"You're all skeptics, hmm?" Reesa leaned against one of the filing cabinets, chuckling, picking a speck of pepper off the bread of her sandwich.

"You would be too, ma'am, if you were one of us."

Doctor Fencer was correct, though she was not one but seven of them. Reesa only nodded, taking another bite and chewing through her silent smile. His mouth turned up at the corner in uncertainty as he watched her. What did he see through that curtain of hair? He would never say.

"I'll leave you to it then, ma'am," he mumbled, turning hunched and moving away.

"Thank you for the sandwich, Doctor," she replied watching his back as he went up the ladder. "It was just what I needed."

As soon as his feet were no longer visible, Reesa shot to the cabinet that contained all the dirt on Big City as it was now. Forget the drill site. What was oil when you looked like a man's dead wife? Fencer had seen her with the oil documents. He wouldn't even know she'd opened these cabinets. She wrenched open the top drawer of the first, A-C.

Adams, Blue, Capell, Cleat all in neat blue ink, and not only that, but between the family markers were individual names. Her eyes flicked over them rapidly. At once a particular label stood out—almost glowing, growing, greying, larger in her field of vision in some insane optical illusion—and with one solid beat of her heart she froze. *Haddox, Merrick Capell.* It was filed out of order. It ought to have been placed with the Hs, and yet, there it was. She stared, unable to send a command to her hand to reach forward and grab it.

Her heart beat her eardrums. Constant popping pressure. Her eyelids receded further and further back into her skull. Opened wide. The acrid air began to sting them. Her hand swept up in one swift motion and whisked the file from the drawer. It sat just in front of a file labeled *Capell, Arthur.* The stable owner. Merrick must have been his daughter.

Reesa took the file and slumped against the cabinet, clutching the papers to her breast. They were dangerous, electric almost, sending little sparks into her body that urged her to open the file and condemning her for doing it. Slowly, she let the file fall from her breast into her waiting hands. She hesitated, then lifted the cover.

Snap—her breath caught in her throat. Like a razor blade. A face stared back at her. *Her* face stared back at her. Well, not her *own* face, but one so familiar, so similar that it could have belonged to a twin or a sister. Merrick Capell Haddox smiled out of a photograph with the very same eyes that viewed it. Her ruby-red hair, tumbling in waterfall curves round her face, was adorned with a veil. The pale pink glow of her skin was far different from the suntanned pelt that Reesa wore, but the features were the same. The same rising cheekbones, the same pointed jaw, the same ski-jump nose. A string of pearls wound round and round Merrick's neck. Reesa reached up to her own neck, searching for them.

No wonder Tombstone hated her.

She flipped to the next picture, another bridal, but this time head-to-toe. White satin pooled around Merrick's feet, a bouquet of peonies caught in one hand. Her hair. She was beautiful. Reesa looked at the next, and the next, unsatisfied, hungry for more. She reached the end of the photographs before she knew it.

The last picture had been taken up the aisle between the rows of chairs in a church. The one a door away from the Big City Hotel on the other side of the seamstress's. She had never been inside it, which was a little dab of heresy for an apostle, but she knew the church. Either way, Merrick stood at the end of the aisle, up on the altar platform, her hands joined across a small space to Tombstone's.

Reesa's heart palpitated. Her fingers lifted to the photograph, set gently down on its shiny surface. She reached back in her mind. She had to be there. She *had* to be. The absolute bliss that radiated from the picture had to be hers. But she couldn't reach it. Just like she couldn't reach the floor.

A tall priest was visible between the couple. She stared at him for a long time, too. How many minutes had passed since she began flipping through the photographs was a mystery, but Doctor Fencer had not come down to disturb her so it couldn't have been too long. Hopefully.

She turned over the last photograph, the one of Merrick and Tombstone and the priest, and found a series of documents on the other side. Birth certificate, social security card, passport, Theocratic identification numbers and travel permits, immunization records, bank statements, everything she would have needed to steal Merrick's identity. No marriage certificate, though. That must have been in Tombstone's file.

The documents were easy enough to scan over rapidly. Nothing she hadn't seen before. After the final bank statement was a collection of newspaper clippings, shriveled and yellowing and every last one from the Big City Press. The clippings were so thin and worn that when Reesa lifted the first one—an announcement of Merrick's birth—from the file, she could see the words on the other side backwards through the paper. Up next was a photograph of a second grade class on a fieldtrip out to the drill site, an obscure girl's face circled in pink highlighter. After that a large number of birthday wishes from the newspaper staff for June twenty-fourth. There were thirty two of them and Reesa looked at every last one.

At last she came to an article that occupied the entire front page of the newspaper. The whole spread had simply been removed, folded up, and placed in the file. Her fingers closed around the edges and began to pull them from one another until the headline was visible across the top:

LITTLE HADHAM'S LITTLE GIRL CERTIFIED PUREST OF BREED

A large photograph of two people and two horses, standing on respective sides of the fence, sat below it. Reesa drew in a breath. That was Indie. She'd dreamed about that horse, she'd very nearly seen it born. She would have known the animal anywhere.

Her eyes wandered over the horses and the people—Merrick and Tombstone. He looked so happy. She had never seen his genuine smile.

The rest of the clippings were not nearly so interesting. Most of them were class announcements of graduation from particular grades, all out of order. Others were further articles regarding the Haddox horse ranch and its success. Strange and silly tidbits that make up a life. Exhausted, Reesa slumped back against the cabinet, letting out a deep sigh.

The file, as it rested against her legs, slipped a little as she sat back and a scrap of newspaper fluttered out, *flip, flip, flip*, and landed face down on the floor. She looked at it. On the back were printed the first panels of several comics from before the war. *Cul de Sac. Garfield. For Better or Worse.* It figured that Big City would be printing ancient cartoons in its ancient newspaper. No syndicate would have sold the rights for anything to a paper with a maximum circulation of a hundred and six.

Reesa reached down and picked the clipping up, turning it over as she brought it to her view. At the top was a photograph, underneath that in bolded script was printed: Merrick Capell June 24, 2267—November 1, 2299. An obituary. Her heart beeps on a monitor. Silver tools, sharp tools. A long, painful slice. A scalpel travels from her bellybutton to her throat. Reesa gasped. Big City put the funnies on the back of the obituaries. Morbid.

She shivered in the chill of the fruit cellar, slipping the obituary back into the file without looking at it again. Not if she was going to see those images as a consequence. She let her hands rest against her knees against the file. Its electricity was gone now, its secrets revealed. The experience, now that it was over, was strangely unfulfilling. Hollow, fatiguing. She shut her eyes for just a moment and leaned her head back against the filing cabinet.

"Everything all right down there, Apostle?"

Doctor Fencer's call shot her straight to her feet, very nearly banging her head on the open drawer of the cabinet.

"Yes!" she called back.

Rustling through the papers, she scrambled to replace Merrick's file in case Doctor Fencer decided to come down and check on her, and as she did, she noticed another file out of place alphabetically. Her eyes locked on it. *Greeber, Benjamin.*

"What are you doing in the A through C," she whispered, slowly slipping Merrick's file into place and reaching for Ben Greeber's. The doctor's footsteps sounded on the ceiling above, his shadow fell over the shaft of light that shone down the ladder. In a panic, Reesa snatched the file and tucked it behind her back, lifting her jacket and stuffing it a quarter of the way down her pants. Fencer's shoes appeared, coming down the ladder. She let her jacket drop and cover the file. When Fencer turned to look at her, she smiled coolly. His eyes flicked to the open cabinet drawer which she had neglected to shut.

"There's nothing on the drill site in there," Fencer said, turning his gaze on her.

"Oh, I know," Reesa replied, going to the cabinet, palms sweating. "I just wanted to get a look at everyone's names." She pushed on the drawer, wheeling it back into the cabinet, but it caught and wouldn't push any farther than halfway. Her breath came faster and she spluttered out another phrase to cover her tracks: "I want to start putting names to faces."

Fencer stepped over. He was going to see. He gently encouraged her to step aside with a slight push and took hold of the drawer himself. He was going to see that she'd taken the file. He braced himself against the floor. He had a perfect view into the drawer and its names. The stiffness of the file pressed against Reesa's back like a board. Doctor Fencer gave the drawer a hard shove and it screeched back into the cabinet. Turning, he looked at Reesa.

"A through C is sticky sometimes."

"Hah…"

The little, nervous laugh tumbled out of her. The wooden file eased against her back. She tried not to breathe a direct sigh of relief, though she wasn't in the clear yet.

"I'm all through," she said. "Would you like help putting these back?"

She stepped gingerly over to the spread of paperwork she'd collected on the drill site. All of the information she'd gathered there had fled her brain the moment she'd opened Merrick's file, so she rapidly scanned the surfaces and gleaned everything she could from the references.

"No, that's all right, Apostle," Fencer answered. He came and stood beside her. "It won't take me long, and I'm sure you've got plenty of other duties to do today."

It wasn't untrue, but Reesa could sense the subtext behind his words. You'll do it wrong and I don't want to pick up after you twice. She smiled. He was, after all, quite right. She stepped away from the pile toward the ladder.

"Thank you, Doctor. You've been so obliging."

"Anytime, Apostle Reesa." He had already bent down and begun sorting the papers into piles by date. "I'm here to help."

"And thank you for the sandwich as well."

"Mm."

That was a dismissal fair enough. She scurried up the ladder, taking the rungs two at a time and popping up in Doctor Fencer's living room. She had to get to Joule.

15

The file scratched against her back as she ran the distance from Doctor Fencer's to the Big City hotel, *swish-swish, swish-swish*. More than once Reesa had to reach back and steady the thing so it didn't pop out of her pants as her hips propelled it upward. She made quite a sight scurrying through the town—half run, half gambol, with a little bit of a limp sprinkled on top. Like a duck with one leg shorter than the other. Heads turned to watch her go, but her brain was swimming with too much excitement to pay them any mind.

Benjamin Greeber was a real person! Not a pile of ashes, not the name of a haunted attraction, not a cover for something else. A *real* person. And she was holding his file. Well, she'd *stolen* his file, but with every intent of returning it. Which made it okay…she figured.

Her feet clomped up onto the porch steps at the Hotel and she slowed her pace before opening the door, passing through the lobby with a polite nod at Shay who did not respond or even acknowledge her, the tenderheart, and taking the stairs two at a time. Joule had better be in their room. Her feet carried her swiftly down the hall where she whipped open the door to their room, went in, and shut it behind her, leaning her back against the wood. Joule was seated on the edge of the bed facing away from the door and he turned in alarm at the sound of her entrance, his blue eyes wide and questioning.

It was only then that she remembered she'd spent the night down the hall. She had not said good morning, or eaten breakfast with him, or done anything she was supposed to have done as his partner. Perhaps hurrying back had not been the best option. She swallowed.

"Where have you been?" Joule asked, getting to his feet.

His voice was peppered with concern and not anger, which slightly eased the pressure building in her shoulders. She stepped off the door and reached behind her back to retrieve Ben Greeber's file. It took a little bit of digging and adjusting as the edges caught on her jacket and pants, but in response she held it up from him to see.

"Doctor Fencer's," she replied. If they didn't have to talk about what happened last night that would be good. "He keeps Big City's records. I went there looking for information on the drill site, but I found this instead."

"What is it?"

Conversation avoided. Reesa beamed and brought the file to the bed where she sat down with it. Joule sat as well and she set it on the mattress between them.

"It's Ben Greeber's citizen file," she said. "There's one for everyone here."

Joule's mouth opened as he took in a breath. "Citizen file?" His eyes went bright as he reached down to pick it up. "So he's real then?"

Reesa nodded, her bouncing head betraying her excitement. "Or this is a very elaborate ruse. Doctor Fencer didn't—*doesn't* know I took it. I don't think he was anticipating my looking through those files at all."

"We should confront Mayor Big City with this right away," Joule said. He shook the file a little in the air triumphantly, then looked at her. "What's in it anyway?"

"Oh—I—"

She hadn't actually looked inside.

"Um."

Think. If every file was the same, then every file must have the same things inside. She'd looked in Merrick's. What had been in there?

"Just his official documents. Bank statements, newspaper clippings, birth certificate. Stuff like that." She tried to shrug. "Stuff it would be illegal to fake."

Joule grinned. "We've got them now."

Reesa grinned back at him, nodding. "I think we do."

Her partner looked down at the file in his hands and opened it. At the top of the documents was a picture of Ben Greeber, a hairy man with a friendly face, and the two of them studied it for a moment before Joule flipped it over. Birth certificate, marriage certificate, Theocratic identification numbers, travel permit. Flip, flip, flip. They looked through the whole thing quickly.

"Seems legitimate to me," Joule said, closing the file and glancing at Reesa.

"Even if it's not we can get them on the forgery," she replied.

"I don't know that we should be trying to 'get them' on anything." He frowned at her.

Reesa struggled not to roll her eyes. "You know what I meant. We have to find a way to make them tell us the truth. I don't want to bring a criminal record down on anyone, but we need answers, and I'll do what it takes to get them."

Joule was quiet for a moment. His fingers traced around the edge of the file. "Where did you go last night?"

Her spine stiffened. "The saloon. I told you that."

"No, after."

"I don't want to talk about it, Joule." She took the file from his hands and stood up. "Let's go."

She started for the door before he could protest. His options were to stay or to go with her, and she could not have cared less which he chose. She yanked open the door and then he was on his feet and the two of them were traveling down the hall in the next moment. He'd better not try to bring it up again on their walk.

Mayor Big City should have been in his office. She exited the hotel and headed north to the town hall. The sun was high in the sky, just beginning to dip down into its arc and start setting. Its rays caught her uniform and lit it up. She and Joule walked to the town hall, two white beacons in the blazing sunlight.

He finally caught up to her at the door. She began to open it and he placed his palm over the edge and shut it, leaning forward to try and catch her eye.

"Can we talk about what happened?"

Reesa opened her mouth to snap back, but he interrupted her.

"Not now! Just…sometime. Later. Can we talk later?"

If it would shut him up, fine. "Yes," she replied. "We can talk later."

That seemed to appease him. He almost smiled, then moved out of her way, releasing the pressure he'd placed on the door. She slipped inside, not holding it open for Joule to follow behind her.

Mayor Big City's voice sounded in the hallway, leaking out the half open door to his office. Reesa knocked and when he acknowledged her, pushed open the door to look inside. Hicks was at his desk, feet propped up on top of it and leaning back in his swivel chair. He seemed surprised to see her.

"Apostle Reesa? Apostle Joule? Is there something I can do for you?"

Reesa stepped into the office, Joule followed close behind her. "We have a few questions we'd like to ask you," she said.

"What about, Apostle?"

Reesa held up the Ben Greeber file.

The mayor's face went white and his feet slipped from the desk.

"So you do know him." Reesa tossed the file onto the desk in front of the mayor and then leaned back against it, folding her arms across her chest, trying her best to look nonchalant. Hicks looked up at her in shock and she looked back at him down her nose.

"There've been an awful lot of secrets since we got here," she said. "I think it's time that changed. Don't you?"

"I don't know what you're talking about," Hicks replied.

Reesa narrowed her eyes. "We're talking about Ben Greeber. And the takers. I've heard them mentioned all over town, and from your own lips I might add."

"I'm afraid I have nothing to say, Apostle," he said, shaking his head.

"What's the point of keeping it secret? What are you trying to hide?"

Her hands flew up into the air and Hicks looked amusedly at them. His gaze flicked back to Joule for a moment—Joule who had said nothing. Reesa turned back to look at her partner as well. He only shrugged and shook his head. They couldn't make him talk.

"I'm going to get to the bottom of this," Reesa growled, turning her face back to the mayor and his desk. She snatched the file from its surface. "It's illegal to forge official Theocratic documents. If you won't talk, I'll find someone who will."

Hicks Grey only smiled, his mouth curling up under his caterpillar mustache. The expression was maddeningly relaxed.

"You go ahead and do that, Apostle."

"Well that was a complete waste of time," Joule grumbled, plopping himself down in a seat and tossing the Greeber file onto the front corner table of the saloon.

"You think?"

Reesa flopped, defeated, next to him. She and Joule could do practically nothing. Their power was an illusion, particularly because that power came from an absent government that had not been present in the region for a century or two. She'd never felt so much doubt in herself, in the Theocracy, before. She wanted to punch someone out.

Chivalry swept by their table, her blonde hair falling out of its bun. "What can I get for you, Apostles?" she asked, absently brushing the loose strands from her bare shoulders.

"Just water for me," Joule answered.

"Nothing." Reesa crossed her arms, and then added, a little more politely, "Thank you, Chivalry."

"Of course, ma'am. I'll be back with that water."

She left them and Joule leaned over the table toward Reesa.

"Don't be angry—"

"You can't just tell a person to *not* be angry."

"—about it. We'll figure this out. Maybe the mayor wasn't ready to talk today, but we have to give it time. We've only been in Big City four days. They barely know us."

"We don't have time to waste, Joule," she replied. "We've got to figure this out now."

"Why?"

Reesa opened her mouth, but nothing came out. Why? She didn't know. But she knew that the more time they spent in the dark was more time in dangerous territory. Something bad was going to happen—just a little inkling at the back of her mind, a silver room—and that made her anxious. Maybe she was just being paranoid, maybe all the secrets had finally just sapped her patience, but either way the sooner they understood what was going on, the better.

"Hello, Apostles. Drinking early today?"

Reesa bristled instantly at the sound of his voice. Her teeth snapped together, she turned to look over, or rather *glare* over, at Tombstone. He gave her an inscrutable toothy smile in response and finished his approach to their table.

"Apostles don't drink," she hissed.

"I'm shocked," he said. "It might actually do them some good."

Chivalry reappeared and set a glass of water in front of Joule. Tombstone grinned at it, the perfect punctuation to his sentence. Reesa rolled her eyes and Chivalry slid her arm around the back of Tombstone's neck to pull herself right up next to him. Evidently, she did not share Darling's trembling adoration of Tombstone or the general wariness of the rest of the town.

"You drinking today, gorgeous?" she purred.

He slipped the knot of her hand. "No. Thank you, Chivalry."

"Oh?" With a huff, Reesa crossed her arms. "It might actually do you some good."

"You let me know if you change your mind," Chivalry said, blowing him a kiss and then gliding away.

Tombstone paid her no heed, taking the seat across from Joule at their table. "What's this one's issue?" he asked, gesturing to Reesa.

Joule started, surprised at Tombstone's addressing him, and glanced at Reesa before answering, "We're just a little frustrated, that's all."

"Frustrated by what? Or should I say 'whom'?"

"Why are you here?" Reesa snapped.

"To talk to you, Apostle," Tombstone answered as if his were the most obvious of intentions. "Why else?"

Reesa stifled a groan. Tombstone was about the last thing she needed at the moment. "What could you possibly have to say to us?" she grumbled.

"You want to know about Benjamin Greeber, don't you?"

A rush rippled Reesa's skin, raising gooseflesh and for a moment all she could hear was the sound of a plane taking off overhead like she was standing right on the runway. Was this guy telepathic? Her shock must have registered on her face for when she snapped out of it, Tombstone was chuckling at her. She closed her mouth, which until that moment she had not realized was open, and glared at him again to no effect.

"Why would *you* tell us about Benjamin Greeber?" Joule asked, evidently just as stymied as Reesa in their new cohort.

"You're in the dark. It's not safe. It'll cost lives in the end," he replied. "I'm in the interest of saving those lives. I'll tell you anything you want to know."

Reesa looked to Joule and found her partner staring, dumbfounded, back at her, expressing exactly how she felt. At least she wasn't alone. All of Big City had its secrets, but Tombstone's had seemed the most shadowy of corners. Here he was offering to spill it all?

"Well?" Reesa prodded when Tombstone did not speak. "Tell us, then. Who's Ben Greeber and why is the mayor so intent on keeping him a secret?"

He shook his head. "Not here. Come out to Little Hadham this evening. Randy will bring you."

Well, that sounded tremendously suspicious. "Why?" Reesa demanded. "So you can kidnap us and hold us hostage?"

Tombstone laughed. "Hardly, Apostle. You're not worth much, alive or dead. I just don't want to see anyone else in the latter situation because you two were ignorant of what we're dealing with."

Her eyes narrowed. Of course he couldn't speak without insulting her. "Fine," she said. "We'll come out to your ranch."

"Reesa—"

"Quiet, Joule. What time should we expect Randy?"

"She'll come by with her coach around four-thirty. That work for you?"

Joule opened his mouth, but Reesa beat him to it, spitting out a snarled, "Yes."

Tombstone smiled. "Excellent. I'll see the two of you around five, then." He got up from his seat and slithered away. Reesa glared at his back until he pushed through the swinging doors and disappeared outside.

"How did he know where we were?" Joule squirmed in his seat. She glanced at him and he held her gaze. "Doesn't that seem a bit too convenient to you?"

She looked away. "I don't care. I want answers."

"I have a bad feeling about this, Reesa."

"You have a bad feeling about everything, Joule."

She tried to make the statement lighthearted, but her chuckle came out a little darker and a little more strained than she'd intended. Mostly the whole thing just sounded passive-aggressive, so she gave up. She didn't have a glass of water to retreat to sipping, so she folded her arms and sat back against her chair, making a pointed effort to look at everything in the room aside from Joule.

An upsurge of exhaustion began in her body, starting with her toes and filling up like a bath. Before too long she forfeited to the fatigue, leaning forward onto the table and cushioning her head in a pillow of her folded arms. Why so tired? She hadn't been up *that* early…

"Are you feeling all right?" Joule asked.

So help her if he asked her that *one more time...*

"I think I'm going to go lay down," she replied, sitting up but getting dizzy and pressing a hand to her forehead. "I'll try to sleep a little before we have to go. What time is it?"

Joule pulled his handheld comm out of his jacket pocket. Couldn't make calls but it could still tell the time at least. "Almost three," he answered.

"Come wake me before Randy gets to the hotel. I'll take the file."

He nodded and she stood and walked carefully to the door. At least Joule had enough sense not to follow her. He could be irritatingly hover-y when it came to being sick. Once, just a few days after their matrimony she'd come down with a light cold, barely more than a stuffy nose, and he'd helicoptered over her for a week, bringing her bowls of chicken broth and supplying packets of tissues at the slightest sign of a sneeze. At the time it had seemed sweet, but Reesa was in no mood for such ministrations now.

Safe in her room inside the Big City hotel, Reesa tucked Benjamin Greeber's file carefully between the mattress and the box spring of their bed, then she kicked off her shoes, shed her jacket, and crawled underneath the covers and squirmed until she was covered by just a single sheet. She could never sleep comfortably unless she was covered by something. Her head against the pillow, she shut her eyes and began a series of deep, deep breaths. Soon thereafter, she was asleep.

Her back aches like some creature has taken a sledgehammer to it and hit her hard enough to bruise and shatter everything, but not to dislocate a single muscle or bone. Like she is broken, but put together. She owed that to the hundred and ten bales of hay she'd had to haul by hand from the yard to the barn after their lift had broken down. Her hands are raw, very near to bleeding. She collapses into a seat beside their bed. If only he was not sick. If only he were here to help her. Tears are in her eyes, their bitter sting making her more apt to cry. Her bottom lip trembles...

But then he coughs. It is always worse when he is asleep—perhaps because he cannot control it while he is unconscious or perhaps because he must lie on his back. Either way it is a miserable sound and it brings forth the tears in full form. She sobs into her hands, unable to watch how his body is wracked and shuddering through the distortion the liquid makes in her eyes. Eventually his coughing quiets and he settles into a heavy, labored breathing.

She rises from her seat and goes to the fireplace, leaning against the mantle and grabbing a poker from beside the hearth. She stabs at the fire absently, throws another log on, all the while listening to his horrible rasping on the bed behind her. Setting the poker down, she runs her fingers over the porcelain elephant on the mantelpiece.

City Ash and Desert Bones

Orrin Fever, that's what Doctor Fencer had called it, but he didn't understand it. Nobody did. They'd boarded them up in their little house, building an adobe foyer around their front door like an airlock to keep the disease inside. Quilts had been stuffed into the cracks around the windows. Had to keep the town safe. Had to keep everyone from getting sick. But she hadn't gotten sick. She'd slept beside him, nursed him, kissed him, and she hadn't gotten sick. She'd felt the fatigue of working the ranch without him, certainly, but never once did she feel the effects of the fever upon herself.

She cannot seem to remember a time when he was well.

A different kind of rasping sounds behind her and she turns. It is her name, spoken on his shredded throat. She goes to him, changes the wet washcloth on his head to a fresh one, mops up the rest of his face. His shirt sticks to him with sweat and he raises a hand, groping absently at the air, searching for her hand.

Instead she climbs into bed beside him, nestling herself right up against his body. She finds his hand, takes it, and holds it against her heart. He is too warm, like a furnace. It's a miracle he doesn't overheat, or dehydrate, losing so much water in his sweat. She presses her face into his neck, kisses him there, then the tears began to fall.

Any moment he could die. Any moment she could be more alone in the world than she already is. He might die. She didn't want to be alone.

She didn't know how much he could sense through the haze. He rarely spoke, only coughed and moaned and did things that sick people do, but then he lifts his hand, slipping it out of the grip she holds on it, and places it on top of her head. He is weak, but he tries to draw her in closer, and she is already as close as she can be. She knows now that he senses her suffering. Both of their suffering.

Her tears quiet and his breathing slows, his arm falling limply on her head. He is asleep. She lies beside him, aching eyes staring at the window until the dawn creeps in through its cracks.

16

That wall of dirt was sure coming on fast. They'd be at Little Hadham before the storm hit, though, Randy could see it just a few miles off. She shifted on the flat cushion attached to the bench where she sat to drive her coach and pulled the collar of her pa's jacket in tighter. Dumb coat didn't have no buttons. What kind of coat didn't have buttons? Good thing her hat was strapped to her head. Wind could've torn it right off.

The girls were running good today and Tombstone had said Messy should be healed up soon. Probably shouldn't pull the coach for a while yet. Randy had noticed that it did take longer to get places being a horse short. Nothing she could do about it though. Didn't trust anyone else's horses but her own. And Tombstone's, but those were for sale and she couldn't go wearing out the goods before their purchase. He probably would have given her one if she'd asked, but she wouldn't ask.

What did the apostles talk about on all these long rides? Or did they talk at all? She seemed to be the only one who had to drag them around though she wasn't alone in having hold of a set of horses and a carriage, but they didn't know that. Didn't bother to ask. She cut them a little slack. They hadn't even been in Big City a week yet.

The coach sailed through the gate in the fence behind her girls. They were on Little Hadham now, gliding past all Tombstone's unused farming equipment and quite a few of his horses. Only the older ones were left out, but they could find their way back to the barn on their own. Little ones had to be gathered up before a storm. She checked the horizon again. The storm was rolling forward like one of those big waves in the ocean after an earthquake. She'd read about it in a weather book one time. Tsunami. That's what they called it. Big brown tsunami cloud rumbling across the desert. Been a while since the last one.

Reesa just looked so incomprehensibly tired, even after her nap. Evidently she hadn't slept well, though that didn't come as a surprise to Joule. She'd been odd—well, she'd always been odd—but more odd, or something, since the pair of them had arrived in Big City. The red rims of her eyes were beginning to betray that oddness, like the color of her hair. She slumped a little in her seat as well. With a flash of her eyes she caught him looking at her.

"What?" she snapped.

Her harshness surprised him, even stung a little. "Nothing," he replied. "You just look tired is all." Someone at some point in his life had warned him never to say that to a woman, but the advice went unheeded.

She rolled her eyes, shifted in her seat and said, "Yeah, well, I feel tired."

"Are you sure you're up for this?" he asked. She looked so run-down there was no doubt this trip to see Tombstone would only wear her out more. Of course they were already mostly there and turning back now would be a waste. All the same, he wanted her to be comfortable.

And healthy. Neither of which she seemed to be at the moment.

In response to his question she glared at him with such a fierce coldness that Joule could not help but try to shift out from underneath its pressure. She knew how to give a good stare-down when it came to it. He said nothing, and she looked away, satisfied by his silence.

That silence lasted for the duration of the ride. Reesa occupied herself with watching things pass by the window; Joule tried to do the same. He found himself sneaking glances at her every so often, just to see if she was still angry, or frustrated, or tired, or irritated, or whatever it was she was. And she was. He didn't dare try conversation with her now and he couldn't exactly leave her alone, either. Their proximity in the coach wouldn't allow for that, so he had to settle for the quiet instead.

The coach came to a stop and the wood squeaked as Randy disembarked above him. Not wanting to tread on Reesa's toes, he looked to her for their next action and she gestured sharply at the door. He opened it, trying not to add to her emotions with a facial expression of discontent as he was only trying to be polite, and got out before she could push him out herself. It was startlingly windy outside the coach. He'd read somewhere in their information packets that Big City often experienced dust storms. This would probably be the first of many he'd have to endure during their ordination. Maybe, just maybe at the end of all of this they could be transferred to Alaska. Alaska sounded like paradise. So cold.

He turned to Reesa and found she'd frozen in the open coach door, her eyes locked on the landscape and Tombstone's shabby house. The far-away, half-gone look in her face was alarming. He took a step towards her.

"Reesa?"

Brown barn. Gravel path. Small house. The ranch from her dreams. She had been here only hours ago in her sleep, caring for Tombstone, curing Orrin Fever. The sable paint peeled around the edges of the house. The pea stones scattered from the center of the pathway, dense in the middle and sparse at the edges like a contracting galaxy. The barn tilted ever so slightly on its base as a blustery breeze blew by. She'd had permanent places in her dreams before, reoccurring ones—any mall she dreamed herself into was always the same mall, any car the same car, but she had never discovered one of those places in her waking life. And yet, here it was. Little Hadham. Exactly like she'd dreamed.

Dust filtered up into the air, gathered into whirling spirals as the wind gathered speed. Reesa took the hand that Joule offered to help her down and stepped from the coach, squinting to shield her eyes from the flying particles, stumbling along on stiff legs. Ahead of them Randy was already standing at the door to the ranch house, her arms sucked into the sleeves of her coat, pulling the buttonless front closed. Apparently she had knocked as soon as she'd got there, for as Reesa and Joule scurried up to meet her, Tombstone pulled open the door.

"Afternoon, Apostles," he said, lifting the elbow of the arm that held the door open to allow room for Randy to scamper in below it. "Just in time."

Huxley'd told the apostles he'd talk, but God knows what for. He didn't have anything to say.

He hadn't any idea what they'd want to know. Hell. He'd woken up that morning with a pit already deep in his stomach at the thought of seeing that female apostle again and then he'd invited her to his house? Idiot. She looked so much like Merrick it made him feel empty.

He stood at the kitchen window, clasping a ceramic mug by the handle, sipping at but not really tasting or drinking a bland brew of coffee. The handle was too small for his fingers, crushing them together in its curve. It was painful, but he didn't adjust his grip. Better to feel discomfort than nothing at all. Looked like a dust storm picking up outside. Lord and Saints he hated it here. He would have left if not for Randy. He had enough for the both of them to leave. Selling expensive horses. Breeding expensive horses. Forcing horses to have little horses with other horses. He could be a monster sometimes. The darkness buried in his heart frightened him more than he cared to admit. Randy wouldn't have wanted to go, though. Her life, everything she knew, was here.

He held the coffee, cool now, in his mouth for several seconds before he swallowed. Why he drank his coffee in the evening he couldn't be sure, but he did. A vain attempt to keep away the nightmares, maybe.

Randy pounded on the door. He knew her knock. He hadn't heard her coach or horses over the roar of the wind, over the sound of his own grief. He sloshed the rest of his coffee down the sink as he overturned the mug before going to the door. Pulling it open, he found Randy huddled in the doorway, hat tied beneath her chin, her pa's coat gathered up tight to her neck, her arms outside the sleeves and in the torso. He glanced at her and then at the apostles as the pair of them trotted up just behind her, their uniforms already streaked with yellow from the dust storm. Here she was. The hollowness began to take hold.

"Afternoon, Apostles," he said. Randy was smart; she slipped inside as soon as the door was open. He lifted his elbow instinctively to give her room. "Just in time."

He stepped aside so the apostles could come in as well, gestured for them to do so. Joule nearly did, but Reesa hesitated—well, she didn't even hesitate, she simply didn't move, so her partner remained where he was in imitation. She looked at Huxley, her eyes distant—off somewhere, in some fantasy. He preferred not to think what that might be.

"Wind's picking up," he prompted.

She started and stepped inside; he thought he saw a little pink in her cheeks. Joule followed right behind her. She came almost to an immediate halt.

"Oh!" she cried, looking around her with intent surprise. She seemed to take everything in, every nook and cranny, every dust-covered object, like she'd seen it before but not in a very long time and had not expected to see it ever again.

But that was all she said. That was all anyone said for a moment. The wind filled the silence. Joule opened his mouth, but Reesa silenced him with an incredible look of wrath like none Huxley had ever seen. Joule snapped his mouth right closed; Reesa looked apologetic but he didn't notice. It was clear then that Huxley would have to be the one to speak.

"Well… Why don't we talk in the kitchen?"

"Yes," Joule said.

Huxley turned, headed toward the kitchen. Joule's stomping steps followed close behind him. He went to the table, removed the dead plant that sat in the middle and set it down on the stove on top of a series of books. He'd put it back once they left. Camilla Shane Grey had given the plant to him several weeks ago in some sort of false gesture of reaching out to his poor lost soul. He'd let it die and was keeping it for her to see the next time she showed up on his doorstep with pity and a plate of cookies.

When he turned around Randy, Joule, and Reesa were already seated at the table. He caught the leg of the chair near him with his foot, turned it backwards, and sat down, resting his arms on the back. To his right, Joule. He studied the apostle—his soap-bar face, the innate sense of righteousness that shone out of his eyes. Reesa, across from him. She wouldn't meet Huxley's eyes. He didn't want to look at her particularly. He only glanced at Randy. He'd spent plenty of time looking at that girl's face. He fed her often enough to claim her as a dependent.

"Where is it I should start?" he asked, leaning forward.

Joule looked to Reesa. "Um…" he said, hesitating to give her room to make her own request, but she didn't meet his gaze. She stared at the table, stiff.

"Start with Ben," Randy suggested. "Ben got taken night before they got here."

Hm. That was a place to start. It was all still so fresh in his mind. That bright red veil of blood that spat out the back of Statia Greeber's head when he'd put his gun up to her and pulled the trigger. The scratches down his arm where she'd clawed at him, begging, were still healing. He had begun to nod, up and down, up and down, gently as he'd contemplated that crimson, killing spatter.

"Ben Greeber…" He took a breath in and then continued, "…had the graveyard shift at the taker hole the night before you two apostles arrived. The hole is what we call the place they live. It's a few miles off of the drill site."

"And it's just a hole?" Joule asked. "In the ground?"

"Yes. With a series of caverns underneath," he answered.

Joule sat back, put his hand over his mouth. "Hmm…" He did not remove his hand, but spoke again. "Continue."

"We keep an eye on the hole twenty-four seven so we know if any of the takers come out. They're dangerous when they do." How did he begin to even cover this topic? "Touch a taker, and the mucus in its skin begins to break down your body almost immediately. It's a toxin."

"And this happened to Ben Greeber?" Joule said. "He…touched a taker?"

Randy added, "Got taken."

"When you're taken you lose your mind first," Huxley continued. "You start attacking people. Friends, family. Doesn't matter. The taken carry the same toxin as a taker does, so they're equally dangerous. Need to be killed. That's…that's where I come in."

That's where he came in and killed them. That's where he came in, angel of death, blazing, burning fire of fury. It was not an easy thing to admit or to talk about. His hands tightened into fists, nails digging into his palms. He was a murderer and it was as simple as that.

Joule raised his eyebrows. "You kill them?"

"It's my job." There was nothing else to say.

"But you know them! They're—they're your neighbors, people you've known your whole life. How could you kill them?"

Huxley brought his eyes up to meet the apostle's. Shielded and hard. He didn't expect a man like this to understand.

"Because somebody has to do it," he said.

Reesa looked up from her lap. "How many?"

Had he heard her correctly? "What?"

"How many people have you had to kill?"

How many?

His mouth snapped closed before he even realized it was open. How many he had killed, how many had he killed. Harvey Shane on watch near the hole, caught in the brush and shrieking, Christine and Mark McCallister outside the church on Sunday, Reginald Rice as he'd clawed his way over the fence, drip, drip his body ran down the chain link, Emily Johns behind the saloon, spattering the clapboard, Shayla French before she'd gone totally mad, foam pouring from her mouth with the blood and the remnants of her stomach, Gerard Shank who didn't go down with the first shot because Huxley had hesitated, whom he'd had to shoot twice through the head and he'd sat up nights for days and wondered if you could still feel pain after you'd been taken, if there was any part of you still you in there, screaming for help, Francis Swallow with his skin mostly on, Ben Greeber in town on the roof of the hotel, the pile of digested insides he was landing on the dirt below without a living brain to hold it together, Statia, Max, and Swan, Ben's family, wife and children, that night in their home.

"Twelve," he said.

Nobody said anything. His twelve ghosts, corpses, ghouls, writhed within his mind, still there. They never left. Empty, he spoke again.

"Ben Greeber was killed the afternoon you arrived," he said. "On the roof of the hotel. He'd been out to see his family before he got to town, attacked his two sons who then turned on his wife. They were killed later that night in their home."

He couldn't say that he had done it. That man with the gun wasn't him. Not really.

Reesa opened her mouth, took in a breath, then said, "How—" but that was all before she stopped and thought for a moment, for a few moments. "How long have the takers been in Big City?"

Huxley shook his head. "Can't say for sure," he answered. "It's possible they've been here as long as we have, though they didn't start killing until a few years ago."

"And they've claimed twelve in that time," Reesa stated, as if she knew.

He hadn't said that. "No."

"More?"

"Two, ah…" Catherine, Randall, Paul, Bravery, Freddie, Cassandra. Merrick. He tried not to rub the bridge of his nose. "Two years ago there was a series of kidnappings. They took seven. Not all at once. We never found their bodies."

Joule butted in. "And the drill site? What do you know about that?"

"Not much, why?"

How like the Theocracy to care more about money, about oil, than about human life. His answer seemed enough to cause a bit of hesitancy in Joule. Reesa jumped in instead.

"What do the takers look like? And who burned down the Greeber cabin?"

Her eyes were wide. He frowned at her. So eager. So…brimming. It was… odd. What was the best way to answer her question so that she wouldn't have another one? He'd never had to describe a taker before though he'd spent the past two years studying them. Everyone in Big City had seen one.

"Takers are…humanoid," he said. "Though their proportions are a little off. Bigger heads, no necks, longer arms. Their only sensory organ is the mouth, which is basically just a big hole in the middle front of the head. They do almost everything through it—see, taste, smell, hear, and they're covered in mucus. They have specialized glands in their epidermis that secretes it. As far as I can tell it functions as some sort of protective layer. Like a beetle's shell, or the blubber on a whale." It all just came out. Just like that. So simple. Two years of work in just a few short sentences. He nearly forgot her second question. "The cabin was the mayor's work."

"I knew it."

Apparently she rejoiced in that. Her partner leaned forward, saying, "And how do you know all this?"

Huxley shrugged. "I was there when he lit the match."

"No—" Joule shook his head. "—about the takers. About…how they work?"

"I'm a biologist."

"No you're not."

Huxley snorted. Of course that soap-bar twit didn't believe him. He folded his arms across his chest. "I am, actually. I studied for several years at the University of the Cardinals back east. I have the degree if you need hard evidence?"

He started to his feet, a bluff move to go get it, counting on Joule to stop him, which he did, waving a hand and saying, "No. Sit down, sit down. Sorry."

Huxley slid back into his seat. "Can't say I blame you. Given what you know about Big City it would be rather odd for one of its citizens to be educated."

The apostle scowled. "That's not what I meant."

"That's exactly what you meant," Reesa laughed.

Joule gave her a glare like the devil himself and Reesa looked away, shamed. Huxley said, "I'm not offended, Apostle. Don't worry about breaking one of your commandments."

Joule looked at him resentfully, but said nothing—it was probably illegal for him to respond or something ridiculous. Huxley took advantage of the silence to explain himself.

"My great-grandfather moved to Big City so he could try his hand at ranching," he said. "He did well enough, but when my father took over the business he decided to expand into horse breeding, so he sent me to university when I was seventeen."

"My pa told me nobody expected him to come back," Randy said softly. "They all thought he was going to be the one to make it out."

"Why did you?" Reesa asked.

"Why did I what?"

"Come back?"

They talked for a long time, Apostle Joule asking most of the questions, but Randy didn't listen. Stupid questions. Stuff that didn't matter squat. What mattered was how to kill a taker and how it tried to kill you. That was what kept you alive. Not all this dumb talk about the hole and how many people had died because Tombstone had no choice but to shoot them. Randy made a comment here or there that didn't matter. Both her parents had been taken during the same series of kidnappings as Tombstone's wife Merrick had. She'd seen most of the taken shootings. Randy knew what it was to suffer. She was just glad she had the job of being the friend of the man who pulled the trigger rather than the man himself. He'd been teaching her though, reckoned she'd probably be the only one fool enough to take his place if anything ever happened to him. She hoped he wouldn't let it come to that, but when people are dying and you're the only one with a gun and the know-how, you don't have a choice. She understood that. Nobody else seemed to.

At once Randy felt a tingling at the back of her neck as her hairs stood on end. *No.* She shifted in her seat, glanced about her, willing that feeling away. It wouldn't go. She knew that feeling. It was never wrong. She looked to the window.

A brownish-blackish form slid into the view. Slowly, strip by strip until its shoulders and head were centered right in the middle. One single drip of slime fell from the top of the gigantic hole in its head to the bottom. Randy couldn't help it. She screamed.

And the taker screamed back.

Everyone was looking at the window now, then everyone was standing on their feet. But not Randy. The taker pounded on the window. Its slimy fist hit the glass again and again. Suddenly, she was moving backwards in her seat. Looking up, she saw Apostle Reesa pulling the chair toward the middle of the room. Apostle Joule hurried to join them. The taker kept hitting the window—bang, bang, bang!

Only Tombstone didn't run away. He stood up calmly from his seat and went to the sink to get a look at the visitor. Apostle Reesa didn't seem to like it much. She dug her claws into Randy's shoulders.

"Lord and Saints, get away from the window!" she yelled.

"It won't break the glass," Tombstone answered.

Glass broke anyways, but behind them. Randy turned slowly to look over her shoulder. First at the rock that lay in the middle of the carpet, then down the trail of broken glass, up the wall, to the window that wasn't much of a window anymore and the taker that was reaching through it. She screamed again. And did not stop screaming.

Die. They were going to die. Death, dead, died, die, dead. She squirmed under Apostle Reesa's grip that held her to her seat, clawing at Reesa's hands like Reesa had clawed at her shoulders. She couldn't really hear herself screaming anymore, but she knew she was. Her vocal chords felt all tingly and hot and shredded. Screaming, screamed, scream. The taker tried to climb in the window, but it got stuck, tipped forward. Tombstone shot it in the head. It started to leak down the wall into the glass. More takers were coming.

They were going to die. Death, death, dead.

Her ma and pa. They were dead, too. Or at least she figured they were. Taker-napped that's what they were. Her ma's chicken soup. Her pa's old tobacco pipe. Randy began to cry.

From that moment forward, Randy sobbed hysterically. Reesa clutched onto her shoulders, forcing the wriggling girl to remain planted in her seat with a little bit of pressure. Her own attentions were stuck on the taker, on the black blood that pooled out of its head all over the floor. Behind it, through the window, three more dark shapes were visible in the storm.

"There are more of them," Reesa whispered. Randy's hot tears fell on her hands with her thrashing. "There are more."

Her eyes flashed to Tombstone. He held a pistol in his hand. He must have. They had to. No. It wasn't. They needed to get Randy out. She wasn't, they weren't. A hard lump of fear in her throat that hurt when she swallowed over it. They had to get out.

"Whatever you do, don't let them touch you," Tombstone said. The quality of his voice was off, soft, a warning, but loud over the roar of the wind. Dirt whistled in through the broken window, gathering in a pile against the sofa in the corner. Huxley stepped carefully toward the window, toward the taker on the other side, toward its residue all over the glass and the wall.

Nails dug into Reesa's hand. She looked down at Randy.

"Ma'am…ma'am, I'm so scared…" The words rasped out like they do when a throat is dry, tight. Reesa had nothing to say.

"We have to go," Tombstone said, turning away from the window decisively.

"Yes," Joule nodded. Reesa had quite forgotten he was there. "We'll be safe in the city."

"No," Tombstone said gravely. "If they're here, they're everywhere." He grabbed a long barreled shotgun off the fireplace mantel, cocked it. The power-up hum was barely audible over the howl of the wind and the takers. "And I'm the only one with a gun."

Boots clomped across the wood to the center of the room. Tombstone offered his pistol. "Here." He set it in Joule's hands.

"I—what? I-I can't take this…" Joule held his hand out as far away from his body as he could. "I can't—I can't shoot a gun."

"Do you want to die?" Tombstone busied himself with other preparations: retrieving another pistol from the bedside table and tucking it into his belt, grabbing his hat and several rags from a hat rack on the wall.

"Well, no—"

"Then take the goddamn gun."

Joule looked at Reesa for back-up, but she could only blink at him. Her partner stepped forward. "It goes against our vows," he said. "We sign a specific non-aggression policy."

"I'm only going to say this once, Apostle," Tombstone growled. He stalked back to Joule. Glared down at him. "Those things don't give a damn about your non-aggression policy. They don't know the meaning of the word. They *will* kill you. No negotiations. I'll take the gun back, and you can pray all you want to your god to come save you. We'll see how well that works when a taker has you by the throat." He slapped a rag against Joule's chest. "Tie this around your face so you don't asphyxiate out there."

Joule let the rag fall to the crook in his arm. "I can't take the gun."

"I don't care."

"I *can't* take it!"

"All right," Tombstone replied, going to Randy and tying a dirty red rag around the back of her head to cover her nose and mouth. "Watch all those people under your responsibility get slaughtered. I can't save them all."

Reesa looked at Joule. The takers howled. At the window. They ignored the body of their fallen comrade, trampling over it, shoving one another. Trying to get at the opening. That little section of skin between Joule's eyes and above his nose drew up into a pattern of wrinkles, his eyes *opened,* pleading. Looking at her. Emptiness whirled inside Reesa like the dust storm outside. Somewhere, in the back of her mind, she was frightened, but it was the kind of feeling that was so dim you couldn't sense it if you focused on it. At the edges of her field of vision, a black circle began closing in.

"Give it to me," she said, and snatched the gun out of Joule's hands before he could object. His mouth fell open.

"Reesa!"

"Tie your cloth around your face and shut up, Joule."

The pistol hummed in her hand. Tiny, buzzing vibrations. Like holding the sound a bee makes. Reesa liked it. Tombstone held one of the last of his rags out to her. She took it, tucking the gun carefully into her belt before securing the cloth around her face. She was a bandit now. A full-fledged old west bandit. All she needed was a train to rob.

When she looked at Joule he was staring at her, his mouth an open trap for flies. She smacked the bottom of his chin, and his teeth clacked together as his jaw snapped up.

"Tie. Your cloth. Around. Your face," she growled.

That sparked a fire in his eyes. His jaw clenched. Good. That was the kind of attitude they needed. Joule lifted his arms, began fumbling with the ends of the cloth behind his head. She turned to Tombstone.

"We're ready."

"Shoot anything that gets too close," Tombstone said, and pulled his own rag up over his nose. "I'll take care of the rest."

"Sable, my horses," Randy rasped. "Sable, my horses, I need my horses…"

"I'll go with you to the coach and you can unhitch them, Randy," Tombstone replied, then looking at Reesa, "You and your partner go to the barn, get Indie. And shut the door when you're done or I'll know who to blame when all my horses are dead." He took a decisive step toward the front door, grabbing Randy and dragging her alongside him. "Meet us back at the coach. We'll ride Randy's team back to Big City."

Joule stumbled over one of the rugs as he tried to follow. "Without saddles?"

"There isn't time."

Tombstone reached for the doorknob, but it jiggled before his hand closed around it. BANG! and the wood rattled in the frame. Knock, knock. They were at the door.

"Damn…"

He hesitated. Then, yanking the door open in one swift motion, he slipped the second pistol from his belt, raising it as the taker followed the sudden pull of the handle into the house. He shot it in the head. A spray of slime and slick burst out the back, spattering the door. Tombstone looked back over his shoulder.

"Let's go."

17

Beyond the door, the world had become one solid cloud of whirling dust and debris. Tombstone grabbed Randy and practically hurled the girl over the body of the taker that blocked the doorway before dashing out into the fray himself. Reesa couldn't bring herself to follow him.

"Well?" Joule snipped behind her, stepping around and stomping to the open door, to the howling storm that awaited them. "You were so eager to go, so let's go."

He snatched her wrist and yanked her forward. Her jaw clenched, fear gave way to frustration. She jerked her arm out of his grip.

"Don't *touch* me, Joule," she hissed.

His eyes went hard. So what? He straightened, cold, but it didn't matter. The wind pulled at the door, swinging it back and forth on its hinges, knocking against the wall one moment and thumping against the body of the taker the next. They had to get out. They had to go. She could have shot Joule then and there and been rid of the stupid cow, but—a tremendous roll of shiver shot down her spine. How could she think such things? That wasn't who she was.

Without another word, Reesa went to the door and slipped past the taker into the storm. A gust pulled her instantly to the right. Her feet slipped on the gravel path. She had wasted enough time already.

"Come on, Joule!" she shouted over the gale.

Her eyelashes fluttered like a panicked butterfly's wings with the tearing of the wind, so she squinted hard and the world became nothing more than a slit in a canvas of dark. A blurry, barely visible slit in which she watched Joule stumble out the door to join her. The second he was out, the pair of them dashed off along the gravel toward the barn. They only had to follow the path.

The wind stole her steps, grasping her leg and shoving it sideways so that she came down in the wrong place. It yowled across her ears whhhhhite noisssssse so she could no longer hear the takers. One could come slopping out of the dust cloud at her at any moment. She kept her gun poised, humming, a hasty heartbeat in her hand, the slit world blurred and nothing but raging dust. Pellets pelted the exposed skin of her hands, her forehead. Dirt conditioned her hair while the wind turned it to tangles. The rag across her face smelled like…smelled like wet dog.

SLAM. She rammed full-body into the barn door. A groan escaped her lips, and she fumbled with her free hand to find the crack where this door met the other one. Joule, a white-blonde blur, appeared beside her—her fingers connected with the crack and she pulled and he pulled and the door creaked open. Joule squeezed inside; she followed suit.

The wind had a different sound inside the barn—tonal, moaning. A ghost. She looked at Joule, streaked with brown and bits of brush clinging to his hair.

"Could do with some eye cover," he said. "Which one did he want?"

He turned to face the barn, the thirty or forty animals that stood snorting and shivering, frightened of the wind.

"The big black one," Reesa replied. "I'll find her. See if you can dig up any goggles."

Muting the gun and tucking it into her belt, she dashed down the row of stalls—horse, horse, horse, horse, there were so many of them she wondered how it was possible that Tombstone had bred them all on his own. When she reached the end of the row, she found Indie, black and clinging to the wall like her own shadow. The horse let out a whinny when it saw her.

"Come on, girl."

Reesa reached up, retrieved a bridle and reins she hardly knew were hanging on the side post of the stable and hopped over the gate into the stall. The animal shied away from her, letting out a snort, but there wasn't any place to go except for the back wall. Indie's bottom bumped against it; Reesa slipped the bridle easily onto her snout. Apparently she knew how to bridle a horse.

Taking hold of the reins, Reesa led the horse forward to the gate which she unlatched and passed through quickly. Halfway up the aisle she met Joule, who held out a pair of plastic goggles, the kind kids at school wear while doing science experiments.

"This was all I could find," he said. He already had a pair on his own face, three in his hands. "I don't know how much good they'll do, but it's better than nothing."

"Thanks."

She took the goggles from him and pulled the elastic back to settle them over her skull. The bridge on the nose was too tight, the bottom rims pushed against her cheeks, but at least she would be able to see. Well, what there *was* to see anyway. With the goggles secured, she pulled her rag back up over her nose and led Indie to the barn door. Joule followed in close pursuit.

"I'll get Indie out, then help you with the door," she said as they reached it. The opening was too small for the massive horse, so she and Joule were forced to roll it open wider.

A burst of dirty wind shot down the aisle, spooking the horses, and they let out a chorus of terrified whinnies. Reesa pulled a reluctant Indie out into the storm, grasped onto the reins so strongly it made her hand hurt. Her nails dug into her palm. Then she and Joule shut the door and took off running, dragging Indie, in what was hopefully the direction of Randy and her coach. Reesa stuck close to the path, fumbling at her belt to retrieve the gun.

A dark shadow emerged out of the dust, the house, and as she turned her head, Reesa caught sight of Randy's coach, her three horses, and the two humans unhitching the animals through a break in the whirling dirt.

"There!" she cried.

Joule only just managed to follow her, but soon they were upon the other members of their group. Two of Randy's horses were loose, the girl herself holding onto the reins, the wind whipping at her hair, her eyes almost completely shut to shield. Tombstone worked to release the last one, but it must have been difficult without the aid of sight.

Reesa grabbed one of Joule's extra pairs of goggles and went to Randy, slipping them on over the girl's face before Randy could register what exactly was going on. She started under Reesa's hands, but relaxed when she saw who it was and the goggles came to rest upon her nose. She reached up a hand full of reins to adjust the fit over her eyes as they blinked open slowly, squinting around the dirt that stuck to her face. When she could see, Randy gave Reesa a firm nod, a thank you. Reesa smiled, but Randy wouldn't see it beneath the rag.

Joule had already given the last pair of goggles to Tombstone when Reesa turned to face them, and the latter was working swiftly now to unhitch the final horse. It came free seconds later, he led the animal over to the rest of them, and passed the reins to Joule.

"Get on!" he shouted.

The words were like a whisper under the gale, but a whisper loud enough to just catch hold of. Joule began preparing himself to jump onto the horse's back without the aid of stirrups, but Reesa was distracted from the attempt by Tombstone as he stepped over.

"You take one of Randy's there," he said, easier to hear now that he was close. "Still got that gun?"

Reesa nodded, holding it up for him to see.

"Good. Randy will help you on."

He held his hand out; Reesa passed him Indie's reins. He took them and then swung himself up easily onto the horse. Behind him, Joule was hanging halfway over his own animal, legs kicking in the air as he tried to get one of them over the other side. Thankfully the horse wasn't moving. So well trained.

A little tapping at her fingers drew her attention and Reesa looked down and saw a set of reins as they were slapped into her hand. Randy shrugged, then rocked up onto her own mount. Reesa hesitated, looking into the big brown marble of an eye protruding out of her horse's head.

"Are you ready?" she asked the animal.

A deep breath, a little prep work with her knees, and she jumped, grasping 'round the horse's neck and hauling herself over in one swift motion. She almost slipped off the other side, but gripping its mane, she managed to stay aloft.

A surprised laugh trilled from her throat. "I did it!"

They were all amount now, even Joule who looked incredibly put out. Reesa smiled at his stupidity, a secret underneath her cloth. How nice it was to be able to emote without exposure.

Tombstone made a signal with his hand, kicked his horse, and raced off into the storm. Randy followed rapidly behind, and with a kick to her animal, Reesa did as well. She checked over her shoulder, and it took him a moment, but Joule soon followed. Slowly, but he followed.

The wall of dust and dirt seemed to go on forever. She ran her horse as if the two of them were on a treadmill. Running, running, running, but always remaining in the same place. The brush that passed by her feet gave her no indication of a passage of landscape. It was like being in an old movie where the set moved, not you.

Just ahead of her Randy's form and shadow were barely visible and she checked over her shoulder constantly to make sure Joule was close behind. It was amazing how easily she found she could grip the body of the horse with her knees, startling how comfortable she felt not only riding, but riding bareback. Her bones felt so accustomed to it, a long life of riding, decades of practice. The constant bouncing was less than pleasant, but she found how simply the cues came to her to guide the horse. Her body had been riding long before it had been her body.

Getting to Big City as single riders should have been much faster than a team and carriage, but the wind hindered them. An eternity passed and Reesa had begun to think she might have entered purgatory, been killed by a taker and, because she'd never quite learned to love Joule, been sent to wait out her salvation, but then a dark grey shadow loomed suddenly upon her and she shot through the back gate into the town. At once, a sound reached her ears over the wailing wind. A shrieking sound. A killing sound.

Takers. And lots of them.

She directed her horse to follow Randy and Tombstone who had come to a stop and dismounted behind the bank. Joule was close behind her. She hopped down, Joule fell off, and she silent and he grumbling they joined their companions in a tight huddle.

City Ash and Desert Bones

"We'll need as many hands on guns as we can get," Tombstone said.
The shrieking chorus was punctuated by human screams.

We swirl through the air in great circumferences, sometimes together in one, and sometimes taken into one another. Around, and round, and around. We gather speed. At first, we laid on the ground—brush growing out of our head like our hair, nappy, footprints of wolves and rabbits, slithers of snakes pressed in to our scalp. Then the wind, and we began to rise. Slowly at first, in short gusts, short sine waves that raised us and lowered us like a sea fowl on an ocean. Then the speed came, and we rose again not to touch the ground, but to spin in the air in a frenzy, in a cloud, up and up and over the desert. Over ourselves. We became not the ground, but the storm.

We roll forward like raging thunder, but silent. The wind speaks for us, makes our howl sound loud over the flat ground that is still us, gathering more of ourselves up. We spin, spiral. We swift through the air forward one moment and back the next, up and down and side to side with the will of the wind, our voice.

We are large. We are infinite. We are the desert in the air.

As we move we touch things. Dark things…sticky things. Things that move slowly across the desert with slopping steps. We stick to them, to their skin, make them not sticky, make them us too. We whip through our hair, the brush, like a wave, like a comb. We hit the little ring of buildings and the building that stands alone beside another building and the frail platform that squats beside the train tracks. We pelt ourselves against those big metal pinpricks in our head, that dig and pull our brains out, except for that they did not succeed, they hit the skull that the sticky things built to keep them out so they could have our brains for themselves. The sticky things are not us, but they are us, for we cover them, their stickiness, and we hide them in our head. They hurt the people who live on our scalp. We hurt them too, when we are the storm.

Inside us, the sticky things attack the people as they have always attacked the people. They kill in the ring of buildings and at the buildings by themselves. Four of the people move quickly, on horseback, through us. We get in their hair, coat the rags they wear over their faces. We could suffocate them. We could get inside their lungs and stay, forever. We have done this before, many times, and we return to us when the people we have hurt are dead and buried. We are all one, but not the sticky things. We are not them, but we hide them.

People run, and scream. We enter their throats, and eyes. The sticky things get them. We are not trying to help.

We are not. But we are.

18

Reesa came around the corner and there was Pip Adams in the arms of a taker, screaming as the thing ripped his arm from its socket and stuck the boy's head into its mouth. Then the screaming stopped, and Reesa couldn't see what happened exactly, but Pip's headless body fell back from the taker and landed on the ground where it promptly began pouring blood into the dirt. The wind whistled past her goggles. The gun buzzed in her hand. The morning before they'd left for Big City she'd had toast for breakfast, toast with butter and strawberry jam.

Someone was screaming. Was it her? She pressed her free hand to her throat to see if sound was coming out while she watched that pool of blood widen in circumference. No, she wasn't screaming. But she should have been.

The taker that had eaten Pip hadn't sensed her yet. It stood relatively motionless over the boy's body, swaying back and forth with the gale. Dust from the storm stuck to its sticky outside, like a mud-pie with dry dirt sprinkled over the top for frosting. Blood dripped out of its mouth hole and ran down its front. At once its head exploded in a shower of blackish-brownish red. Reesa jumped, whipping around.

Tombstone stood behind her, lowering his gun.

"Shoot them when they're occupied," he said. "Another twenty seconds and you'd have been next."

She turned back and stared, *stared* at the two headless bodies now lying on the ground. What was that ragged sound? Was that her breathing? Her blood rushed around in her head, in her ears, competing with the noise of the wind, the beat of her heart pounding, pounding. The gun began to tremble in her hand, more than just its power-on humming. She nearly lost control of it, nearly dropped it in the dirt, but she turned to look at Tombstone and he steadied her.

"Your partner and Randy are evacuating everyone they can find to the shelter under the church," he said, grabbing her hand and pressing it firmly around the gun. "I'll need as much help as you can give me getting rid of the takers."

Her head bobbed up and down, nodding furiously as tears began to sting her eyes. This sick sort of nausea mixed with fear and panic bubbled in her heart and rose in her throat.

"Your gun's fully charged so don't worry about running out of shot." He cocked his shotgun and tucked his pistol into his belt. "Aim for their heads."

And like that, he was gone—dashed off into the cover of the storm. All around her Reesa could hear shrieks and screams, human and inhuman, doors slamming, windows shattering, all around her a panic she couldn't see. Never in her life had she felt so totally alone, so helpless. She looked down at the gun in her hands. She wondered if the Theocracy would punish her for using it, considering the circumstances.

A resolve sparked in her breast. She was an apostle. It was her duty to see to the well-being of Big City. She *would* help, she was determined, but she wavered when she looked back to Pip, or what used to be Pip, and then all she wanted to do was throw up.

She took a deep breath, and started forward into the storm.

"*Our hallowed, holy Father who resides in Heaven with all glory, sacred be thy name and works and blessed servants upon this land.*" The apostle's prayer flowed from her lips without effort. "*May Thy will be done through humble hands.*" A dark shape formed in the whirling dust. "*May Thy plan for Thy children come to pass.*" Reesa drew near it, held up the gun. "*May we, your obedient apostles, be given the strength to aid in Thy divine labor. Hallowed, holy Father, help us to serve Thee by serving Thy people.*" She took aim, the figure turned, her pulse picked up, beat, beat, beat, in her ears. "*Bless us with Thy strength. Amen!*"

Her finger began to squeeze down on the trigger when Darling came exploding out of the storm to meet her.

"Apostle Reesa! Reesa!"

The girl threw her arms around Reesa's neck and clung desperately. Reesa's face felt suddenly cold as all the blood ran from it. Darling. She was about to shoot *Darling.* Suddenly she didn't feel so confident with a gun.

"Get to the church," Reesa managed to squeak. "To the basement."

Darling clutched at her neck, suctioned tightly around her body. "The alarm—the alarm didn't go off, we had no idea they were coming, nobody could see them in the storm so nobody could set off the alarm."

Reesa pried her off. "The *church.*"

She gave Darling a firm, but gentle push in the general direction of the church as best she could calculate in the confusion of the storm. She hadn't been able to tell it was Darling ten feet in front of her, there was no way she could be certain where anything was. But they'd come in between the bank and the stables and she'd only gone straight since then. If she squinted she could maybe make out the shape of the fountain. Darling would not let go of her arm.

"*Let go.*"

Darling obeyed.

"Now go. Tombstone and I will get the takers." She winced. That sounded so stupid. She had no idea in hell what she was doing. It didn't seem to matter to Darling. The girl looked at her with wide eyes for a moment, drawing in strength it seemed, and then with a firm nod, she turned on her heel and ran. How could she stand to keep her eyes open in the storm?

Kicking down the Pratts' front door, Huxley burst in, shotgun level with his shoulder, taking aim at and shooting the first thing he laid eyes on, which fortunately for him was a taker. Unfortunately it had been chewing—if you could call it chewing—on Derek Pratt's arm when he'd found it. He didn't really hear the screams. He just reached down and covered Derek's eyes.

"Forgive me," he said. Then he shot him through the head.

If Big City made it through this attack, there would hardly be even a semblance of a population. How long had the takers been here before he arrived? Evidently there had been no time to sound the alarm. How many people were dead? He could count two for certain, and two was two too many, but he knew in his heart there were more. He could feel it. It hung heavy in the air.

He searched the house and could find no one else. He left Derek's body where it was. He would clean up later, when all this was over. As he left he hesitated in the doorway, shut his eyes, took stock of what he could hear. Wind mostly, but underneath that a current of cries and shouts. He went in the direction of the loudest one.

Across the street was Freddie Dunstan's house—his wife's house since Freddie had been kidnapped along with the others. Screams reached his ears, and a pounding like something slamming hard against a wooden door over and over again. Huxley came upon the porch and a taker which he shot without a second thought. It slumped against the door. The frame was just about to give way.

He stepped carefully onto the porch, avoiding the puddle of taker and shouting over the wind, "It's dead now, but it's blocking the door! Go around to the back, and I'll meet you there!"

Hysterical tears of relief burst out from inside. "Lord and Saints, Lord and Saints—thank you, Tombstone, thank you!" Feet trampled over wooden boards, running, and as soon as he heard them start to move he dashed down from the porch and went around the back of the house as he'd said he would.

As he arrived, Desdemona Dunstan hesitantly opened the door, checking for takers. When she saw Huxley, she threw the door open and pushed her daughter Georgianna without pause into the storm, stepped out of view for a moment, and reappeared ushering Arabella, Freddie's aging mother, along with her. Georgianna ran to Huxley immediately and he met her halfway where she grabbed onto his arm and did not let go. She wasn't much younger than he was, but she stared in terror with the eyes of a child.

"Apostle Joule and Randy are gathering everyone to the church," he said, coming upon Arabella and Desdemona and offering his free arm to support Arabella's other side. "It's right next door. Do you think you can make it?"

Desdemona nodded, tears streaking her face, dirt getting stuck in those tears. "Yes, thank you, thank you so much, we'd be dead now, if, if…" Her bottom lip began to tremble.

"Hey, it's fine. Just focus on getting to the church."

It was slow going with Arabella, but the church was less than twenty feet from the house. He led them around back to the cellar door that was planted in the ground. Thankfully the thing was thrown open. He detached himself from Arabella and Georgianna took his place.

"I'll be back as soon as I finish searching the rest of the houses," he said.

Georgianna looked at him, her eyes glittering with fright, and nodded her thanks. He couldn't find the strength to nod back. Randy's head popped up just as the Dunstan women disappeared.

"Who isn't accounted for?" Huxley asked.

"All of the ranchers," Randy replied, "Biddy, Rake, and Pip Adams, the Sullivans, Edward Shank and his boys, Seville Swallow, Callum and Nana, and Derek Pratt."

"We can't do anything about the ranchers," Huxley said, shaking his head. "I'll do my best to find the others." He could tally the dead when they were dead. No sense in counting now. "Where's Joule?"

"He went with Gig to the Sullivan house," Randy replied.

Huxley nodded. "Did you check the Adams's?"

"Yeah, we got Richard and Frenchie from there. Germain and Dilla, too. They said Rake and Biddy were headed uptown when the storm hit."

Well, Huxley could account for Pip. He'd watched him die. That didn't bode well for the kid's parents, even if they were still alive somewhere.

"I'll head for the bank, then," he said. "Maybe I'll run into them on the way." He pulled his pistol from his belt and handed it to Randy. "You seem like you've got your head back. Shoot anything that isn't human."

She took the gun and looked at it for a moment in her hand.

"I'll be back as soon as I can."

Randy nodded, a curt gesture. He nodded back and left her there. The winds were beginning to slow. He edged around to the front of the church. Edward Shank and his boys were probably stuck at the bank, Seville in the jail. Joule and Gig were accounting for the Sullivans. He couldn't be sure about Callum and Nana but he would check the smith shop, Biddy and Rake Adams must have gotten separated from their son. The ranchers, though. Damn. There was no way he could get to them. If as many takers had attacked the other ranches as had attacked his, they were all dead.

He stuck close to the buildings so he'd have a landmark in the whirling cloud of dust and debris and worked his way swiftly up toward the bank. As swiftly as was safe. Takers weren't fast, but they were tricky. He strained his ears, listening for the sucking sound of their sensing so he could shoot before one even had a chance to move.

Suck. A taker emerged from the space between the hotel and the newspaper office. As if on a swivel it turned its head toward Huxley. *Snap.* He shot it straight through. The shower of slime and insides that accompanied his shots had long since ceased to affect him. He moved on.

Deep in his heart somewhere, something began to twist, something painful, something he couldn't do anything to ease. *Suck, snap.* His sternum grew heavy. Another taker. His breathing gained pace. Behind him, *suck snap*. Lord and Saints they were everywhere. He was approaching the jail now, no takers pawing at the outside. He shielded his eyes and stuck his face against the glass to get a look in the front window.

Seville lay on the table, head toward the window, a taker rooting around in his intestines. Huxley shot them both through the glass.

We begin to die, falling from our voice and with our voice until we once again meet ourselves on the ground. We have moved much, hurt much. We have hidden sticky things against our will. We have brought this death for we were party to it.

We no longer have anything to say for ourselves, to let the wind say. The whistling, howling, whirling sensation is gone. We are ourselves on the dirt. We are not the storm.

Human red, sticky thing black, it runs upon our scalp. It stains us, marks our sin. Their bodies lie heavy upon us. Soon they will lie heavy within us.

The sticky things turn back, sticking quickly across our scalp back to the hole they have dug into our brains. We wish we could swallow them up, close the hole and trap them inside our brains until they wriggled and died. But we cannot. We can only move with the wind.

The wind ceased slowly and then at once and the dirt it had been carrying sifted down from the air. Suddenly, Huxley could see. And there was Reesa, collapsed to her knees in front of Biddy Adams's slumping body at the bottom of the steps to the town hall, a pool of muddy blood inching its way toward her as if magnetized by the white of her uniform. A taker lay not far from her, writhing on the ground and howling. Looked like she shot it through both legs. Huxley finished the job. He looked at Reesa.

"Get up. Let's go."

"I-I...do it—couldn't..."

"Get up."

"I couldn't do it."

Her eyes flashed—wild and hungry. She stared up at Huxley with such complete desperation, such abject horror, that for a moment she no longer looked human.

"I couldn't do anything!" she screeched.

Huxley grabbed her by the collar and yanked her up. She made a little choking noise. "Get on your goddamn feet," he hissed.

The door to the bank burst open and Edward Shank's boys Seth and Junior came running out, supporting their father between them. Blood and mucus dripped from a wound in his leg, his head lolled back and his skin a sickly green.

"He's been taken," Seth said.

"I can see that," Huxley replied, still clutching on to Reesa's collar.

"Lord and Saints, can't you do anything for him, Tombstone?!"

It had been a long time since he'd tried one of his antidotes. But it had been a long time for a reason. Reesa began to sob. Seth and Junior begged him with their eyes. A little ripple passed over Edward's skin. Reesa's knees went weak, her body going limp, and Huxley dropped her, let her collapse back into the dirt. Seth and Junior didn't even look her way.

"*Please,* Tombstone," Seth whispered.

He set his eyes like stone. He would regret this.

19

Tombstone dumped Reesa with the others in the basement of the church. Joule came running through the crowd to meet them, catching Reesa as Tombstone practically flung her out of his grip. She didn't even try to squirm away. She let her head rest against his shoulder.

She'd come through the dust and Biddy Adams had been standing on the town hall steps, clutching her shawl around her neck, panicking. Reesa had started to go to her, but the sight of a figure in the storm must have startled Biddy, for she had shrieked and scrambled away, right into a taker that had appeared out of thin air and grabbed onto her and *scratched*—long, deep lines of blood that ran instantly, and Reesa had hesitated—just for a moment, her finger on the trigger—just long enough for the taker to open a vein in Biddy's neck and for the woman to begin choking on her own blood.

The basement was hot, and dusty—dark, filled with sweating and fear. Little cracks of light shown through the clapboard ceiling that was the floor of the chapel above them.

"Is she all right?"

"She's seen some things, that's all," Tombstone said. "You find the Sullivans?"

"Yes, but—"

"Randy! Get over here. Let's go."

She had shot twice, but only hit the taker's legs.

Randy appeared, Tombstone gave her some sort of summary of the events with the Shanks who were waiting outside in case Edward infected anyone else by accident. Randy listened. Reesa didn't. Joule's shoulder smelled like soap.

"I'll leave that gun with you in case they come back," Tombstone said as he turned to go. "But you'll probably want to give it to someone else."

His eyes flicked disapprovingly down at Reesa for a moment—not a bit of sympathy in them, not a bit of warmth, not a bit of hey-I-know-how-you-feel-let's-feel-together. Maybe he didn't know how wretched she was inside. Maybe he felt worse. That gun suddenly weighed like an anvil in her hand, pulling her down, and she slipped out of Joule's arms and followed her hand to the packed-dirt floor.

"Reesa!" Joule got to his knees and leaned into her face. "Careful. Are you all right?"

Was she all right? Was she *all right?* Of course she was not all right. She'd watched Pip's head get bitten off and then wandered around in the storm on high-alert, seeing shadows in every swirl of the dust, until she'd found the poor dead boy's mother and then *she'd* died too, right in front of her eyes, and Reesa had just *stood* there, like a damn useless old stump. She stared at Joule, saying nothing, her eyes about to burst.

Joule snagged her into a hug, and boy did she try to wriggle out this time, but he clung on tighter and there was nowhere to go. Reesa went limp, slumping against him, the gun finally trickling out of her fingers and clattering onto the floor, its impression etched in the palm of her hand, down to the crosshatch detailing on the grip.

A crowd had gathered around them, or rather turned around to face them. All was silence in the absence of the wind.

"Are they gone, then, Apostle Joule?"

He had to crane his neck around to see who had spoken. "What? Yes, I suppose so."

"They're gone, everybody!" the same voice shouted into the crowd. "Give it another half hour and then we'll get outside."

A little bit of the tension hissed out of the shelter like a deflating balloon. Shoulders softened, quiet conversations struck up, bodies shifted and Mayor Big City waded through until he came to Reesa and Joule.

"Where's Tombstone?" he demanded.

"He went back to his ranch," Joule replied.

"Edward Shank got taken," Reesa mumbled into Joule's shoulder.

"What'd she say?"

"She said Edward Shank got taken. Tombstone took him back to his ranch to see if he can do anything."

Hicks grunted in response.

"If you hadn't kept us in the dark about this, we might have been able to help," Joule snapped. He stiffened and Reesa had to change the distribution of her weight to keep from toppling over.

"Help?" The mayor's cheeks puffed out and crimson crept in.

"You lied to us and now people are suffering. We could have done something. We could have helped." Joule was very nearly getting to his feet and Reesa was slipping against his uniform, clutching on, holding him down.

Hicks looked at her. "Apostle Reesa, were you any help?"

Pip's blood ran red down the side with the missing arm while the taker held him firmly, squeezing, lifting, until his head was inside the taker's, and then his head was gone. Reesa did not answer.

"You wouldn't have been able to change a goddamn thing, Apostles." Hicks's red, red face began to chuckle, and those chuckles began to turn into laughter, and the laughter turned into guffaws until tears ran down his face and his belly rolled in contortion with his sudden strike of good humor. Bending over, he picked up the gun at Reesa's side. "Not a damn thing." And he burst into laughter again.

"*Stop it!*"

Reesa found herself on her feet, found her vocal cords searing from the painful screech. Startled, she realized it was she who had made that sound. Hicks Grey stared at her, so did everyone else. She stood her ground.

"Your people—*our* people have suffered, and you laugh? Show some respect."

Joule reached up to grab her hand. "Reesa—"

She slapped him away, actually *slapped* his hand and it made a great crack in the air. He was going to remind her of the commandments. He was going to tell her she could not stand up to Hicks, but she didn't care anymore. She'd seen two murders she should have, and could have, prevented and suddenly telling off a rat bastard in a cowboy hat didn't seem like such a big deal.

"We could have changed things today," she said. Her voice sounded so powerful, so commanding. It felt good. "If we had been prepared, we could have changed things. I watched two people die today, Mayor Big City—people I could have saved if I'd been told what to expect."

He took one step toward her, lowered his head right into her face. The individual hairs of his mustache bristled. The pores on his skin poured sweat.

"I've seen more death then you could ever imagine, Apostle," he hissed. "I only laugh to keep from losing my mind." He laughed then, sharp and barking, just a single laugh. It pierced her ears. "I got blood enough on my hands, Apostle. Welcome to the club."

With a grunt, Mayor Big City turned—the people parted like a sea to let him pass—but Reesa wasn't finished with him yet. She took a step, but that step turned into a powerful leap that sent her off the ground, her arms outstretched, soaring for a moment until she hit Hicks's back and *snap!* her arms closed tight around his neck.

Seven different voices screamed in her head, some of them making their way out into the air as she struggled to hold onto Hicks with one arm and the fingers of the other scrambled around like a giant spider to reclaim the gun.

"We're in here, *we're in here*, and we're all dead how do you think that feels? Huh, do you? You got no damn sense of yours in that fat old melon! I-just-I-just-I-just—I just want to go home! *Huxley!*"

131

"What the *hell*?!" Initial shock worn off, Hicks tossed Reesa easily from his shoulders. She landed in the dirt, *smack*. When she looked up Hicks was pointing the pistol at her face, his eyelids peeled back far over his eyes so that they were white and bulging.

"Mayor—"

"Don't move! Don't move or I'll blow your brains out!"

Reesa closed her lips. A ring of empty space had formed around herself and the mayor. A ring of people, dirty people, exhausted people who stared at her in terror. She and Hicks were alone in the space. Even Joule had scurried away. When she'd landed in the dirt, he had not come to her. What must she have looked like from the outside? What had come over her?

"I'm sorry," she said, and hung her head. A curtain of ruby-red hair fell around her face, a place for her to hide a moment. Her mouth opened, a painful, silent scream flowing out. Tears stung her eyes, grew fat, and fell to the dirt as she had. In the silence that choked the church's basement, she could hear her tears as they met the floor—*pat, pat, pat*.

"Everybody go back to your houses," Hicks ordered, keeping the gun trained on Reesa. "If there's a dead taker in your house, go to the neighbors. Don't go near them. If there's a dead neighbor in your house, leave them. Gig and I will see to clean-up. Go."

Nobody moved.

"*GO!*"

Everyone hurried toward the exit, staying well-clear of Reesa. Not one of them crossed over the line of that invisible ring. A few men paused near the mayor, said something about wanting to assist in the clean-up. Hicks nodded, told them to wait outside. Sent Gig out with them. Soon, the basement was empty and the three who remained regarded each other uneasily.

"What's the matter with you?" Hicks hissed.

Reesa managed to choke out a wavering, "I—I don't know." She sniffed and wiped at the string of snot slipping out of her nose. "I'm sorry—I'm so sorry, I don't know what happened."

"I'll be damned if I do!" Hicks looked at Joule. "She ever do something like that before?"

Joule should his head. "Not since we've been partners, no."

"Hm."

Hicks considered Reesa a moment. His eyes dug into her like a pair of railroad spikes. She couldn't find the strength to raise her head.

"You going to attack me again?"

"No, sir."

"You going to attack anyone else?"

"No, sir."

"You'll understand if I don't give you the gun back?"

"Yes, sir. I won't object, sir."

"Good." Hicks flicked the power-down switch on the side of the pistol and tucked the thing into his pants. He placed his hands on his hips and looked between the two of them for a moment before puffing out a gust of air and shaking his head. "She's all yours, Apostle Joule. Keep her in line."

He turned and tromped up the steps and out the hatch. Joule stayed silent, stunned probably. Reesa couldn't explain what had happened, how could anyone? Her shoulders began to shake. Other voices had come from her mouth, voices that were not her own. She'd lost it, just straight up lost it and *attacked* the mayor. Good lord, that was a terrifying thought. Joule would have to tell Cardinal Cyatan about it in their report. She would make herself scarce that evening.

"What on *earth*, Reesa?"

She kept her eyes on the floor, shook her head. "I'm sorry, Joule, I don't know what came over me…But there's no excuse."

"You think?" He scoffed, a short-sharp "Ha!" that stung. "You assaulted a government official, Reesa! What would you have done if you'd been able to get your hands on the gun? Shot him?"

That *had* been her objective. She wouldn't admit that to Joule though, so she shook her head again. "I really don't know."

She glanced at him and he rolled his eyes, shaking his head as well and crossing his arms. His goggles and the cloth that had covered his face during the storm hung around his neck. A layer of dirt coated his skin like make-up, caked into his uniform as well.

"We'll have to buy a lot of bleach," she said.

He looked at her. "What on earth are you talking about?"

"Never mind."

"No, tell me."

"I said never mind, Joule!"

"Why are you always like this?" he snapped.

Reesa's brows pulled together. "Like what?"

"Pushing me away, never explaining anything to me like it's too complicated and I won't understand."

That dolt. "You hardly ever understand!"

"Well that's not my fault if you won't *tell* me anything! For heaven's sake, Reesa I'm supposed to be your husband."

What?

Reesa blinked.

…What?

"I'm supposed to be your husband…" Joule looked at the floor. "I just want to help you. That's all. Please, let me help you."

Her…husband?

Biddy Adams. She had had a husband. His name was Rake, if she remembered correctly. He was probably dead, too. Probably dismembered somewhere up on the surface waiting for someone to find his body, waiting for Gig and Hicks to come by with their cart and shovels and scoop away whatever was left, waiting to join the remnants of his wife and child. Reesa's blood ran hot, color rising in her cheeks, heat radiating from her skin. A family *murdered*. She would make those bastards pay. She would make them *pay*.

"I'll kill them all." She punched her clenched fist down on her leg.

"I'm sorry, *what?*"

"The takers." She turned to Joule, her lips curled back around her teeth in a vicious smile, a predator's smile. "I'm going to kill them all."

She popped up onto her feet and hurried for the open hatch, a lust for blood rolling through her veins—not red blood, no, not red, but black, black *taker* blood, she would see it run like the River Nile, a Moses on the banks.

Joule's hand brushed her hand and he tried to snatch her and keep her still, but she evaded him and started up the stairs two at a time. First she would get the pistol back from Mayor Big City, then she would hunt down Tombstone and make him show her where those monsters lived, and then she would shoot every last one of them. In an ideal world she would have liked to paint herself with their blood in the pattern of victory, but if she did that then the toxin would invade her body and make it digest itself, so she'd have to settle for less. A laugh bubbled in her belly and then burst forth from her lips before many others joined it. A disharmonic chorus like a hoard of demons giggling, many kinds of laughter all slipping from her open mouth at once. She reached the top of the steps. The world started to tilt, then spin. The ground came toward her swiftly and she met it with a crack.

Slick, warm blood began to run down her forehead where she'd cut it on a rock. "I'll kill them all," she whispered, giggling, and fell under.

It was debatable whether or not a lethal injection was a better way to die than a bullet out the back of your head. If he screwed up the chemicals it could have been agonizing. But how was anyone supposed to know really? You didn't come back from death to report to your friends how it had gone for you. All Huxley could say was that Edward's was the quietest death he'd dealt out. Maybe he should start carrying needles in his holster instead of a gun, but either way, he'd still be a killer. Either way, Edward was still dead.

Huxley stepped back from the metal slab table where Edward's body lay in his basement lab, the wound in the man's leg still festering, growing, the taker toxins feeding greedily. He'd keep the body if Ed's boys would let him. It would be an invaluable study specimen.

Seth and Junior slumped in the corner, tired, exhausted, terrified, fatherless. Seth would have run of the bank now, not that there was much money that needed running, but as the oldest he'd inherit Edward's position. Huxley crossed the short distance to them.

"He's gone," he said. "I'm sorry."

A clock ticked on the wall. The room was white and spotless, a wall of books and plants and herbs and tools and containers lining one wall. Two rows of metal tables like the one where Edward was spread out filled the space, were littered with glass tubes and notes, incubators where Huxley had been growing his ineffective antidotes. He bent down to be level with Seth and Junior who leaned against the wall, their legs pulled up against their bodies and their arms draped over their legs—helpless fetuses in a world crammed with death.

Huxley drew in a breath. "Can I keep his body?"

Seth raised his head slowly, bloodshot and red rimmed eyes glaring. "*What?*"

"I know what that sounds like, but—"

"*Keep* his body?"

Seth shot to his feet, stuck his face into Huxley's, a menacing tilt to his teeth and jaw. He grabbed the collar of Huxley's white coat.

"Seth—"

"No!" He tossed Huxley back, then stalked after him. "What kind of son would I be, uh? 'Stead of giving my father a proper burial I let the town freak poke around his dead body? No, never. I can't—I won't."

Huxley backed away, but Seth followed him wherever he went around the room—his nostrils flaring, angry sweat pouring into his eyes, very much a minotaur. Huxley wove backwards through the labyrinth of tables.

"You could *save lives*," he said.

Seth didn't give a damn about that. He bolted forward and grabbed hold of Huxley's shirtfront, yanking him into his face and snarling. Seth could inflict whatever pain he wanted, Huxley couldn't afford to lose this chance to have a live specimen to work with.

"If I can study the living toxin, I might be able to come up with an antidote that *works*. Please—"

"NO!"

Seth gave Huxley a violent shaking. From the corner, Junior's calm, quiet voice issued forth. "Stop it. Let him do it, Seth... For godsakes, let him do it." He stood up and looked at his brother with a worn, weary face. "Dad would have wanted to help."

"And what if he doesn't help, uh? What if the freak *can't* make a cure?"

Freak. Huh. Seth's grip on his shirt did not ease. His eyes bore down on Junior who, having nothing to say, hung his head. Seth reset his gaze on Huxley and *glared*. Huxley wasn't sure what expression was constructed on his own face, hoped it was one that wouldn't piss Seth off even more.

"Can you make a guarantee?" Seth asked. "Keeping his body means a cure?"

Huxley shook his head. "Of course not."

"Then why should we—"

"Because there's a *chance*, and right now that's all we've got."

They regarded each other for a long moment and eventually Seth released his grip and Huxley was free. The seconds ticked by on the wall clock. When the takers had come for Merrick, they had taken Huxley, too. Snatched the pair of them right off the ranch at the end of the day. Huxley didn't remember much about it—just hazy pictures of things, snapshots of terrified feelings. For whatever reason, they hadn't wanted him. Kept Merrick and dumped him on the surface. Gig had found him wandering out in the desert on his way to watch duty at the hole a few days later. Everyone assumed he'd been out there burying Merrick's body. And nobody would say it to his face but he knew they blamed every single one of the kidnappings on him after that. He'd tried to redeem himself but it was difficult to wash your hands by dipping them in blood.

"It'll be a few days until you can arrange a funeral," Huxley said. "You can store his body here, in the lab. So he won't infect anyone."

"And you can mutilate him in the meantime."

"No."

"Damned if I'll leave him here! I don't trust you, Tombstone, sure as hell."

All this coming from the son who had begged him just hours before to save his father. People get angry when things don't work out, throw little fits like children who didn't get their way. Well, Huxley hadn't gotten his way in years and nobody saw him complaining. His patience had worn razor thin, but he wouldn't disrespect the wishes of the dead or the grieving.

"Take him, then," he said. "If you want to run the risk. But you should leave him here. I won't touch him."

Seth held his eye, making that familiar face Huxley knew all too well as the face someone makes when they're trying to decide if you're a liar. He'd never quite understood why people made that face at him so often. He always played it straight, but perhaps that *was* why. Nobody wanted what he said to be true, so they searched for a lie to wrap a blanket around their unease and put it to bed. Huxley was a lot of things but a liar wasn't one of them.

"I'll leave him," Seth said, "but I'll be back for him and I swear to God if there is one hair out of place on his head, I'll kill you."

Huxley conceded. Seth could *try* to kill him at least, but there wouldn't be a need. He would keep his promise. Maybe Derek Pratt's family would let—no. He'd shot Derek. Seth and Junior would be the only ones remotely inclined to let him keep their dead relative as a specimen. He'd go to sleep that night and pretend that if someone asked him to let them keep Merrick in order to study her, he would say yes. He'd drift off deluding himself into believing that he'd let the greater good of all Big City prevail, but what he wouldn't give for even a little piece of her to bury. He looked at Seth, shut his eyes, and nodded.

That toxin tickled. From the wound in his leg the dead Edward Shank felt a little more of the world than he ever had alive: a fine dusty breeze that slithered over the surface of the earth like a snake breathing out its warm, warm breath, the soft quiet dripping of the sink onto Randy's pile of rusted silverware, measured steps, careful steps, the chuck-scoop of shovels lifting sticky taker bodies from the dirt and piling them into a cart, the wild space-journey of the earth, spinning so fast its inhabitants couldn't feel it, traveling so quickly through the void of outer space that no being or object ever occupied the same space twice in their lives, the large lonely cities full of people on the other side of the planet, exhaling a ring of smoke and smog into the nuclear air. Through the wound Edward felt what he never felt in life, the desperate beauty of a dying world clinging to a ledge for survival.

He felt his boys, curled up in the corner like a pair of hunting dogs. He felt them snap when Tombstone tried to talk. He felt them fight, spitting and raw, making the wrong decision but holding to their values all the same. They fought over him, over his body, his dead body. Over the shell that used to house his spirit. That crawling, tingling, tickling in his leg let him feel all this, like how a taker senses the world, he guessed.

He felt his boys stamp their feet out of the basement, Seth's nose huffing, fists clenched. Junior followed close behind him, placed a hand on his brother's shoulder that Seth threw off. He felt Tombstone, his eyes closed, standing, then sinking to his knees. He wouldn't touch Edward's body. He'd given his word. Tears began to fall from Tombstone's eyes. Edward felt them when they splashed on the ground.

Through the wound, Edward felt Tombstone rise as his sons passed out of his house and into the desert where Randy was waiting with her coach and her horses and her sink full of dripping silverware. The skin of those horses was like fine silk, covered with beautifully bred hairs, but sullied with the dust of the windstorm. Where their hooves touched the dirt there was an exchange of energy, a little electric feeling. That's what happened when a living thing touched the earth, clinging as the planet and its people hurtled through space. Edward felt that.

He felt Tombstone as he leaned against a metal table. Sensed vials that bubbled and vials that grew tiny microscopic little things, sensed the books and all the ink and paper they contained, all the information, all the weight. He felt as Tombstone came near his body, looked down upon it, his brown eyes shining like the Lord Himself. He felt the needle entering the skin of his forearm, felt the whisper-sweeping coolish numbness that swept through his body and lifted him up out of his shell like an oyster. He'd never eaten oysters, but he could feel them now, clinging to their rocks where the tide comes in and out, clinging in groups, growing pearls. A pearl grew in his own mouth, starting as a bit of sand until he covered it, smoothed it, making the irritation stop but creating a nuisance in its own way until some diver would pick him up, pry him open and steal his treasure. Tombstone would not pry. He was a man of his word.

As he felt, he felt that Tombstone was not Tombstone, but Huxley. He'd forgotten that boy's name. Such a soft name. Such a soft name for such a hard man. Edward wrapped his arms around the boy, the alone-boy. Huxley went to a silvery sink on the far wall, removed his gloves and goggles and apron and dropped them into a solution of disinfectant. They floated, the apron especially until it gathered water and slowly drifted, drifted, drifted to the bottom and covered the goggles like a shroud. Huxley covered Edward with his own shroud, a ceremonial sheet of plastic, a container for Edward's tickling wound. He went upstairs, then, flicked off the lights and left Edward in the dark.

The boy went to the kitchen sink. Cold crept into Edward's limbs. The boy leaned over the sink. His arms began to shake. Edward began to shiver. It was a peaceful shiver, full of the music of the desert at night—the howling of wolves and the scampers of rabbits, the creaking of crickets that people pretended was the most beautiful of all sounds, the sweet whisperwind that sprinkled dust like fairy magic, the chattering of the brush at what went through it. In that lilac night, Edward sensed the movement of underground things and aboveground things, the foolish vainish plottings of the human race: the positive illusions of self-concept. The false belief that we have more control over our lives than we actually do and to have unattainable expectations for the future.

His boys would come back for him. They'd find his body covered in its beautiful shroud and they'd take him away to burn him and bury his ashes in the desert. They'd give Huxley the eye and never know how he suffered. They'd go forth, thinking that tomorrow would be a better day in spite of all they'd experienced. In spite of all they knew, they'd think highly of themselves, of the world, and believe that they occupied a permanent space upon it, when in fact, no being ever occupied the same space twice.

20

Where had the bed come from, and the soft light? What about the bandage on her head? The sheets pulled up to her throat? Reesa snapped out of sleep like flipping a light switch. She was off and then she was on—her eyes were open, her breathing paced, her mind alert. Her forehead stung when she scrunched it up, bits of sticky medical tape pulling on the skin around the bandage and the cut itself disturbed.

Joule wasn't in their room. She was still dressed in her uniform, just minus the jacket which was hanging on the post at the end of the bed. Judging by the yellow-orangey light that slipped easily past the curtains it was evening. When had it gotten to be evening? She got out of bed. She went to the window.

There, in the middle of the square, five bodies lay, out baking in the sun. They were barely bodies. Limbs missing left and right. Mudcakes. The small one on the end without a head, that was Pip. Reesa *seethed*. A bit of foam fell from her lips and pattered onto the windowsill.

"I'll kill you for this," she whispered.

All at once Tombstone rode up on his big black horse and Joule stepped down from the hotel porch where Reesa had been unable to see him. The mayor and Gig were close behind, and aside from a small clean-up crew that worked down the way on the taker lying on the steps of the town hall, the four men were the only ones out on the street.

"What's the damage, Tombstone?" The mayor tipped his hat back from his forehead and wiped at the sweat with a handkerchief.

Tombstone shook his head, swung down from his horse. "They got to every ranch house," he said. "Thirteen in all, including the ones who died here in town."

In a place like Big City, thirteen may as well have been a thousand. Who? Reesa slammed her fist into the windowsill. Who else had they killed? Those bastards. She wished they had fingernails so she could pull them out one by one.

"Any news here?"

"Callum and Nana are still unaccounted for. Found Seville where you left him. Derek, too," Hicks replied. "This is a fine mess, Tombstone."

Tombstone lowered his gaze. The brim of his hat shaded his face from view.

Hicks looked at the sky himself, tucking his thumbs into his belt loops and sighing. "I don't even know how to begin to clean this up."

This was her chance! Reesa scrambled away from the window, barely dodging the edge of the bed as she passed it. She threw open the door, ran down the hall, down the stairs, out the door and leapt off the porch.

"We have to fight back!"

She had appeared suddenly and practically pounced on them. The men started, jumping back, looking at her with the wide eyes of surprise. She'd come out of nowhere. None of them said anything, so she kept going.

"We have to fight back. We can't let them do this to us and get away with it. What kind of message would that send?"

Her eyes flicked from Joule, to Gig, to Hicks, to Tombstone.

"We have to do *something*. We have to make them *pay*."

"Reesa, what on *earth* are you talking about?" Joule took a few steps towards her, his arms prepared to take hold of her shoulders, so she side-stepped him and he was forced to follow as she found her way into the little ring the others formed. He called after her. "Reesa!"

"The takers, we have to get them. Smoke them out, bury them all alive, I don't care, but we have to do *something*."

Her pulse had quickened and her chest rose and fell heavily with her excited breath. A spark in her eye of vibrant color, she looked at each of her companions in turn. She was serious, they *had* to know that, and she let them know, giving them each a good, hard stare out of her wild, wild eyes. Tombstone opened his mouth.

"For once, I agree with the apostle."

Really?! A squeal of joy sounded in Reesa's throat. She covered her mouth. Covered her smile. Shouldn't look too happy. Hicks and Gig regarded Tombstone with a mix of frustration and surprise.

"What?" The mayor adjusted his thumbs in his belt.

"She's half-crazed, but she's right, Hicks. We can't keep doing this. We can't keep losing people the way we did today." Tombstone shook his head. "We have to do something."

"And what do you propose we do, huh? We don't *have* weapons, Tombstone. Most of these people have never even held a gun and what's a hoe or a shovel going to do against a taker, huh? Nothing. Goddamned nothing, that's what! We can't fight them, Tombstone. We don't have the means."

"Besides, we have a non-aggression policy," Joule said.

Reesa looked at him. "And people died because of it."

His eyes flicked to the ground. Reesa looked away. She'd just let the guilt of that last comment sink in a little bit.

Tombstone picked up the thread. "We have the means, we just have to do a little thinking. Talk to everyone, Hicks, I'm sure they'll agree with Apostle Reesa. They'll *want* to fight back."

Her skin tingled when he said her name. He hadn't said it with malice or mocking and for whatever reason the intonation made her soar. She'd like to fall asleep to that at night, just his voice saying her name—over, and over, and over again.

"Can I help you, Apostle?"

Tombstone looked down from right above her, an eyebrow raised. She'd tipped toward him in her dreamy state and was very nearly leaning against him, would have been if he hadn't stepped back from her. Oh, all she wanted was to kiss him. That, and the takers dead. Perhaps both at the same time, the two of them covered in black blood, ardently embracing. Her arms began to reach up toward him.

"Reesa!"

Joule grabbed ahold of her then, pinned her arms behind her back in an awkward position like that hadn't been his goal initially. She snapped out of it. Tombstone was giving her a look. They all were. She turned red. What the hell— no, not *hell*, *stop* it for god—*heaven's* sakes! Her jaw tightened. What was *wrong* with her?

"Reesa, are you all right?" Joule peered around from behind her into her face.

She blinked, breathing. "I...I think so." She looked at him though, looked at him and said with her eyes *don't let go of me*. She didn't know what would happen if Joule let go. Not just yet, anyway. He seemed to understand, softening his grip but keeping his hold on her wrists.

Satisfied that she was contained, Hicks resumed the previous discussion. "What should we do, Tombstone?"

He shrugged. "Hold a meeting. We need to know how everyone else is feeling."

"Like they've been through shit and hellfire," Hicks replied with an angry snort.

"I don't doubt that, but we've all been through the same. We need to know if they're willing to fight, Hicks. And see if anybody has an idea *how*."

Hicks pursed his lips, mulling the thought around and around in his mind as his eyes rolled about from side to side. Eventually with a sigh he conceded the point, lowered his head and shook it. "You're right," he said. "I'll spread the word. We can meet tomorrow."

Reesa pulled at Joule's grip. "Tonight! It has to be tonight!"

Hicks looked at her. "Apostle, these people have lost family today. Daughters, mothers, fathers, brothers. I ain't about to disturb their grieving. It can wait."

"The more time we take the more time we give *them* to reform their ranks and attack again. We don't have time to waste. Please." She looked hard at him. "*Please.*"

Hicks glanced at Tombstone. He nodded once and Hicks looked to Gig who glanced at Tombstone himself before nodding as well. Hicks sighed, turning his gaze on the dirt before Reesa. Her heart beat in her ears. *Say yes.*

"All right, Apostle."

Reesa squirmed joyfully and Joule's handcuff hands tightened around her wrists, but she wasn't about to wiggle away. She held the corners of her lips down with some effort, trying not to smile. It was not a time to smile, but she couldn't help feeling that she'd won somehow. The mayor stood shaking his head and staring at the ground for some seconds while she waited eagerly for further instructions.

"We'll spread the word. Meet tonight around seven at the church. Don't make anybody come who don't want to." He flicked a stern glare Reesa's direction. "But let them know that it's important. Tombstone, will you tell the ranchers?"

He nodded. "I was going to head back out to help with clean-up anyway."

"Gig, you take the west row, I'll take the east row. Apostles, you'd better stay in your room until seven o'clock. Gather your wits. Understand?"

Reesa nodded. "Yes. Thank you, Mayor Big City."

"Good. Let's go."

The group broke up, Gig heading west for the house where Darling's family lived, Hicks east toward the Dunstan home, Tombstone lifting himself up onto his horse. He looked so lovely when he did that. Reesa kept her eyes trained on him as Joule led her back inside the hotel and Tombstone gave Indie a kick and headed off.

They looked like a horde of orphans out of a Dickens novel, but everyone showed up for the meeting. Huxley watched them as they filtered in. His arms crossed in front of him, he leaned against the side of the church right by the entrance and took roll as his neighbors took care not to get too close. By the time the apostles came jogging up from the hotel, all of Big City was present and accounted for—all that remained, anyway.

"Is everyone inside?" Reesa asked, breathless and excited. Her eyes shone like a kid on Christmas.

Huxley nodded. "Everyone but the two of you."

"Well, we're here now, so let's go." Joule, looking irritable, ushered his partner inside. Poor guy, having to stay locked up in a room with Reesa for hours.

What *did* they do with one another? Huxley didn't think he would ever figure that out. He grabbed the door and pulled it closed behind him.

The biggest room in Big City was the chapel of the church, and as she came to her seat right at the front in the first row of chairs, Reesa couldn't help but wonder if everybody typically attended services on Sunday. It was such a close-knit and tiny community the whole town would know if you weren't at church. And they'd probably start formulating rumors why.

Joule adjusted her seat and instead of telling him not to, she sat down and was quiet. Hicks stood just a few feet beyond them at the altar, Gig at his side. Tombstone came up, whispered something, and the mayor nodded. They were ready to begin.

As Tombstone found his place, Reesa caught wind of a hissing whisper that passed to him from the audience: "You better not have touched him, freak, or I'll have your head." She turned to see who had spoken and noticed Seth Shank. His face was an angry mask of flesh, red and contorted and glaring at Tombstone.

Tombstone looked at him once, and Reesa couldn't see his face, but whatever the expression upon it, Seth shut right up. A gavel cracked on the pulpit as Hicks called everyone to attention.

"I'm sorry to do this to you folks after the day we've had, but Apostle Reesa is right when she says that we don't have time to waste. We need to fight the takers and we need to do it now."

All was silence.

Reesa had expected a general hubbub like in a movie, voices talking about what had just been said and public protestations, something, anything, but there was nothing. Hicks's moustache pulled across his lip as he made a half-frown with his mouth At the back of the room, somebody coughed.

"I don't know how it would be possible, and that's why we're meeting. We've decided, as town leadership, that something needs to be done. We just don't know what…"

"We were hoping you'd have ideas," Gig put in.

"Floor's open." Hicks smacked the gavel against the pulpit.

For a moment, no one moved. The air was pregnant with expectation, with the waiting for someone else to stand up, with the anticipation that someone would, but not wanting to be the first, but wanting to put an end to the terrible silence and the uncomfortable shifting, waiting. Finally, at the back Shane Grey, the mayor's own son got to his feet. His hat clutched in his hands, he kneaded the felt for a moment before speaking.

"Tombstone has guns. He could teach a few of us to shoot."

Randy popped up on the other side of Tombstone. Reesa hadn't noticed him sit down by her. "Tombstone only has five guns," she said. "That's not enough."

"It's a start," Hicks replied.

"Ain't he been teaching you to shoot, Randy?"

She looked back at Shane. "Yeah. And when the time comes, I'll do it." She smacked back down on her seat, braids swinging, jab stinging, and Shane Grey's face turning an embarrassed red. She folded her arms triumphantly.

Hicks took over once again. "Can we use your guns, Tombstone?"

"Of course. Randy and I will each take one."

"Leaves three. Any volunteers?"

Reesa's hand slipped from her lap and began an ascent into the air. Joule grabbed it before it could get high enough for others to notice. She blinked at him. She hadn't been raising her hand. The room was quiet, nobody else volunteering.

"I'll teach you," Tombstone said. "I'll make sure you know how to use it before we do any fighting." He glanced ever so imperceptibly at Reesa—just the spark of a millisecond—but she saw it. Was he thinking of her failure? Was he thinking of the people she could have saved? She wouldn't have been surprised if he pinned their deaths on her, but the way he looked at her, even in that tiniest flicker of time, made the guilt come swarming in like a nest of furious wasps.

"I will," Shane said.

Fortitude Downs stood up not far from him. "So will I."

"Good. Anyone else?"

Timidly, next to the mayor, Gig raised his hand. "I am the deputy-sheriff after all."

Hicks gave them all a look-over and then a firm nod. "Thank you, gentlemen. You can talk to Tombstone afterward and work out the details." Shane and Fortitude took their seats, and Gig would have, and probably *should* have sat judging by the pallid look on his face, if he'd had a chair, but as it was he remained standing at the front looking faint. Darling stood up then.

"Randy's right," she said. "It won't be enough. We need more than just guns."

"What else can kill a taker?"

"Is there any way we can get more guns here in time?"

"We should use what we've got. We have to be quick."

The debate continued. Reesa tried to stand up, but her hair caught in the joint where the top of the chair and one of the wood bars that made up the back rest met. Just one single strand. It pulled as she sat forward. "Ow!" She spun around, yanked it from the joint.

"What?" Joule whispered beside her.

145

"My hair's caught in the chair." She settled back against it, then leaned forward and it happened again, just one strand. "See?"

Joule made a face at her. She ignored him, pulling her hair from the joint and getting to her feet. Sprung-up conversations ceased as eyes turned to look at her.

"We have no idea what we're up against," she said. "Not really."

Hicks narrowed his eyes. "What are you saying, Apostle?"

"How many takers are there? Do they have a weak spot? What are their living habits? Do any of us know?"

Silence again. Apparently, no one did.

"We can't attack until we know." It would be foolish otherwise. Even in her rage, Reesa understood that simple fact. Only an idiot rushed in, and when that idiot was the prey and not the predator, things could get messy fast.

"Well, then, what do you propose we do?"

"Send a small group to gather information. They could go tomorrow, just two or three, while the rest of us prepare."

"Go where?"

"The taker hole."

Well, *that* got the reaction she had been expecting earlier. The entire chapel erupted into a spray of shouts and curses, cries and whispers. The taker hole, was she *insane*? That was suicide. Suicide for certain. Reesa sat down. She had nothing else to say. She would let the debate—though it was really more of a shouting match now—run its course and accept the outcome, whatever it may be. *Crack! Crack! Crack!* Hicks slammed the gavel against the pulpit. The room got quiet, but the air still hummed with frenzied whispers.

"Apostle Reesa," Hicks began. "I know you ain't been in these parts long, but around here, folks have a sense of mortality, and ain't none of us fool-dumb enough to climb down into the taker hole and go looking after death."

A hubbub of affirmation. Citizens nodded, passing glances her way that said she belonged in a straightjacket. Tombstone stood.

"I'll go," he said. "I've been before."

Hicks stared. So did Reesa. So did everyone else. Apparently at least *one* of them was fool-dumb enough, but whether death was looking for Tombstone or Tombstone looking for death, Reesa didn't think they would find each other. He looked right at Reesa.

"I'll go and the apostle can come with me."

Her mouth fell open. His face did not soften. In fact, it became a little stonier.

"Make good on what you owe these people."

Reesa looked away. She owed these people a family. She owed them Pip and Biddy Adams. How could she even begin to repay that debt? What about

Tombstone? What did he owe? How many lives had he taken? But then, how many had he saved? She didn't have a choice. Finally, she nodded. She would go. She had to go.

"If Apostle Reesa goes, then so do I," Joule said.

Hicks's mouth fell open. "You're all goddamned crazy!"

At once an enormous gust of wind burst out of the sky and slammed into the church, letting out a great wail like a chorus of a thousand lost souls as it whistled over the roof and through all the eaves and cracks. The building began to shake, then the stained glass in the windows shattered, sending a shower of colored, tinkling shards over the whole congregation.

Reesa raised her head. When had she lowered it? Glass fell out of her hair.

Around her was a sea of duck-and-cover bodies, littered with shards of glass like snowfall. The hills of their backs and heads began to shuffle, glass shifting off and away and clinking to the floor. Soon everyone had straightened up for the most part, but nobody moved from their seats.

"Is everyone all right?" Hicks called. He himself nursed a cut across the forehead that dripped blood down his face.

A few murmured in reply, others held their hands to cuts like the mayor's on their arms or heads or necks. Nothing looked too serious, thankfully. A breeze moaned through the open windows.

"Let's get outside."

The congregation obeyed, shedding more glass from their backs as they moved carefully toward the door. They tread lightly, but each step sounded crushing and cracking and clinking. By the time the back of the chapel had emptied out and it was Reesa's turn to follow, the glass that lay all up and down the center aisle had been crushed to powder. Sharp powder. The reason why mothers wipe the floor down with a wet rag *and* vacuum after one of their children has broken a dinner glass. She tried to step only on her toes and went up the aisle.

That seemed the end of the meeting. Once outside people began to scatter, returning to their homes, whispering at one another through the purple twilight. Nothing had been decided. Not really. They had no plan. No weapons aside from Tombstone's guns. Reesa watched them go, wanting desperately to corral them and shove them back inside the chapel and demand they find a solution and *now*. She managed to keep herself stuck to the steps.

I don't want to go back.

I do.

If we go we can find...

She turned to Joule as he emerged from the front door. "Did you say something?"

He made a face. "No. Why?"

City Ash and Desert Bones

Reesa shook her head. "Never mind." The breeze blew again, pricking up the hairs of her arms in gooseflesh.

21

Huxley looked at his shadow. Sunlight traveled ninety-three million miles unobstructed until it hit him—ninety-three million miles, and he was the first thing in its way. He wasn't sure whether that thought made him feel lonely or significant. The morning had come and gone and with the afternoon he'd left Little Hadham with three horses packed up for an overnight expedition. He'd ridden them into town, taken them to the fountain and let them drink if they wanted, and it was then that he'd noticed his shadow. A flat, grey form of himself bending over the rocks and the ground, him the only thing for ninety-three million miles.

The apostles were supposed to meet him. He wasn't sure how he felt about taking them down into the takers' caverns. He'd been twice before himself, but hadn't gotten far. Always better to go with a partner, but with the partners he'd assigned himself he might have been better off alone.

Maybe they'd get killed down there and then that would be two less to worry about. Two incompetents that didn't know they *were* incompetent. That was the worst kind. Everybody else stayed out of the way, understood their powerlessness. The apostles meddled and assumed they were helping. What was wrong with them? Nobody else had a god complex. With the exception of himself, perhaps.

Randy came out of the stables and gingerly over to him. "You're really going, then?"

"I've got to, Randy."

She took Indie's nose in her hand, stroked it. Didn't say anything.

"I can't go alone and the apostles are the only ones dumb enough to go with me. I need answers—*we* need answers."

Two years ago, when they'd come for him and Merrick, theirs had been the last of the series of kidnappings. Six others had gone before them: Catherine first, then Bravery, Parson Paul a few nights later, then Freddie Dunstan, and finally Cassandra and Randall Jack, Randy's parents. Nobody ever thought that the takers might have been responsible. Up until that point, they hadn't seemed all that intelligent, hadn't done any harm. But Huxley knew. The moment he looked up and saw them surrounding his house, he knew. And from then on they'd attacked once a week.

Beyond their arrival, he didn't remember much of the experience. It was all hazy and displaced, like a dream when you just *know* someone is your mother though she has neither her face nor her features, when everything makes perfect sense until you wake up and try to talk about it. He remembered trays of tools…a lot of takers hissing at each other…being strapped to an angled table, but it came out of his memory all misty. Some days he could have sworn he remembered Merrick being strapped to a table not far from him, others he wasn't so sure.

What he *did* remember was being suddenly dumped in the desert. One minute he was underground, the next stripped down and abandoned in the hot sun miles away. Gig had found him wandering around, half-dead and dehydrated, when he'd come out for watch duty at the taker hole.

Everybody said he'd killed Merrick after that. Blamed the other kidnappings on him as well. He let them. He lived in a nightmare. Part of him hoped that he actually was dead or dying in the desert somewhere and that all of this terrible reality was an illusion.

"You think you'll find answers down there?"

"I don't know."

Randy's hand slipped from Indie's nose. "I hope you do."

He could only nod in reply.

Across the way, the hotel front door swung open and the apostles emerged in their ridiculous white uniforms. How many of those did they have? He'd seen the pair of them made filthy more than once and laundry was not an easy thing to do in Big City. Camilla Shane Grey was the only one with a washing machine. She made people pay out the nose to use it.

They stepped out into the sun, the light glinting off the three gold bands on their shoulders. Shadows leapt out behind them. Huxley did not hail them, but let the pair make their way on their own. Maybe if he didn't call them over, they'd change their minds and go back inside. Joule hovered around Reesa like a nervous hen around her only chick. Reesa ignored him. What a bizarre couple.

"You think they're really married?" Randy whispered.

Huxley snorted, but the apostles were upon them and he could not reply.

Reesa smiled a little, folded and unfolded her arms. "We're ready," she said, folding her arms again, deciding against it, and letting them hang at her sides.

Nervous was good. Nervous meant a little less likely to get killed in the long run. Fear was adaptive. A proto-human with the good sense to run when something rustled in the bushes, that was a proto-human who survived, the one who passed down his genes. That was why people were afraid of snakes and spiders, tasted poison as bitter. Human beings were little more than specialized perception machines, but if you perceived only what was critical to your survival, did that mean there were things out there, places, creatures, colors that one could neither feel nor see nor sense? What Huxley saw as reality was only a loose construction of what *actually* existed. A chill swept over his skin. He looked first at Joule, then Reesa.

"You're sure you want to do this?"

Reesa nodded. "Yes."

She understood the direness of their situation, at least. He assumed she did anyway. The apostle was so foolhardy it was difficult to distinguish enthusiasm from capability.

"We stick together, all right?" He grasped the reins of the horses he'd packed up and brought for them, passed a set to Joule and a set to Reesa. "I'll be the only one armed. I'm leaving the rest of the guns here with Randy and the others. In case the takers come back."

His companions nodded. Randy shifted nervously beside him, his pistol in a holster at her belt. She knew what she was doing. She could shoot. He wasn't so certain about Gig or Fortitude or Shane, but he would have to trust them. A dark part at the back of his mind almost longed for someone to get taken while he was away, and for one of the new recruits to have to take care of it. That part of his mind wanted to pull someone else into his personal hell. Though he didn't really think that would make it any less lonely. He grabbed Indie's reins.

"Let's go, then."

Joule figured he hated horses just as much as the average person and he tried not to let it irritate him how easily Reesa took to riding one. She just settled right in like it was nothing, like she'd been doing it her whole life. He sat stiff on his own animal, holding the reins as lightly as he could manage so as not to annoy the beast by tugging. When they'd first set off, Tombstone had told him to kick the poor creature and Joule had barely given it more than a nudge, his feet getting caught awkwardly in the stirrups. Thankfully the thing had just decided on its own to follow Reesa and Tombstone as they set off. Joule let it do its own thing, trailing a little ways away at the back.

The glint off Reesa's hair was lovely in the afternoon sun. When Joule had opened his match document, he had been surprised to read her name, see her picture. He'd known so little about her, having only paid attention to the women in training to be oil techs like him, having assumed he would be paired with one of them. He supposed it made sense to match him with a public relations specialist. He wasn't particularly adept when it came to other people. Reesa was. She seemed to understand him, though he didn't understand her, which was remarkably frustrating sometimes. She was different now, though, from when they'd married. Something about this place had gotten under her skin.

His horse stopped walking, bent its head down into the brush, and began eating the plant with flapping lips. Joule tugged on the reins, but it pulled back and his grip slipped and the animal succeeded, slurping up its snack. Up ahead of him, Reesa and Tombstone were getting further away.

"Um, Tombstone?"

He did not hear. Joule called louder.

"Tombstone!"

The man looked back, saw the dilemma, and immediately turned Indie around while Joule himself turned red in the ears.

"I can't get her to stop," he said once Tombstone reached him.

"You have to be firm," he replied.

Joule looked at him. Those had to be the least helpful instructions he'd ever been given in his life. Tombstone simply looked back, nodded at the reins once with his head, and said, "Pull."

Joule pulled. He pulled as hard as he could and the dumb horse pulled back. He nearly had her up and moving, but the second he relaxed his arms, she dipped straight down into the brush again and started eating. Reesa snickered. Joule glared at her though the effect was probably lost over the distance.

"Here." Tombstone moved Indie closer and took the reins from Joule's hands. He gave the horse a good, hard yank that looked almost effortless and its head popped right up like a jack-in-the-box. "Now give her a kick and let's get going."

He wheeled Indie away and Joule kicked his own horse to follow, sufficiently hard this time evidently as it hopped to attention and hurried after Tombstone.

This was stupid. Stupid, stupid, stupid. Spending a night out in the desert all exposed. Why anyone in their right mind had ever enjoyed camping was completely beyond him. Joule barely wanted to spend the night in the safety of their rickety hotel room, much less out in the wastes with the rabid rodents and the poisonous bugs. Why couldn't they have left that morning, been back before nightfall? Nobody ever bothered to explain anything to him.

Then there was the whole business about the takers. Whoever heard of going underground to chase out an alien you didn't know how to fight? Come to think of it, were they even aliens? Joule had never considered the fact before. Where had the takers come from? He gave his horse a kick to catch up.

"Where exactly are we headed?" he asked once he was close enough to Tombstone to be heard.

"The taker hole is due north of Big City," he replied. "Quite a ways past the drill site."

"Why aren't we running the horses, then?"

Tombstone chuckled. "We're in no hurry to get there, Apostle. But we may be in a hurry to leave."

That didn't sound good.

"Takers are least active in the early morning," he continued. "Which is why we're camping overnight."

"How long will it take to get there?" Joule asked.

"Can you still see Big City behind you, Apostle?"

Joule glanced back. "Yes."

"Then you've got several hours yet."

With a sigh, Joule settled in for the long haul.

Huxley smiled privately at the sight of Joule dismounting his horse. The apostle was just as stiff as he was stuffy and collapsed in the dirt almost as soon as he was free from his stirrups.

The Big City camp had been relocated since Ben Greeber'd been taken, more west of the Hole than south now. It was only a circle of cleared-away scrub with a pit in the center for a fire. The brush actually made surprisingly good cover since it came up to the knee. You could lie down and not be seen until someone was right on top of you. Of course, the horses were not so easy to hide.

"Where's the hole from here?" Reesa asked. She swung herself down with surprising ease and led her horse into the circle.

Huxley pointed northeast. "That direction," he said.

The sun was just beginning to dip below the horizon.

"Very far?" She hauled her pack off the back of her horse and went to help Joule do the same, though her partner brushed her off and stumbled up to do it himself.

"Walking distance," Huxley replied. "We'll eat, set up a watch, and then go to sleep. We'll head out to the hole about four." He went to Indie and untied the straps to his own pack to lift it off her back.

Joule's face went a little white. "AM?"

"No, Apostle, four PM. Half an hour ago." He rolled his eyes.

"Why so early?"

"If you'd been paying attention, you'd remember that I said the takers are least active in the early morning. So unless you want to up your chances of getting killed, we're going at four AM."

Joule opened his mouth, but Huxley pulled a box of matches from his pack and hurled it at him. It hit Joule's chest with a satisfying rattle. Joule barely managed to catch it.

"Just shut up and start a fire."

The camp was stocked with firewood, piled up along the top half of the circle. Some of the pieces were old wood and boards from the Big City buildings, but the rest of it had to be shipped in by train. No trees in the desert and the scrub burned too fast. Joule went to the stock and picked through it delicately.

"How can I help?" Reesa asked, approaching Huxley carefully from the side, her arms tucked behind her back.

"Set out the sleeping bags," he replied. "I'll tie the horses down."

She did so, making a triangle along the inside of the circle while he secured Indie and the others to a post hidden in the scrub. Out of the corner of his eye, he watched her struggle for a moment to decide whether to place her sleeping bag with the head facing Joule's or his own. In the end she flipped one of the bags around, so everyone's head was at someone else's feet.

Huxley watched Joule try to start a fire for about as long as his sanity would allow before just doing it himself. Wasn't this guy supposed to be some kind of genius? Top of the class and he couldn't even start a fire. Huxley muttered to himself as he built up a base of kindling, sprinkled it with lighter fluid, and lit a match. Once the flames took to the kindling he fanned them with a paper plate from his pack until they took to the larger logs.

In the meantime Joule had pulled up a log from the pile and sat on it, his elbows propped up on his knees. "What's for dinner?"

"Oh, I only packed food for myself."

"*What?*"

"I'm kidding, Apostle. Keep your pants on."

Joule glared at him but there was so little bite behind the bark that it only made Huxley smile. He reached over to his pack and pulled out a plastic bag with three fat tinfoil wraps inside it, like oversized baked potatoes.

"It's just beef and vegetables," he said.

"You have beef here?"

"Of course we have beef. What? Did you think this was 1845?"

Joule folded his arms and huffed. "Could have fooled me."

Huxley laughed out loud. The sound seemed to startle Joule. "This is the worst thing that's ever happened to you, isn't it?" Huxley chuckled. "Eating beef out of tinfoil is worse than going down into the taker caverns."

"No, that's not—"

He laughed again, waving him off. "It's fine, Apostle. But own up to it."

"Well, it's easy for you. You don't know any different."

"Ah, but I do. I lived in what you'd call 'civilization'. For four years." He shrugged. The city simply hadn't suited him, he supposed. He took the tinfoil wraps from the bag and tucked them carefully into the embers around the base of the fire.

"Did you like it, though?" Reesa asked, pulling up a log for herself. "I've heard New Boston is a beautiful city, and the University of the Cardinals is a great school. Did you like it there?"

"It was…complicated. And not to say that life out here isn't complicated, but…it was complicated in the wrong ways."

He glanced at her and the thoughtful expression on her face. She seemed to agree. Neither of them pried after that.

It took a little over half an hour for their dinner to cook and the sun was out of sight long before Huxley fished the wraps out of the fire with a stick. He waited for them to cool and then passed them around. The three ate in relative silence, Joule picking through his vegetables like a grumpy kid. When they were finished, clean up was easy, and it was already starting to get cold, so he suggested the apostles get to sleep. He'd take the first watch.

Joule was quick to slide into his sleeping bag. "What should we expect when we go down there?" he asked as he settled in, looking up at Huxley like he was his scout master.

Huxley shook his head. "I really don't know."

"Haven't you been down before?"

"Don't remember much of the first time, second time I didn't get far. We're going in pretty much blind."

Joule frowned at him. Huxley was tempted to tell him if he made that face it would stick like that, but he kept the comment to himself. By then Reesa was in her sleeping bag as well, snuggling down into the bottom.

"I'll take next watch," she said.

He nodded. "I'll wake you."

Soon, Joule was snoring. How could Reesa stand to sleep next to that bag of bones every night? He was so absurdly loud. Huxley shook his head and chuckled to himself. The fire began to burn low. He'd let it. Easier to see in the distance without the help of the light.

Reesa stirred and her little voice slipped out of her lips. "Tombstone…" she said. He thought she'd been asleep.

"You know my name's not Tombstone, right?"

He glanced back over his shoulder at her and smiled. Startled, she looked at him, her eyes wide and surprised in what was left of the firelight. He laughed at her expression. She blinked at him.

"But everybody calls you Tombstone."

"I know. They have since I was eight."

"What's your name then?"

"It's Huxley."

Her breath caught in her throat. She was quiet for a long time, then whispered, "I like that much better than Tombstone."

He smiled to himself. "So do I."

The stars were incredible—a thousand, a million pinpricks of light littering the sky like glitter tossed by some tiny god-child across space and time. This far out Reesa could see how the stars were different sizes, varying shades of brightness, clustered together in groups, and diverse colors. That vast purple and nebulous rift the Milky Way tore through the sky, dividing its hemispheres like the great corpus callosum of the world. At the horizon, the slight ebb and glow of the nuclear haze still covering most of the desert could be seen. It was a new moon, just a grey disc hanging among the stars. She didn't want to close her eyes.

Their fire had long since burned down. Joule lay at her feet, bundled in his sleeping bag with the face part cinched around his chin so that the spiders wouldn't crawl in. How could he possibly sleep like that?

She could sense Tombstone—no, *Huxley's* awake presence not far from her, sitting up on a log, his rifle leaned against his knees. She felt so warmly secure knowing he was on watch, knowing that it was his eyes that scanned the desert for danger, that it was his hand that would pull the trigger to protect them. The warmth spread from her heart through the rest of her limbs and she drew in a deep breath, smiling gloriously up at the glorious sky. This was where she belonged. She could feel it in her bones.

Part of her wanted to talk to Huxley, the other was comfortable in the silence. He didn't know she was awake. He didn't seem to notice the sky like she did, but then again he had been looking at it this way his whole life. Then it struck Reesa, very firmly and square in the middle of her mind. She had been looking at the sky this way her whole life, too. And not only one life, but many lifetimes, some of them short-lived. She *knew* this, but she did not understand how she could possibly.

Puzzling up at the stars, she fell asleep.

Be-YOU-tiful Princess is the theme of the daddy-daughter dance this year. The Big City Youth Events Council opted out of the annual sleep-out because Mayella French broke her leg at the last one. He always thought that girl was a grade-A twit. Now everybody has to dress up in poof and sparkles and get twirled around by their pa. And of course he'd have to do some of that twirling. Why'd everything have to have a theme? Princesses weren't practical unless they'd been raised in the woods by animals. Then maybe one could argue they had a few life skills.

Randy is as ready as she's ever going to be, looking more starched-up than pretty in one of Cassandra's old dresses, her arms hanging at forty-five degree angles above her sides. Can't put them down, apparently. She's miserable, but they have to go. Everybody has to go to everything because that's what you do in Big City. No bones about it. Cassandra's taken Randy's hair out of her braids, brushed it, made it look nice and shiny.

"You ready to go?" he asks.

She gives him a glare from the devil himself and he sets to laughing.

"It'll be all right," he says. "I won't make you dance."

"I'll break both Mayella's legs and then she won't be able to dance either," she grumbles. "I miss the sleep-out."

"Me too, sweet pea. Me too."

He places a hand on her head and she sighs. Cassandra comes out of their bedroom then, camera in her hands, gushings pouring out her lips. Oh they look so precious and she just can't get over it, and oh! Randy you look so lovely in that dress!

He smiles and poses for the picture. He knows she'll never get Randy into a dress again.

Midway through the night, when she woke, Reesa found herself at the mouth of a deep, dark hole. She stared down into it, a diver hovering over the edge of a drop-off into the open ocean. A great unknown lay before her, under the ground. She could feel it breathing up at her. Its breath tugged at her curiosity and pulled her inside.

Dirt trickled in behind, knocked loose by her feet as she squatted and slid them forward until her legs dangled over the edge of the hole. She scooted until only her palms gripped the rim and then dropped down. It was only a little ways to the bottom, but when she landed, a shock went through the soles of her feet in a painful vibration. She stood, and the three or four feet between herself and the top of the hole probably should have alarmed her, but didn't. That adventurous breath was whispering at her from down the tunnel. She followed it.

Darkness engulfed her as she left the ring of starlight, and it held her eyes until they adjusted. There was only tunnel to look at, a smooth packed floor and rough-hewn walls, angled carefully down to hell. For a moment, a wave of heat whirled across her face and arms, but it was gone so quickly she could not be sure if it was real.

"Reesa!"

Jolt—she whipped around, heart racing, ears pounding. What-was-that-who-was-there? Through the dim she saw Huxley straightening up from his landing.

"What the hell are you doing?" he hissed across the distance, coming swiftly forward to meet her.

She didn't, or rather *couldn't* answer. He reached her, stared down at her intently though she could barely distinguish his features. His eyes were shiny like two silver dollars, and when she didn't speak, he gripped her arm. It almost hurt.

Still wordless, she turned, slipped her arm from his hand, and headed again down the tunnel, leaving him no choice but to follow her. She moved quickly and he cursed at her, hurrying to catch up.

"Your partner's out there without a watch," he whispered.

She glanced at him. He was hunting around in his pack for something. She didn't answer.

"You got up, but you looked asleep so I followed you. You came straight here."

Yes. She remembered that now. Traveling across the desert in a straight line, pulled like a magnet to this place. The breath whooshed around her again and she smiled, careful to keep her face away from what little light the open hole still provided this far down the tunnel.

"Hang on a second," Huxley said.

His fingers tapped her gently on the shoulder and she paused at the foreignness of that feeling rather than because he'd asked her to. Whatever he'd been looking for in his pack, he'd found it. A box of chalk, apparently. He took out a piece, a perfect white cylinder, and handed it to her, taking one for himself as well.

"So we know what way we've been," he said, holding up the chalk and then placing it on the wall. He nodded at her to proceed, so she did, and he followed, scraping a white line into the tunnel as they went.

Together they walked for a long while without change. Always the slight downward angle, always the gentle scratch of Huxley's chalk against the wall, their soft footfalls. The darkness grew heavier, heavier. It became particles, tiny ones, but they were many and they came for her. Heavy tiny particles of darkness that slipped into her eyes and her nose and her mouth and her hair, making it hard to see, hard to breathe. Her fingers began to shake, little movements like the ticking of a clock, and the heavy tiny particles swirled around them, crushing them under their weight. She tried to draw in a breath, but the particles came in with it and she choked, gasping. Her heart reared like a spooked horse, gasping, gasping, and her knees gave way beneath her.

Opening her eyes, she woke up. Huxley stood above her, held her in his arms at an awkward angle. Had he caught her when she'd fallen? Had she fallen? Where were the stars?

"You all right?" he asked.

She took stock: feet, legs, torso, middle, neck, head, arms. It was all there, all accounted for and as far as she could feel, uninjured. She nodded and he helped her to stand.

"Where's Joule?" she whispered once she was on her feet.

He let go of her, and she couldn't be sure, but it looked like he made a this-woman-is-crazy face at her through the darkness. He went to the wall, set the chalk against it, and started moving forward.

"Back at the camp," he said.

Reesa hopped to attention and followed him closely down the tunnel. "Why?"

"He's asleep."

"Nobody's on watch then?"

He stopped and turned around and she crashed into him. Looking up, she found him looking down, not quite scowling but raising an eyebrow. His sudden proximity made her heart beat a little faster. She took a step back, swallowing and turning her face to the ground. Thankfully in the darkness he couldn't see her blush.

"*You* got up, Apostle," he said. "I followed *you*."

"What?"

"Twenty minutes ago you rolled out of your sleeping bag like a walking corpse and came straight here. I had to follow you. Now we're down here, so we may as well keep going."

He started away again, but she grabbed his sleeve. "What about the takers?" she asked. "Aren't they active now?"

"They're just beginning to wind down," he said. "It's nearly three."

He had a gun. He would shoot if he had to. What would happen then? She'd never studied much about firearms, not many apostles did, but she suspected that setting off a gun in such close quarters was bound to be dangerously loud. And it would echo. Perhaps she shouldn't rely on Huxley.

"We should go back," she said.

He shook his head. "We have a narrow window. Going back and waking Joule would waste too much time."

She only had his word for it. "Why didn't you wake me for my watch?"

"You got up on your own," he replied. "Remember?"

Again, she had only his word. Still, he'd never lied to her. He, the shadiest, most mysterious and dangerous man in Big City, had been the only one to play her straight. Sometimes she hated the human race. She hated their selfishness and that their sense of self-preservation was stronger than their charity. She hated how blind they were to their own psychology. Sometimes, she just hated *people*.

"I don't remember," she said. "But I believe you. What's our window?"

"Most of them start going into their sleep cycle about now," he replied. "Those that do will be completely out by four. The cycle lasts about an hour, then they start coming out of it slowly, like they went in. We'll take our time getting down there. Maybe some of the bastards will have turned in early."

159

Reesa nodded. "We have a little more than two hours then."

"There will be sentries," he said. "Keep an eye out for them."

How did he know all this? He said he studied them, but could she really be sure? He seemed to have so much detailed information, so many things it seemed impossible to know, particularly when everyone else in Big City behaved like the takers were this great anomaly they knew nothing about. How, and why, did Huxley know so much?

"Follow me."

The chalk met the wall once more and again they moved downward into the earth.

As they traveled, what little light had come in through the hole was lost or too slight to be detectable. All was darkness and the scritch-scratch of chalk on packed dirt. Reesa had only the sound of Huxley's feet against the floor to follow, and even then he was practically silent. The surrounding black amplified her own noises—noises that would have seemed soft in any other environment—while it muffled his. Her ragged breathing seemed to ricochet down the tunnel and back at her, the shuffle of her clothing and the tap-tap-tap of her feet. Like a traveling circus come to town. She covered her mouth and nose with her hands.

The decline leveled out abruptly. Ahead of them she thought perhaps she saw a split in the tunnel, two different archways and paths to choose. But the dark on dark was difficult to distinguish. Huxley selected the left one.

"Once we're certain they're asleep, I'll get the flashlight out."

She hoped it wasn't like the one Randy had had.

The decline into the earth continued in the left tunnel, a little steeper than before. The path began to wind, snaking through the gloom like the belly of some great serpentine beast. More than once it forked again, snake-tongued and split into multiple pathways. She could sense the shift in the flow of the air across her arms with the change in the tunnels. At each turn, Reesa followed the sound of Huxley's footsteps, straining her ears after him.

Her eyes began to weary at the lack of light, hurt from searching for it, so she shut them. The world looked the same with them open. Besides, she was only following with her ears. Until she had a flashlight in her hand, her eyes would be useless down here.

She stepped with confidence across the unobstructed ground. Aside from the darkness, the journey was easy. Nothing had been seen or heard from the takers. What had she been so afraid of? Nothing could stop her. She was—wait.

Reesa halted. She could—no, she wasn't sure. She covered her own mouth again to quiet the sound of her breath. Yes. Silence. She could no longer hear chalk scraping the wall. She couldn't hear Huxley's footsteps either.

She opened her eyes but of course that did nothing. Darkness of darkness and all was darkness—*umbra umbrarum, et omnia umbra.*

He was gone. She was alone.

What-was-she-supposed-to-do, what-was-she-supposed-to-do? He-was-gone, he-was-gone, he-was-gone. She didn't have a flashlight. She didn't have the courage. He-was-gone-and-she-was-going-to-die. Fearful tears stung her eyes. Her heart rose up into her throat, so large and afraid for a moment it felt like it might pop into her mouth and she'd be forced to throw it up. The breathing which had before been ragged, picked up into a windy cacophony of panic. Her hands tried to stifle the sound, but it only made the air harder to catch. Her head felt sort of…floaty. Her foot came down strangely on the floor and she faltered, falling against the wall.

Then she took off running and could not stop.

22

Parts Room.

That's what it said. The meaning of those vague scratchings on a silver plate mounted on the wall flicked across her comprehension. How had she come to be here, standing in the blinding light of fluorescent bulbs? How did she know how to read those markings? She had run and run, panting and panicking, down switch backs and through corridors until she'd seen this light. At the end of a long tunnel. She'd headed for it, unsure if she was walking into heaven or hell. It had turned out to be just another hallway. Overhead, the lights flickered. Reesa went inside.

The room—the *Parts Room*—was small, perhaps ten foot square, and lined on every wall by filing cabinets just like Doctor Fencer's fruit cellar. These cabinets were spic and span and neatly marked. The takers must have spent a lot of time cleaning. Reesa turned a little circle in the center of the room, eyes scanning over the labels. None of them jumped out, that is until—

Project Pilot Documents.

She halted in her turning. Had she actually seen that? She was stepping toward the cabinet before she was sure, and a tug at the back of her mind said, *no, NO,* but she paid it no heed, or at least her body didn't—hand reaching out, gripping the metal handle on the cabinet drawer, pulling it open.

It slid smoothly, silent, like rolling across butter. She pulled it all the way out and blinked at what lay inside. Files. Files and files of paperwork. Her fingers skimmed the label on the first file and the paper felt…different somehow, thicker like plastic, sturdy. In short, it wasn't paper. But it looked like paper. How odd for the takers to keep documents the same way humans did. She touched each file in turn, rubbing the labels and the scritch-scratch writing between her thumb and forefinger. When she came to the last one, she hesitated.

Reesa.

That's what it said.

The label said her name.

It said, *Reesa.*

She snatched it out of the drawer with whip-crack arms, opened it, and began pouring over the writing, waiting for something to jump out, waiting for the meaning to flash across her consciousness…but nothing happened. The lines remained incomprehensible lines.

Her ears swam and she shook out her head, but the effort did little to clear the fuzzy feeling. She flipped through the papers in the file—it was quite extensive—but even on the second, then third round, she could understand none of it. Had she only imagined her understanding before?

Ding!

What was that?! She'd been staring hard at the papers and the little chime made her jump, tip the file, and send the papers fluttering all over the floor. She gasped, dropped to her knees, and scrambled to pick them up. Were those footsteps? She heard footsteps. Her blood pounded in her ears. Her trembling fingers struggled over a few of the papers, but managed to grab them all up. Clutching the file to her breast, Reesa shot to her feet and looked for a place to hide, but there was nowhere. In a panic she crammed herself between the filing cabinet and the wall with the archway. She squeezed her eyes shut, and listened.

All was quiet.

Ding!

The chime again.

She opened her eyes, and there at the back of the room was a door she had not noticed when she came in, just an outline in the stone wall. A panel on the wall beside it was perhaps the only indication that the outline even *was* a door, and that panel lit up with green light each time the chime sounded. *Ding,* green, *ding,* green.

Reesa slid out from between the wall and cabinet. She untucked her shirt, slipped the file halfway into her pants, and tucked her shirt back in around it for safe keeping. She was taking it with her. Her name was on it after all.

Coming to the door, she paused. How was she supposed to open it? It didn't have a handle. She pried her fingers into the crack of the outline, looking for lord knows what and finding nothing. She pursed her lips and took a step back. The panel continued to chime. It had buttons. A code, perhaps…?

She raised her hand to the panel and it went *ding-ding-ding!* She jumped back, a lock clicked, and the door popped out of the wall just enough to allow someone a purchase on its edges. Cold air flowed out, caressing her ankles.

Well? Should she go inside? Should she wait for Huxley? Her fingers decided for her, reaching out with the rest of her hand and pulling on the door. It swung toward her, releasing a great draft of cold air as it opened. A light clicked on inside. Silvery walls lined with boxes and buckets on silvery shelves. It was chilly, like a giant refrigerator. Reesa went in.

All was silver, a sea of silver. Her breath poofed out in clouds in front of her as she breathed. The cool of the air raised goosebumps on her arms. She looked around. It was about the same size as the anteroom. A weird smell floated through it. Chemical. Preservative?

As she stepped closer to the shelves of boxes and buckets she realized that they, too, were labeled. Single words she had no trouble identifying. *Femurs. Ribs. Small Intestines. Tibia.* The tiny box on the end of the shelf said *Eyes.*

Dear lord.

She stopped, stepped back, stood in the center of the room. She had been here before, on several different occasions. Her distorted reflection wriggled across the walls and shelves and boxes and buckets as she turned a tiny circle. How many times had she been here? And why? She stepped toward a set of shelves.

The smell was stronger there—not quite rotting and not quite not. It smelled... sweet, but also pungent, like a loaf of rye bread. The strange labels stood out to her once more—*Lungs, Livers, Nails, Kneecaps.*

She came to a box labeled *Hair* and before she really knew what she was doing, she took it from the shelf and worked at the lid. It popped off with a hiss of air tainted with that particular odor and she cracked open an eye to peer inside. As expected, there was hair. Lots of hair. Gathered and bound into neat piles of blonde, piles of black and brunette. Wigs, apparently.

Reesa breathed a sigh of relief. Just wigs. That was all. But...at the corner of the box... Copper glinted at her. Copper like she'd seen before. She reached inside, took hold of a few hairs and lifted carefully until the entire thing came free. Beautiful copper-colored hair gathered into a ponytail hung from her hand.

This hair. It belonged to Callum.

She hurled the hair back into the box, strands of it flew up into the air. Her breath stuck in her throat, the strands tried to cling to her, but she stumbled to her feet and struggled to the door, knees weak, but she gained strength as she went and soon she was running. Callum's hair. She left the hall behind her. That was Callum's hair. Up the switchbacks, the light fading. That was Callum's hair in that box. A great shudder traveled down her spine and settled in her stomach, where, at the top of the switchbacks, she stopped and threw up. Huxley's beef and vegetable meal made its reappearance, and even after her stomach was empty of it, she continued to retch, bringing up bile, then nothing. Her hands shook with the effort, her face coated in a cold sweat. Her gag reflex triggered again, but she pushed it down and pushed herself from the wall, running weakly once more.

It didn't matter where she went as long as it was away from Callum's hair. She could feel its presence down her back, reaching out for her. Her skin crawled. He was coming for her.

She ran through the cavern, ran down another tunnel. She ran, taking turns at random, scurrying down and down, then up, then down, anything to lose the following feeling. It did begin to fade eventually, after several minutes of running, several minutes of ridiculous evasion. Out of breath and heart beating quick, Reesa paused and leaned against the wall.

Only after she stopped did she realize she had not marked her path. Only after she stopped did she realize she no longer had her chalk. Only after she stopped did she realize she was lost. Only then did she remember she'd left the box of scalps and hair in the middle of the floor open and rifled through. The takers would find it. And they would know she was there.

23

By the time Huxley realized that idiot woman was no longer behind him, she could have been half way to China. When had she slipped away? *Why* had she slipped away? Damned if he knew. She was batshit crazy. He'd been a fool to think she'd have the sense to stick with him. The information gathering expedition had turned into a rescue mission. Luckily for Reesa, the takers were still asleep. At least for now.

He stepped carefully but swiftly down the tunnel, chalk trained on the wall, flashlight dim but at the ready. He scanned for traces of Reesa. He'd given her chalk, lord only knew if she'd have the sense to use it. He hoped she did. And he hoped that he would find whatever marks she might have made. Otherwise he might be forced to leave her in the tunnels.

Something glinted up ahead in the beam of the flashlight. He switched it off and hurried forward, sticking close to the wall. As he approached, he discovered a metal pillar, small enough for him to get both his hands around that jutted out at a bizarre angle from the roof of the tunnel and passed through the floor. He flicked the flashlight on and looked the pillar up and down. A sound… Was that…rushing? He pressed his ear against the pillar and the rushing sound grew louder. This was a pipe. He looked down the hall. There were more up ahead, stuck through the earth like giant pins through a pin cushion.

As he went deeper, the packed dirt and rock of the tunnel walls gave way to thick metal sheeting. He rapped his knuckles against it, but it barely made a sound. It must have been incredibly sturdy. He kept going.

Some ways down, something caught his eye. A bizarre dent in the metal, pushed inward toward him and the pipes, extending downward from the ceiling, all twisted and cone-shaped and bent, like the end of a drill. No, not like. It *was* the end of a drill. An oil drill had struck the other side of the wall and the wall had stopped it.

Oil. Oil was running through those pipes.

He turned around and flashed his light down the hall and it reflected back at him from all those angled metal tubes. No wonder nobody had been able to access the Big City reserves.

At the end of the tunnel he entered a cavern and a tiny inkling pricked at his senses. Reesa had been this way. He was about to step forward into the cavern when a harsh hissing sound reached his ears. Takers.

He ducked against the wall and flicked off the flashlight. From across the tunnel, a vague light appeared, swinging back and forth as if being carried. Takers hissed at one another through the gloom. He peered around the edge of the archway, slowly, slowly.

A group of three had gathered across the cavern, each of them holding lanterns, all of them hissing about something on the floor near the entrance to another section of the tunnels. Huxley could not make it out from the distance, but whatever it was it had them excited. They hissed in short spurts, talking, he supposed, over one another. It sounded like they decided on something and moved off, *suck-stick, suck-stick* down the tunnel they had gathered around. Huxley waited until he could no longer see their light to peel himself from the wall and hurry toward whatever they had been talking about.

He didn't dare turn his flashlight on. He simply dashed across the cavern to the archway and knelt down to get close to the floor once he'd reached it. Dim taker lights ran in strips along where the wall met the floor, but he didn't need them. He could smell immediately what the takers had been talking over. Vomit. Human vomit. Reesa's vomit.

Sharp hisses sliced up through the archway and reached his ears—*suck-stick-suck-stick-suck-stick-suck*. Damn, they were moving fast. He shot to his feet and raced to the next nearest archway and ducked around the corner just as the three takers reappeared, the light of their lanterns swinging and throwing great shadows onto the wall.

He listened as they spoke, unable to understand a word of what they said, but gathering a sense of frustration and urgency. So Reesa wasn't down that tunnel. He poked his head around the corner briefly to make sure she wasn't passed out and with them. No, just three takers snarling at one another. If Reesa *had* been with them and conscious, no doubt she would have tried to reason with them and bargain her way out. She was stupid like that. Their hissing grew, and with a few final spurts, the takers parted ways, one of them coming directly for his hiding place. He had no choice but to bolt down the tunnel.

He sped through the dark, marking with the chalk only when he took a turn. The takers wouldn't be able to see the chalk on the wall, but they would be able to hear its scrape, taste its dust in the air if he traced it along the wall as he ran. It would be enough to guide him back out. Hopefully.

The taker's lantern light never appeared behind him, but he could hear it, sucking air into its mouth, lifting its sticky feet, searching, so he ran until its sounds went silent.

Coming around a bend, Huxley paused and covered his mouth to quiet his own breathing. He shut his eyes, put all his energy into his ears. He couldn't hear it. The taker, for now, was off his tail. Turning his flashlight on to its lowest setting, he took a brief look around.

For the most part, it was just another tunnel, but this one must have been one of the lesser used. Bits of the ceiling were crumbling, having let down little showers of dirt and rocks which had not been swept up. The takers were notorious cleaners, and they wouldn't have let this tunnel go unchecked unless they never used it. He stepped carefully down the hall, avoiding the piles of dirt and rocks and the inevitable crunch they would make when his boot came down. It made travel down the tunnel rather tedious, but if he had not been going slow, he would not have noticed a lengthy scratch along the wall.

He caught it in the beam of his flashlight for a millisecond, and doubled back. Was it? Yes. He placed his fingers on the wall, felt along the mark. Someone had picked up one of the rocks and scraped it along the wall as they moved. Reesa had come this way. He had to get to her before that taker.

His pace quickened and he kept his flashlight trained on the wall, following the undulating wave of Reesa's trail. It was possible she was still alive. The markings he followed were a good indication of that, but given Reesa's track record, he wasn't so sure. What was the punishment for getting an apostle killed? Pretty severe, probably.

The scratch went around a corner and he followed it. Why couldn't she have just stood still? He'd lost her near the entrance, and she would have been much easier to find if she had just sat there. In fact, he probably would have come across her on his way out. But no, she had to go running around and puking and alerting the takers to their presence. She had to save the day, be the hero. Huxley had learned a long time ago that there were no such things as heroes and villains.

A dim light appeared, shivering and dancing around a turn just ahead of him, so he flicked off his own. He poked his head around the bend and, was that a human figure against the wall? He squinted. A trick of the light? At the other end of the tunnel, a long, dark shadow cast onto the wall, shuddering as the light shifted, grew brighter, bigger. The human figure pulled away from the rock, heading toward the light. Yeah, that was her.

"Reesa!" he hissed, and shot forward, pushing her back against the wall and covering her mouth with his hand.

She let out a little muffled squeal, and then glared at him once she realized who it was. The light was bright now. It had arrived. He gestured with his head to the light and taker that appeared in the mouth of the tunnel, its own mouth gaping open in the middle of its head. The color drained from Reesa's cheeks. Drip, drip.

With a quiet *slorping,* the taker's feet picked up and set down and picked up, moving stickingly down the tunnel. One step. Another. Reesa grew icy, stiffening in his grip, and compressing her body back against the cavern wall. Huxley followed suit, breathing deliberately.

Stick...suck...stick....suck. The creature passed in slow time, a slime-covered lantern grasped in one of its three fingered hands. He'd never really thought about it, but what in the hell did it need a lantern for? Wet rasping filled the air as it breathed through its mouth. He couldn't see it, his back to the tunnel, but Reesa could. He tracked its progress watching her eyes. The pupils in their hazel irises. They were so wide, glittered with terror. Merrick's eyes. He just couldn't get that idea out of his head.

She tried to shift beneath his arm, but he pushed her a little more firmly. It was right behind them now. Couldn't afford to move. If it sensed them, they were dead.

Stick...stuck, sti—

It paused. Directly behind his back. The hairs on his neck rose, standing on end in tiny pinpricks of gooseflesh that spread throughout his whole body. Rasp, rasp—it tasted the air, breathing in deep, breathing in long, sensing it was not alone. Reesa squeezed her eyes shut, her heart beat fast and strong, he could feel it in her shoulders where he gripped her. Don't move. Rasp, rasp. Figured he'd go down like this.

The rasping stopped. The taker resumed its footsteps. The lantern light and the taker disappeared around the bend down the rest of the tunnel. Huxley waited, his head turned toward it. The light grew dimmer, dimmer, dimmer, swaying and flickering with each of the taker's steps until it disappeared altogether. The rigor mortis stiffness plunged out of his limbs, leaving a trail of exhaustion in its wake. He let his hand drop from Reesa's face.

"It's gone," he said softly, looking down at her.

Her eyes had already locked on his face, a familiar expression reigning over her features. He knew that look. He knew what followed that look, but he was still stunned when Reesa lifted onto her toes and drew his mouth to hers in a kiss.

He was. Alone. So alone. He was starving and he hadn't realized it. He went rigid for a moment at her touch, shock sending a ripple from the crown of his head to his heels, but seconds only passed before he recovered. He didn't want to soften, but he did, he did, God help him, and he couldn't stop himself. He kissed her back.

He felt the jolt of surprise go through Reesa's body. He lifted a hand to touch the side of her face, the back of her head. The other slid around her waist. He pressed her warm, weak body between himself and the rock. Alone. Starving.

Merrick had always told him he had clever lips. He knew what he was doing. He held her to him, kissing her mouth, her neck. He lost himself for a moment in the fire that spread through his limbs, in the furious kiss after kiss that he pulled from her lips. Another and another and another, on and on. Her hands around his back, in his hair, everywhere. It was too much.

He drew away, drawing in a breath deep and steady. Her shoulders lifted from the wall, but he tamped his forearm across them and pushed her back against it. She opened her mouth.

"Huxley, I—"

"Don't."

Her lips fell together, closed. She looked at him. Her hair tumbled in disheveled impressions around her face. Her hazel eyes. The heat behind them. Flushed cheeks, pink. Her mouth turned up slightly at its end. Merrick. Resistance was pointless. He fell to her again, pressing his lips against hers and reveling in the feeling of her pressing back.

So long. It had been so long. Two years of nights alone, two years of repressed agony. After the takers had stolen Merrick, he'd turned himself off. Unfeeling. Cold. Nothing had changed. He'd broken, that was all. But he couldn't take it, not a second more.

He had such clever lips. She'd imagined, dreamed, *remembered* what it was like to kiss him, but not a bit of it was as gratifying as experiencing it in reality. Her body had taken a risk without consulting her brain, and yet when he'd held her against the wall to keep the taker from detecting them, her lips on his was all she had been able to think about. What had followed when the taker passed had been instinct.

She followed him back along the line she'd etched with the rock she'd found on the ground, then his haphazard Xs at junctions in the path, to the cavern, back to the archway that marked the chalk path they'd sketched onto the wall, their trail of bread crumbs that lead to the three-foot opening into the ground and the caverns. He hadn't spoken since they'd started on their way, but he had let her lace her fingers together with his. His hand was warm, soft and strong. Long, beautiful fingers.

Huxley. His name. The sound of it made her want to take his face in her hands and kiss it off his lips. She could not have picked a better name herself. She would never call him Tombstone. Never again.

They rounded a corner and starlight flooded the cavernous tunnel. Just ahead, a shaft of light—dim, twinkling—shone onto the rock floor. The entrance, now exit. She let Huxley lead her until they were standing beneath it, a million pins of light sparkling overhead.

"In the city, you can't see stars like this. The lights block them out," she whispered, shifting toward him unconsciously, pressing her body against his arm.

"New moon tonight," he replied.

She looked at him and his eyes were locked on the sky. There was so much behind those eyes. Pain, misery, wisdom. His were eyes that had seen and experienced more than any pair of eyes should have to, and it shone—like the tip of the iceberg into his consciousness. He felt things deeply, happy and sad at the same time.

He removed his gaze from the stars and tilted his head down at her, his expression indecipherable. At least he didn't look at her with as much hatred as before.

"I'll lift you up," he said, slipping his hand out of hers and moving to the side.

She stepped up to him, right along the edge of the wall and therefore the hole above her. It wasn't too far to the top. Just a few feet above her head. Huxley's hands fell onto her waist and she smiled, glow spreading across her cheeks. She could have just fallen back against him and stayed in the tunnels forever in his arms.

He counted to three, she gave a little jump, and he lifted her easily enough, her torso popping up over the edge. She reached out and grabbed hold of the deep-rooted scrub and pulled herself up and out, Huxley adding a boost to her feet as she did.

The sound of the night air was entirely different than the sound of the tunnels. Out in the wastes it was open, the echoing of crickets going on for mile after mile into eternity. As she straightened and turned to offer a hand down to Huxley, a pack of wolves took up their howling chorus, distant, but loud all the same.

"I hope they don't think Joule is a snack," she said, taking hold of Huxley's hand and helping to pull him up over the edge as he climbed. "He's wrapped up so nicely. Like a giant burrito."

Huxley laughed. Not the dark chuckle she'd heard in the past, but a genuine laugh—a beautiful, lyrical sound that made her heart swim. He gained his footing over the side of the hole.

"I don't think the wolves will be interested in your partner," he replied. "Too soapy."

Reesa smiled, moving toward him, but he stopped her.

"We should get back," he said. "Joule's asleep without a watch."

He didn't wait, but started off immediately in the direction of their camp. She scurried to catch up, her pant legs tangling in the brush as she waded forward. Pulling, snagging, it was slow progress. Huxley was so practiced, picking his way through expertly just ahead of her. She had no idea where they had left Joule and their own sleeping bags. That was what Huxley was for.

When they made it back, the fire in the center of the clearing had completely burned down and Joule was asleep and snoring right where they'd left him. Reesa wanted to kiss Huxley good night, but she didn't dare, and he didn't say anything to her. He just climbed into his sleeping bag and turned over. She followed suit and fell asleep wondering if takers had dreams.

24

When Joule woke up, it certainly wasn't four AM, and it certainly wasn't Huxley doing the waking. It was the sun, peeking up over the edge of the brush and lighting up his face. He blinked his eyes open, and when he rolled over—*ah,* his spine ached from its night on the ground, though that rotten bed in the hotel had probably helped ease him into this particular situation—Reesa and Tombstone were asleep, curled up in their sleeping bags.

What?

He squirmed his arms up through the confines of his sleeping bag and worked with cold and swollen fingers to undo the knot that cinched the opening of the bag around his face. It was slow going until he got some feeling in his fingers. Once the knot was undone he wiggled out, stood and stretched, then went to Reesa. He squatted and shook her shoulder.

"Hey… Reesa… Wake up."

She drew in a breath and let out a little groan that turned up at the end like a question. She rolled over and squinted up at him.

"Joule? What time is it?"

"Why didn't you wake me up? We missed the window."

She rolled over again and pulled her sleeping bag up under her chin, saying, "We went without you."

What?

He…he didn't even know how to respond to that. He sat back in the dirt, a little stunned. They went without him *where?* And more importantly, *why?* Behind him, Tombstone awoke at the sound of their voices and started rustling around. Joule turned on him.

"Why didn't you wake me?"

Tombstone mumbled something and put his face in his hands. Before Joule could snap at him and tell him to speak up, he said, "Look, Apostle. I'm not entirely sure what happened last night, but your partner got up in the middle of my watch and sleepwalked all the way to the taker hole. I had to follow her. When she came out of it, it was too late to go back for you."

Then he'd been here, out in the desert, alone and exposed without a watch. He could have been devoured by wolves! The thought made him shiver. He almost wished he had been—or at least maimed a little bit. Would have served them right.

"You went without me."

Tombstone started rolling up his sleeping bag. "Yes."

"Then...we're done here."

"Yes."

Joule swallowed, swallowed again to try to get the lump of anger out of his throat. He had ridden a horse for hours through the waste for nothing. He'd slept on the ground for nothing, eaten Tombstone's weird tinfoil meat for nothing. God in heaven he hated it here. Hated it down to his very core. Big City, ha! He hoped it burned. Why couldn't they have been assigned to Alaska like he wanted?

"We can pack up and go, or we can eat out here," Tombstone said as he stuffed his sleeping bag into its sleeve. "Which do you prefer, Apostle?"

Neither, was what Joule wanted to say, but he didn't. "Let's pack up."

"It's a long ride back to Big City."

"I don't care. I want to get out of here."

Tombstone shrugged, tied up the strings on his sleeping bag, completely unaware that with those words, Joule had come the closest he ever had to breaking a commandment. Apostles shouldn't speak that way, ever. Turning away, Joule covered his mouth. Was this what it felt like to be Reesa? It was awful. He went back to his sleeping bag and began brushing the dirt off before he rolled it up. Behind him, Tombstone stepped over to Reesa and nudged her with his foot.

"Get up."

Reesa groaned at him.

"Your partner decided he'd rather go than stay. Get up."

He gave her another hard nudge and this time she sat up, sending one dagger of a glare at the back of Joule's neck like a knife-thrower. Joule tried to ignore the feeling.

Together Joule and Tombstone packed up the camp, scraping ashes out of the fire pit and restacking the wood pile while Reesa stood stiffly by, her hair a mess around her head. Tombstone secured their packs and sleeping bags to the horses and they were ready to go.

Joule accepted his horse's reins as Tombstone handed them over. "Did you at least find anything down there?"

"Most of my time was spent looking for *her*," Tombstone answered, gesturing over at Reesa with his head, "but I think the takers may be responsible for the oil shortage. They've got pipes and stuff down there like I've never seen."

"*Really?*"

Joule looked over his shoulder in the vague direction of the taker hole. Oil? Those monsters were after the oil? All of a sudden a desperate desire to go down in those tunnels and take a look for himself overwhelmed him. What kind of tech were they using? How much more advanced was it than their own? Had they been here since the beginning? Since the reserves were discovered and drilling was planned? Since that first drill hit the ground and dug until it could not dig, spinning out of control without ever having brought up a single drop of oil? He suspected that they had. They *must* have been.

"You all right, Apostle?"

Joule snapped out of his reverie. "Fine. I'm fine. Let's go."

He waved his arm for Tombstone to get on his horse, then braced himself for his own mount. He slid his foot into the stirrup, *one, two, three*, and jumped, swinging his leg haphazardly over the other side of the animal as he pushed down on the stirrup and rose. He came down roughly, but he made it. So help him, he would never ride a horse again.

When he looked to his companions, they were ready to go. Tombstone took the point position and started off, leading the three of them through the brush. Even as his horse started walking, Joule's stomach began to grumble.

Reesa had completely forgotten about the file she'd stolen from the takers until Tombstone had come and forced her to get up and the thing crinkled against her back. She'd slept with it tucked into her shirt and pants. She let her horse fall behind to the back of the trio and once she was certain the men weren't looking, she pried it out and brought it around so she could look at it.

The paper was warped and wrinkled now—she'd been sweating as she ran—but she had no intention of ever trying to return it to the takers so she supposed it didn't matter if it looked pristine. She stared down at the yellowish outside of the folder, the little tab on the top marked with two of those crosshatch characters. *Reesa.* She knew those markings were her name though they no longer appeared to her as such.

Did the takers have a file on everyone in Big City or was it just her? If they had a file on everyone, how did they know she and Joule were even there? How much did they understand about the workings of the government? The file raised more questions than it answered. She opened it and began carefully thumbing through the pages, letting her horse follow Joule and Tombstone at its leisure.

Each paper was inscribed with the markings—the same markings she'd seen on the wall. There was no doubt this was a language, a language of which she had some strange fundamental understanding. Nothing popped out at her as she looked over the pages, though she did notice some patterns.

The first seven documents in the file seemed to be of the same nature. Each of them was marked with a large print across the top and the organization of the groups of characters on the page looked identical. As she compared them, Reesa began to notice distinctive words, words that were the same across all seven pages. At the end of the seven pages, some kind of log or diary began. A different sort of marking—numbers, she supposed—separated long blocks of text. This went on for twenty or thirty pages until she hit the final page that matched the first seven. She continued to stare at them, study and try to decipher, clear her mind and let that comprehension she'd experienced in the caves take over. It didn't work.

None of them spoke the entire ride back to Big City, and when they arrived, the atmosphere was entirely different than when they'd left. Even from some distance away, Reesa could hear music. *Music.* It had been six days since she'd last heard music. For whatever reason she had just assumed they didn't have such frivolities in Big City. But as they drew nearer it became clear. A band was playing, a bouncing happy rhythm that echoed off the buildings around the square. People were talking cheerfully over the music, calling to one another and laughing. Reesa had never heard so many happy sounds coming from the citizens. Up until then she might have said they were incapable of it.

Huxley entered first through the open gate, passed between the bank and the stables to enter the square. Reesa hurriedly tucked the file away against her back once more, finishing just as her horse exited the alley between the buildings. The square was full of people—probably as many people as were still alive in Big City—jostling about, setting up tables and chairs, hanging even *more* strings of lights from building to building, carrying covered plates of food out to a long buffet table. A bandstand had appeared overnight, a rickety structure set up at the foot of the town hall steps, and several fellows practiced atop it, sending their jolly music out into the air. It made even Reesa feel a little livelier.

She kicked her horse to catch up to Huxley. "What's going on?"

"The Bicentennial," he replied. "I'd forgotten it was today."

Nobody seemed to notice their return. They were all so wrapped up in their preparations for the celebration. Big City turned two hundred that day. It *was* kind of exciting. Reesa smiled down at the gathering, watching them scurry about gleefully from task to task. At the foot of the bandstand, Reesa spotted Mayor Big City. She pointed his direction.

"There he is."

The three of them steered their mounts over to the town hall, swinging down as they arrived. Hicks did not look particularly pleased to see them. Reesa couldn't blame him. She and Huxley and Joule were the buzzkill for the day. He'd probably hoped they'd die in the taker tunnels and he'd never have to deal with them again.

"You're back," was all he said.

"Hicks, I think we should consider sending out a larger party to conduct a second investigation," Huxley answered. "There's—"

"Let's talk about what you found later, hm?" Hicks waved a hand at him. "Right now, Big City needs a break from the takers."

"A break won't make the dead any less dead." Huxley stared flatly at the mayor.

"No," Hicks replied, "but it will make the living a little more alive. We'll talk later, Tombstone. Right now, what Big City needs is a party."

"What Big City needs is a new mayor."

The words were out before Reesa had any idea they'd been in her mind.

"Excuse me?"

Her mouth hung open, a few sounds stammered out, but Reesa had nothing to say for herself. She was in direct violation of a commandment and her apostolic vows. Hicks eyed her from beneath the brim of his big black hat, squinting a narrow, angry squint, hands on his hips. Joule stared at her in shock and she looked just as shocked back at him. Only Huxley didn't appear in the least bit surprised. *He* seemed to agree with her.

Reesa stepped toward him. "I'm so sorry, Mayor Big City, I don't know why I said that."

Hicks stepped back. "Oh, I think *I* do. The truth comes out at last."

"I apologize, really, I do, I—"

"Save it, Apostle. I don't give a rat's ass about you or your government, and now I know we stand on equal ground. I like it that way. Makes things simpler." He didn't *look* like he liked it, glaring fiercely at her.

Reesa didn't know what to say. She could apologize left and right, up and down, but it wouldn't make a difference either way. She pursed her lips. The damage was done. There was nothing for it. Turning her gaze on the dirt under the mayor's shoes, she nodded. She nodded and she turned away, heading for the hotel. Hicks and Huxley stayed where they were, Joule followed after her.

"Reesa, where are you going?"

He caught hold of her hand and this time she didn't pull it away.

"Back to the hotel, Joule." She couldn't look him in the eye. He was a model apostle, always had been. He didn't deserve to be stuck with her, all the pain she'd caused him.

"Is there anything I can do?"

"Why don't you stay and help set up?" she suggested. She knew that wasn't what he meant. "Save some face. I need to go lie down." She squeezed his hand and smiled somewhat sadly. Joule looked back at her, nodding eventually.

"All right. If that's what you want."

"It is."

He nodded again, looked deeply at her, then let their hands slip apart, going back toward the mayor as Reesa hurried away. She couldn't bear to look at him.

The music continued outside, but all the joy had gone from Reesa's heart. Tired. That was all she felt. An exhaustion weighed down on her shoulders like a bag of flour, growing heavier and heavier the more she tried to lift it. Her back ached from sleeping what little she had on the ground and her stomach growled at her, empty and hurting. She ignored it, entered the hotel and went straight to her room. Once the door was closed, she collapsed upon the bed.

Poke—the file jabbed into her back. She sat up. The file. She removed it. *The file.* She brought it around in front. *Reesa.* Her name, clear as day across the tab. She could read again. She opened the file, and started with the first page.

Across the desert, deep underground in the darkness, a sensor went off that had not gone off for nearly a year. Long enough that they had counted the test subject a failure and removed her name from the list.

Now she was right on top of them.

How had she come to be there? The human settlement was not supposed to have the government liaisons. It was why they had positioned her in the government in the first place. What was she doing so far west?

Her light blinked on the panel. She was in the human settlement. Perhaps it was she who had emptied her stomach on the floor in their cavern. Perhaps it was she who had picked through the box of the human hair. When one came back from retrieval and reported her file missing, they knew it was she. She had come back.

They had no way to know what returning had done to her brain. The signal was weak, her location scarcely readable. Had memories awoken in that blank darkness? Had she remembered who she was? They had no way to know. They had only one choice. She would have to go.

They would destroy her, and the human settlement as well.

25

The Big City drills had not been touched for two hundred years. As the afternoon of their bicentennial birthday slipped through the sky, the underground things which had stolen their bounty became aboveground things and began stealing *them*.

Hissing and scratching filled the air like the whirl of a shaft plunging down into the dirt. The aboveground things worked swiftly, buckling their knees, bringing them down, the great bastions, the reason Big City existed, the failures. They brought them down and they dragged them through the dirt to a great basket in the ground. One drill went into the basket with a load of heavy boulders; the others lay in wait.

The basket began to turn with the wide panel in which it was mounted, aiming at some tiny flashing dot that showed on a panel deep underground.

They were ready. Joule had been little help setting up, carrying a few plates of cookies from the Dunstan home to the buffet table. The ladies had swarmed around him like honeybees, taking whatever work he'd started on out of his hands and cooing at him for being so sweet. He didn't feel sweet. He felt useless.

Nobody asked about the taker tunnels. It was like they knew he hadn't gone down, like they knew he didn't know anything. Like they could see the useless written across his forehead. He wanted to crawl into bed and lay there for the next forty years. This was what his life had become—carrying cookies for backwoods women who wouldn't let him do anything else.

Mayor Big City mounted the bandstand platform and called everyone to their seats in the square. The Dunstan women cooed again and grabbed Joule and made him sit by them. He wished he'd gone with Reesa. Mayor Big City cleared his throat, and then leaned into the microphone.

"My fellow Big City-ans, today our beautiful town turns two hundred!"

A round of whoops and hollers and applause went up in the crowd. The small crowd. The entire city. Joule clapped, and as he clapped, he saw a strange vision, a vision of what this place might have been if the drills had struck oil. A rich, opulent, shining city, reaching toward the sky with great silver spires, full of people, rich people with rich things, philanthropists, no poor among them. He saw himself, a bright white beacon of an apostle, head of the drilling operation, savior—at least for a time—of the world with the oil he brought forth from the well to let it drink. Oil was the true living water. Oil was the lifeblood of the earth. The glittering city faded from his eyes and he saw only the town hall, falling to pieces before him.

"We've lived our entire lives in this city," Mayor Big City continued. "Been raised, raised children, buried parents. We've seen hell, and we're still standing."

Another chorus of cheers. Joule did not clap this time. Thirteen bodies were sequestered away in Doctor Fencer's basement. He could hardly call that standing.

"Big City, be *proud* of your heritage." Hicks cast his arms out in front of him in a wide, sweeping motion. "Be *proud* of your blood. Be *proud* to be born and buried in such a place as this one. Happy two hundredth birthday, Big City!"

The band struck up, their music echoing loudly through the square, bouncing off buildings and reverberating back to Joule's ears three or four times before he finally tuned it out. People got up and started to dance. He glanced up at his and Reesa's window at the hotel. He wondered if she was asleep.

Up in her room, Reesa could hear the mayor's speech, the band as well when they started playing, but she wasn't listening. She was reading through her file. She was reading through a nightmare. Her heart beat fast in her throat—pounding, pounding.

The words were so clear.

The aboveground things were having trouble with the great basket. Their read on the flashing dot was constantly changing—it was hither and thither over and over again. They hissed around, giving orders, orders to shut down their signal scrambling machine, the machine they used to block the human settlement's telephone.

The machine whirred down into a powered-off state. All the crackling interference diffused from the sky.

Across the desert, in the human settlement, a comm unit exploded with undelivered messages and voicemails that had lain dormant. A man in white with yellow hair heard its ringing, buzzing, beeping, heard its cries for attention and attended it. He alone seemed to have heard its call.

The flashing dot flashed less now, now that the signal scrambling machine was quiet. The great basket no longer gave the aboveground things any trouble. They aimed it at the coordinates of the little flashing dot.

Each of the first seven pages had a heading. Each of those headings was a name. A name that she recognized, a name that she knew. The name of someone who had lived in Big City. Someone who had lived in Big City and disappeared long ago—two years to be precise.

Each of the seven pages had a list. A list of pieces. A list of organs.

Page one, *Catherine Shane*, aged 61, taken January 6th, 2299, parts used in model: skeletal structure (note: not skull), occipital lobe, glandular system, diaphragm, larynx

Page two, *Bravery Downs,* aged 9, taken April 18th, 2299, parts used in model: parietal lobe, kidney (2), gallbladder, inner ear (2), esophagus

Page three, *Paul Hatfield*, aged 36, taken April 21st, 2299, parts used in model: temporal lobe, stomach, bladder, trachea, rectum

Page four, *Frederick Dunstan,* aged 49, taken August 9th, 2299, parts used in model: spinal cord, brainstem, cerebrospinal fluid, intestines (large and small), pancreas

Page five, *Cassandra Jack,* aged 28, taken September 14th, 2299, parts used in model: frontal lobe, skin, veins, arteries, blood (type O+), muscles (lower body), vocal cords (50%)

Page six, *Randall Jack,* aged 34, taken September 14th, 2299, parts used in model: lungs, liver, spleen, bone marrow, tongue

Page seven, *Merrick Haddox,* aged 32, taken November 1st, 2299, parts used in model: skull, cerebellum, heart, sex organs, muscles (upper body), vocal cords (50%), heart, eyes, hair

Merrick Capell Haddox. Huxley's wife. Everybody had said she had Merrick's eyes and hair. She did. The very same. Pulled from a corpse and planted in her. Her hands shook. A sharp, slice-cut from the bottom of her belly all the way to her ribs, disassembled, disassembled, disassembled. Another cut, another slice, another cut, through her memory seven times. Seven times. It happened over and over just as it *had* happened to the people who were part of her.

How could this be true?

Her breath stuck in Bravery's throat. Merrick's heart pounded in Bravery's ears. How could this be true how could this be true how could this be true? Catherine's bones, wrapped in Merrick's muscles, covered in Cassandra's skin—fingers. Those fingers lifted the page and Merrick's eyes looked down at the journal entries.

November 2nd, 2299—The model is assembled and is not rejecting any assigned parts. It has been treated with the appropriate chemicals to cease possible decomposition. It will remain in refrigeration until all wounds are healed. This

model is the most striking of the seven. When the test run is through, if this model is still in operation, I should like to have my mind plumbed into it. This model will be my new body. There is talk of placing it into the government for the test run.

I was hesitant when the idea of building human suits was proposed, but now that I see what progress we've made, I am happy. Before, when we had not scrambled their pieces, they had been recognized by other humans, and their minds had rejected our tech. These models are obedient. They will allow us to move freely among the humans once they are complete.

November 3rd, 2299—The model is complete. All wounds have healed. Her artificial personality and understanding of our language is being plumbed in. We have decided to call this model Reesa after the earth-river that runs nearby.

November 5th, 2299—Plumbing is complete. It may take several days to bind, but Reesa will open her eyes when she is ready.

November 8th, 2299—Reesa has not yet woken up. I am worried that the plumbing might have destroyed the brain matter. There is no way to be sure without opening her up. I will not do that until I am sure she will not open her eyes.

November 10th, 2299—Reesa woke up today. She is very lovely. Her artificial personality has stuck well. I believe that is the reason why it took so many days. She likes to talk. She talks at me all day as I do my work. Soon, she will begin to walk.

On and on like that for twenty-seven pages. Like a mother's journal of her child. A taker mother.

Tears streamed down Reesa's face. She went to the window. She lifted her shirt, dared to open her eyes and look down at her stomach. It was faint, but it was there. A thin white line from her abdomen upward. A scar. The faintest scar left on Cassandra Jack's skin through which they had pulled out her insides and stuffed her full of someone else. Reesa was wearing Randy's mother's skin. Reesa was not Reesa, she was Catherine Bravery Paul Frederick Cassandra Randall Merrick. Her entire life. It was a lie. She didn't want to live it anymore.

Like a signal going right into her skull, Reesa snapped to attention at the sudden awareness that she was being tracked. They had found her—their machine, their Frankenstein's monster.

At that very same moment a whistling sound cut through the air and seconds later the church erupted in a shower of wood and glass when one of the Big City drills landed on top of it.

Joule heard the whistling long before it passed overhead. His ears perked, he listened to it a moment, curious. The Big City comm was still flooding with emails, error messages. He'd heard them making their notifications from out in the square in spite of the music and gone in to check it out, but there was no way he could possibly sort through all. Following the whistling, he went to the front window of the town hall just in time to see an enormous heap of metal and stones come crashing down from the sky onto the church.

His heart beat once—sent ice into his veins. Time slowed for a moment like it does when you're not sure if what you're seeing was real or a dream. Wood and splinters spiraled through the air in twisting ballet arcs, deadly dancers. They floated, spraying outward from the point of impact like the splash of a rock dropped into a pond. As they neared the ground, time seemed to speed, they hit, sprayed outward again when they met the ground. *Snap.*

His heart beat a second time, and he made a dash for the door, threw it open, and threw himself down the steps. All of Big City had turned to the church, but they were too stunned to move. Joule ran into their midst shouting words he could not understand. Nobody looked at him. They all looked instead at the body of Darling, lying in the settling dirt in front of the church, pierced through with a beam of wood.

Another whistling hissed through the sky, another drill appeared as a black dot rocketing toward them. The sound became so loud Joule had to cover his ears along with everyone else. The drill grew larger and larger, nearer and nearer. The notion to run pricked up in Joule's mind, but his legs would not obey. *BOOM,* the town hall erupted as the drill smashed through its ceiling. The impact knocked him to the ground.

Everyone *screamed.*

A panic went up, gushing into the air like blood and everyone scattered, yelling and crying and weeping and wailing and gnashing their teeth.

Death was imminent.

Death was upon them.

His vision swimming, Joule stumbled to get to his feet. His ears rang having never heard so loud a noise in all his life. As he turned he saw through the dust the remains of what had been the town hall only moments before, the great legs of a drill sticking out of it like spears through a chest. He coughed. He stared. He stood still while people rushed about him. The neck of a guitar poked up through the rubble, its owner crushed beneath and bleeding. The band was gone. He didn't even know their names.

Randy still had Tombstone's gun, but you couldn't shoot a drill out of the sky with a pistol. You couldn't shoot a drill out of the sky with anything. The takers were doing this. She was certain.

Terror bubbled in her throat, but she shoved it down. Made her sick, but sick she could handle. Spilling her guts wouldn't do any good. Jess Blue was running around next to her like a chicken with its head cut off. Randy snatched up her sleeve in an iron grip and yanked.

"*Stop it*," she hissed.

In the middle of the mayhem, two little girls regarded each other. One about to die, the other, more unfortunate, about to live on. From the rubble of the church, a taker struggled to its feet. Followed by another, and another. They came out of the drill.

Randy caught sight of them only seconds before one came barreling down on her and Jess. She'd never seen a taker move so fast. Before she knew what happened, the taker grabbed Jess from behind and stabbed her through the back with a plank of wood. Jess's eyes bulged, looking at Randy. She gasped and gurgled and fell to her knees, looking at Randy.

Randy stared down at her.

Blood began to pool at her feet.

Takers crawled like worms from the insides of the drills.

The taker made a grab for her—the gun snapped on in her hand—a shot went off—her finger on the trigger—right through the taker's head.

She couldn't keep her sick down anymore. Doubling over, Randy retched. She felt a hand on her back and *snap!* she popped up, whirled around, and readied to shoot what had touched her. It was Tombstone, jumping back and putting his hands up as she pointed a gun at his chest. She lowered the weapon immediately, tears came to her eyes.

"You can't cry, Randy. Not yet."

All around them was the hissing of takers, the screams of her friends. Big City was dying. The day had finally come. The dominoes had started to fall long ago.

She swallowed, forcing down the sobs that hiccupped in her throat, wanting out. She spit on the ground to get the vomit taste out of her mouth. A thought passed through Randy's mind, an image of herself shooting Tombstone. An image of the bullet entering and exiting his body in the same instant. An image of him falling down backwards and dead. It scared her. She clutched onto her gun.

"I'll go north, you go south. Kill as many takers as you can."

His hand was on her shoulder one second, then gone along with him the next. He ran right for the town hall. Crazy bastard.

Not knowing if she would ever see him again, Randy turned and walked toward the church. The gun trembled in her hand, but she gripped it hard. She wouldn't cry. Not yet.

Their radar was trained on her—Reesa could sense it, *she* was their coordinates, a little sting of electricity inside her head like a wasp trapped in her skull. They were aiming the drills, their damned Trojan horses, at her. Only this Troy had not accepted the gift willingly.

With Merrick's eyes she watched the destruction from her bedroom window. With Bravery's ears she heard the shouts and screams. Cassandra's blood rushed fast through her veins, flushed her face. When would the next wooden horse arrive? Down on the street she saw Randy and Huxley, parting ways with their guns in their hands. A thought struck her. At the top of the lightbulb of buildings, the town hall caught fire. She would stop the signal.

Her feet carried her away from the window. She floated across the room. Her hand opened the door and she floated down the hall, down the stairs, across the lobby to the front door. When she opened it, the screaming, howling, whistling of the outside grew louder. Flames crackled to life on the wind. Dust rose into the air, dust and smoke. Through it she saw Joule, a beacon in his white uniform.

He ran to her. "Reesa! Thank god you're safe!"

"I have to get to Tombstone," she said. She put out her hand to push him away and the hardness in Merrick's eyes made him back off. She walked again, on her borrowed legs, walked through the smoke and the dirt and the death.

She could barely see. Chairs were scattered across the square and she had to pick her way through them. Screams whistled on the wind around her, filling her ears with surround sound, echoing off the buildings and amplifying tenfold. People stumbled through the wreck of chairs in every direction—left, right, north, west, south, east, inside, outside, even up and down it seemed. The takers chased them, quick now, quicker than they had ever been. Gig fell in front of her as she moved. A taker fell on top of him. She moved on.

Huxley had gone toward the town hall, toward the second Trojan horse, so that was her destination. Rubble littered the ground in front of it—blood covered rubble, band covered rubble. The takers ignored her as she went. They had no other choice. She was certain then. They needed her alive.

Smoke stung Merrick's eyes, made them water. The fire that had taken hold of the town hall crackled and snapped, sent up sparks. It was only a matter of time until it caught the bank and the jail in its ravenous grip and burned them as well.

Out of the corner of her eye, Cookie started to run to her, but a taker caught his arm, pulled him back, ran him through.

She caught sight of Huxley by the light of the flames, standing in front of the remnants of the town hall steps, waiting for takers to emerge from the fallen drill so he could shoot them. Dirt and dust whirled around him.

The wind had picked up fiercely.

"Tombstone!" she shouted over it. "Tombstone! Huxley!"

He turned at the sound of his name, regarded her with some surprise. His face was covered in dirt and sweat, blood from a cut on his forehead.

"I'm the beacon!" she shouted.

"What?" He came toward her.

"I'm the beacon," she said again. "They're aiming the drills at me."

He squinted at her. "What are you talking about?"

"Because, I... They. They made me."

His eyebrows drew together and he frowned, bereft of comprehension. She didn't know how to make him understand.

"Catherine, Paul, Bravery, Cassandra, Randall, Freddie, Merrick, your wife, I—I'm *them*. I'm pieces of *them*, Huxley. The takers made me."

Joule grabbed her shoulder, turned her sharply around to face him. "What are you talking about? That's insane, Reesa!"

"This is Merrick's hair, Huxley," Reesa said. She looked back at him over her shoulder. "These are her eyes. I found the documents in the taker tunnels. I'm telling the truth."

Merrick's...hair? Huxley could see it now. The blood drained from his face. She wasn't lying. He could see it now.

Two years ago they'd taken him. They'd taken him and Merrick and they'd taken her apart and they had rejected him and somehow he suddenly knew why. The fever. Orrin Fever. They couldn't use him because he'd had the fever—his organs would have infected everything they touched.

Reesa looked at him. "Please, shoot me, Huxley."

Why did everyone always beg him to shoot them?

"No."

"Huxley, please. It will stop the signal. Shoot me."

How many people had begged him to shoot them?

"*No.*"

"Huxley!"

He was done. He was broken. He couldn't do it. Not anymore. He couldn't shoot Merrick, even just pieces of her. He couldn't do it.

"No," he whispered. His gun fell loose in his hand.

And before either he or Joule could react, Reesa grabbed the gun, tore it from his hand, and fired a shot into her borrowed brain.

The shot rang out and reverberated through Big City and for a moment, time stood still, then the pieced-together parts of seven different people collapsed in a heap on the dirt.

"*NO!*" Joule screamed.

Unable to get a breath in at all, he stumbled forward, falling to his knees beside his wife—his and Tombstone's wife. He gathered her up into his arms, unaware of, or perhaps welcoming in his shock and despair, the blood that spilled from her shattered skull to stain the purity of the whiteness of his uniform. He hugged the lifeless body to him as the sanguine river ran through her hair, tinting it a deeper ruby than ever before. He couldn't speak. His throat was a knot in his neck.

Huxley recognized her now. Merrick's hair, her eyes—dead again—open and glassy and *dead* in her skull. He recognized Cassandra's skin, the pattern of freckles behind her ear. How could he not have noticed? How could he not have seen? They'd—they'd been right in front of him the whole time.

He lingered a few feet away, watching Joule clutch onto pieces of Freddie Dunstan and Parson Paul, pieces of Randall Jack, pieces, pieces, pieces. His hands began to tremble. The tremor traveled up. Through his arms, into his shoulders, down his body with a shattering shiver. Fingers that did not feel like his own found their way into his hair where they grabbed and pulled. Pain as a means of holding onto reality. *This* was reality. This was *reality*.

A cry, a sob, a whimper, a great and terrible roar was building inside him but he could not find a way to let it out, so there it remained, twisting his throat tight and clawing at the edges of his soul. He was six feet underground, cold coins on his eyes to keep them closed, sleeping fitfully until the second coming. He could not blink. He was empty.

A mile off, an ill-aimed drill tower fell from the sky. Its impact rattled the planks of Big City. Reesa had stopped emitting her signal.

He got up—couldn't remember falling to his knees, but he got up. "Joule," he said, but the apostle ignored him. "Joule."

Joule continued to sob, blood on his hands, on his face, everywhere.

"Let go of her," Huxley ordered.

"No."

"Do it, Joule."

"*No!*"

"Goddamn it, Joule, *do it!*"

Huxley reached out, gripped the back of Joule's collar and *ripped* him off of

Reesa. The apostle choked, reaching up toward his neck, towards Huxley's hands, but Huxley didn't care. He pulled Joule to his feet, shook him something fierce. Joule moved to fight back, Huxley slapped him clean across the face.

"You listen to me," he growled.

Joule regarded him in shock and terror, his eyes watering with the sting of the slap, wide, tears rolling out from their corners, cutting clean salty paths through the blood on his face.

"She stopped the signal. She stopped it. You—you need to, you need to do something. This is our only window. You—call. Call someone, call for help. Do it, Joule. I'll take care of the rest of them…"

The apostle slipped from his grip, stumbled. Joule fumbled around in his pockets until he found his handheld comm, began punching buttons with shivering fingers. Huxley was satisfied. He could leave Joule to it now.

When he turned around to face the town, his heart stopped. Takers…were everywhere, with everyone. They flowed throughout Big City on a high tide. One by one his friends, his family, were murdered and all he could do was watch, frozen, outside of time. The speed with which the takers moved was incredible, but Huxley seemed to sense every minute motion—every piercing of every person with every block of wood. He hadn't known them to use weapons before. Look at all the new things he was learning.

Behind him Joule started hollering garbled sentences at the comm.

Huxley had to do something, but it was all too late. Two years too late. Ten minutes too late. Hardly anyone remained to fight back. Through the smoke and the dust he caught sight of Hicks, his children and his wife and his father gathered around him. Huxley called out, unsure of what he said, but the seven of them came running toward him, right into a trap—an ambush. They passed by the fountain and six takers leapt out of the rubble and fell upon them.

He heard their screams—each individual voice, each tone. They blended in the air in harmony. Sweet, Hicks's youngest girl, fell from her father's arms as a taker grabbed him round the throat.

Huxley's legs carried him swiftly across the distance to the fountain where he snatched Sweet up from the ground and lifted her into his arms. She screamed, screamed right in his ear, but he could barely hear her. His vision began to darken around the edges.

It was then he started shooting indiscriminately. Shot after shot after shot went off in his hands. His gun grew hot, too hot to hold, but it was far too late for that. He kept going. He kept shooting. He'd shoot until he was dead and even then he'd make sure to keep his finger on the trigger, maybe his corpse would take out a few more.

Something grabbed onto his sleeve.

He whirled and pointed his gun right at Joule who shrieked and put his hands up.

"I-I reached them. They're, they're coming," he said, his knees shaking. "The Theocracy, the military, they're on, they're on their way."

Huxley lowered his gun. He heard other shots—Randy, probably. He'd given weapons to Fortitude and Shane and Gig. Shane lay at his feet now, next to his father, eyes open, not a shot fired. Useless. Huxley wanted to kick him, call him worthless, blame his death, his family's death on him, but for Sweet's sake, he didn't. Her tears ran down the back of his neck. She clutched onto him in a choke hold.

"How soon will they be here?" he asked. His voice was not his voice.

"Minutes," Joule gasped. "That's—that's all. They're flying in."

"Here."

Huxley dumped Sweet into Joule's shivering arms, pried his unused gun out of Shane's dead grip and handed it to him as well. Then he turned and headed toward Randy. If anyone was going to survive today it was going to be that ratty little girl. He wouldn't let them take her from him. He'd die first.

Takers flew at him, he shot them down. He walked over bodies—Gig, Cookie, Desdemona, Darling—and kept walking. Big City was gasping, the dying throes of its very last breath. The ground seemed to tremble with its effort.

He fought his way to Randy across hours, across minutes, across years, killing anything that got in his way, unsure in the haze really if they were human or taker. He never seemed to get closer to her, she was always just out of his reach, then, just as he had found her, just as his eyes beheld her through the clouds, a great rocketing boom sounded in the sky. He fell to his knees, ready to die—another drill, another hoard of takers to kill—but looked up in time to see the tail end of a white jet disappearing from his field of vision.

It was not the takers. It was the Theocracy. It was God.

26

Soldiers fell from the sky like snow, radiant as the stars in their white uniforms, their sparkling parachutes ballooning out above them. Their clouds, their bright white jets, sprinkled more and more of them upon Big City. They landed in the dirt and the smoke and the blood, and they were not dirtied. They cooled the ground where they walked. Cold, they lifted their guns, their icicle spears, and they put an end to the demons of hell with blast after icy blast. They moved through Big City—a healing balm.

Only there wasn't much to heal.

They chased the demons out or shot them down, but it was too little too late. The town ran red with blood. The crystal fountain, once white, spurted red up into the sky, bodies drowning in its base. There seemed little sign of life.

They found the apostle who made the call huddled by the fountain, a girl child cradled in his arms. Tears warped his face when he saw them. He struggled to his feet.

A commander stepped forward to speak with him. A team of nurses rushed to his aid.

"Apostle Joule?"

He nodded. The nurses pried the girl from him. She began to wail.

The commander eyed him. "Where do these demons come from?"

"Out in the desert. Due north of here," he answered. "There's a hole in the ground. That's where they're based." A nurse wiped blood from his face. He was filthy.

"We must get out there. Re-route a few of the bomb jets."

"No, you can't—you don't—"

"We must exterminate these creatures."

"No, I mean the oil! If you bomb near reserves of that size, the potential explosion would be devastating. And if it didn't explode, it would most certainly light the reserves. If it starts to burn, there's no way we can get to it. We need that oil. Please, listen to me!"

But they shook him off their sleeves.

"Re-routing jets now, sir," said an attendant at the commander's side.

189

"Very good."

Apostle Joule stared at them, hollow faced. The commander ignored him and stood resolute, his hands behind his back.

"We're picking up a signal, sir," the attendant said. "It appears to be hostile. Orders, sir?"

"Scramble their airwaves."

"Very good, sir."

They used the signal to pinpoint the demons' location, hone in on it, make their aim precise. Apostle Joule was half-crazed, but if for some reason he was speaking the truth about that oil, some kind of precaution was a necessity.

In the air, the jets having already passed over the signal coordinates circled back around, prepared their aircraft to release their missiles.

"Fire at will."

An explosion shook the ground at once like an earthquake—rattling the buildings and knocking soldiers over. The reaction was too strong to have come from their bombs alone. *Far* too strong. They'd hit the reserve.

"Report," the commander snarled into the radio.

"We can't see anything, sir. Too much smoke."

"Tell me what you see when the smoke clears."

"Yes, sir."

Several minutes of radio silence passed. The commander stared strongly in the direction of the town hall—stared over the rubble and the bodies and the fire. Stared until his eyes no longer saw much of anything and only his hearing mattered. The memory of that great and terrible rumbling shook his legs still. Had he made a mistake? He could not afford to make mistakes.

"The smoke isn't clearing, sir," came the voice through the radio. "We're sending a ground team down."

The commander glanced in Apostle Joule's direction. The man stood with his head hung in agony or shame. He knew then what the report would be. He waited for it all the same, praying to God that the ground team wouldn't say what he already knew they would say.

"There's a fire, sir. At the bottom of the impact crater. It smells like oil."

A sharp hiss issued from the commander's lips. The oil. It was over then.

"Put it out!" he roared into the radio.

"You can't," Apostle Joule said. "That fire will burn until the reserve runs out. There's no way to stop it now."

The commander glared at him. "We can try."

"You can try. But it won't do you any good."

Joule walked away.

"The fire isn't responding to extinguishing, sir. I don't think it's possible to put it out."

The commander hurled the radio at the ground. Pieces of it scattered everywhere as it met the ground and broke. Mistakes.

Several of his men had found dirty little people hidden in the destruction and brought them into the square, to the commander. Three or four. That couldn't be it, could it?

"Scour the area," he ordered. "Find all the survivors."

He had thought perhaps he could save Big City, exorcise its demons and put it to rest. But now, now as he looked into the eyes of burnt and burning, shivering people pulled from the rubble he could see that nothing would rest. Not in Big City and not in the memories of it either. His rescue mission had turned into an evacuation. There was nothing left here for them but death.

Behind him the bloody fountain still poured red into the sky.

27

Nearly five hundred years spent in the direct and blinding rays of the sun had dried Big City out good—every last semblance of moisture evaporated away over time and left nothing but husks of buildings, husks that when filled with bodies and set ablaze burned fast and hot like kindling. Huxley half-hoped some stray spark would find its way into the scrub and set the whole desert burning for miles. Make the hell it all felt like a little more corporeal.

He threw the match himself. Not many people left to bury the dead. From one hundred and six, eleven. Himself, Randy, Seth and Junior, Chivalry, Marty Shane, Georgianna Dunstan, Timothy Swallow, Rachel Rice, Howard Blue, and little Sweet Grey, the mayor's daughter. They alone remained to gather their goods and pack up to leave. They alone would walk away from Big City, board a train, and be taken away. Their belongings would be the only ones going into cardboard boxes, their animals the only ones left behind and missed. Big City was dead now—just a dusty memory at the back of eleven minds.

The heat of the flames licked his face with a hundred broiling tongues, but he didn't move away. He let it singe him, write its memory all over his skin.

They'd chosen the saloon to set ablaze, stack the bodies in. Took him and the others nearly three hours to find everyone and put them inside. Sweet had started crying when she found her daddy beneath the bleeding body of a taker. Those white suits from the military had tried to help, but they wouldn't let them. It was theirs that were dead. Nobody else's.

All those loaves of funeral bread Cookie had baked for the town meeting still sat in neat rows in the dark of his kitchen. Huxley and the others carried every last loaf out and set them in front of the blazing building, stood to watch it burn. Huxley clutched a loaf in his hands. Reesa would never know how like a premonition her choice in refreshments had been. Cookie at least would have appreciated that he'd baked his own funeral bread. Nobody could bake it like Cookie...

He hurled the loaf in his hands through the front window of the saloon. The glass shattered and flames sprang forth from the new opening. Dead. They were all dead. Everyone. He didn't save them. He couldn't save them. That scream that had been building in his body since Reesa had killed herself finally rose to the surface and the force of it sent him to his knees in the dirt, shredded his throat. Hot tears stung his eyes. Merrick. Merrick was in there, burning. In the end he hadn't even been able to save what remained of her.

Rachel started humming. The others joined hands behind him. Eleven. That was all. Hardly worth saving. He wished they were dead—himself included—but he shoved that thought to the back of his mind in a hurry. He couldn't afford to think like that.

A hand touched his shoulder. Expecting Randy he looked up and found Joule looking down at him—the white of his uniform orange in the firelight, his blonde hair red. He offered his hand and helped Huxley to stand. For a moment, neither of them said anything. What did you say to the man who had also lost a wife today?

"The soldiers are ready to help pack up," Joule said. "You can all take whatever you want. There's room for it."

Seth and Junior nodded. Sweet started to cry.

"Go with them to your houses. Just tell them what you want boxed up. We won't leave until you're ready."

The survivors scattered slowly. Rachel took Sweet under her wing and walked her to her house. The others followed suit. Huxley had to push Randy to go without him. He couldn't turn away. Not yet.

"I'm sorry," Joule whispered once the two of them were alone. "We should never have come to Big City."

Huxley shook his head. "It's not your fault. Not really."

"All the same."

Huxley turned and regarded him for a moment. Joule looked back, for the first time not flinching under his gaze. The apostle knew now what it was to see death, what it was to be powerless in the face of it. Huxley could respect him for that.

"Where are they taking us?" he asked.

"Alaska," Joule replied.

Sparks flicked up, caught hold of the blacksmith's next door. Soon, the whole lightbulb ring of buildings would be little more than ash and bones.

"All right."

Joule left him then. He turned to face the burning buildings. He'd left Big City before, to go to university, without any intentions of coming back, but the wind and the land and his heart had pulled him, and he'd returned. This was his home, though he hated it, and it was nothing now.

His heel slid in the dirt as he turned and began to walk away, the heat of the flames falling from his face. Indie and the others, they would have to remain here.

He'd make sure they had enough to eat, could get out of the barn. He looked back over his shoulder one last time at the row of loaves of bread in front of the saloon. The shadows of flame danced around them like spirits, cast long shadows from out their backs.

Alaska was no place for horses.

About the Author

Laurel Myler is a graduate of the University of Utah where she studied Psychology and Latin. Her hobbies include watching TV, playing fetch with her cat, collecting model ships, and eating sushi. On the weekends she moonlights as a Howard Jones impersonator. Her work has been performed at Westminster College and the Great Salt Lake Fringe Festival. This is her first novel.

www.ingramcontent.com/pod-product-compliance
Lightning Source LLC
Chambersburg PA
CBHW031454260626
47154CB00017B/2686